ZORAH

THE ADVERSARIES

K. EMERSON

EDITED BY: LAURA M. MORALES

Forastero Press LLC
Denver, Colorado
Identifiers: ISBN 9781737293606 (international edition)

Cover design by © 2020 Laura M. Morales
Map and Cover Illustrations by Larissa Wolf
Interior Graphics and Illustrations by Valeria Wind

Second Edition printed in 2021
Printed in the United States of America

To the source of Infinite Wisdom, from where all revelation and inspiration is granted to us. And, to a world, I don't entirely understand, but for which I'm forever hopeful.

It is with absolute gratitude and appreciation that I want to thank everyone involved in the completion of the first release of the ZORAH series, The Adversaries.

First and foremost, to my wife, editor, and translator, Laura M. Morales, for her unconditional support, insight, and endless hours of dedication to this literary work.

Many thanks to our Illustrator, Valeria Wind, for her incredible talent and enthusiasm. Thanks to our friend, Stacey Kilpatrick, for her graphic insight and expertise. Working with them was both exceptional and rewarding.

Thanks to our families and friends for their constant loving encouragement and their ongoing support. Special thanks to grandma Elvia, for always pushing us in our search for greatness; we cannot thank you enough for continuously believing in our project.

Also, thanks to our friend, Carol Wilcox, for helping us "getting there." Thank you to my students for their relentless cheers during the publishing process.

Finally, to the readers and all who have been a part of this journey, to whom I owe my passion for writing.

Alzamak
Aversa
Orioto
Burh
Gémeaux
Olu
Ghalaban
Land of Tenshia

It is 2120 A.D.

...and drought threatens the survival of the citizens in wealthy nations.

Hundreds of outcast territories have been called "purgatories" by the financial Elite who now rules planet Earth. Those wretched places are saturated with people the secluded and flamboyant new society discards. They are all segregated by impenetrable high-technology barriers erected by the new global government called Societas est Numerus—also called The Society of the Number or S.E.N.

Most of the population in the purgatories work ceaselessly to maintain the superb quality lifestyle of the cities inside the ruling countries. Poorly paid labor, extended shifts, and living conditions below human dignity are all the people experience in the afflicted areas.

People out there, work sunrise to sunset, not knowing the human race is coming to an end sooner than expected. The planet's drinking water is rapidly running out, and soon there will be none for the rich nor the poor. Rain seems to be a memory; it stopped falling four years ago and appears to be gone forever.

Desalinating the oceans is no longer an option

since the water has been exposed to hazardous pollutants after decades of plastic waste. To make matters worse, all the ice left in the poles and glaciers around the world contains large amounts of radioactive residue as a result of constant nuclear experiments.

Present circumstances render a direct threat to the population inhabiting the purgatories. The cruel Elite is considering a way to get rid of them soon, for, in a few months, the treasurable liquid will be depleted. Global governments strive to ensure their water supply for as long as they can, no matter the cost.

Finding underground water deposits in remote corners of the southern hemisphere is humanity's last hope. In the meantime, the selfish society the Elite designed ignores the fact that they will die of dehydration if the precious resource is not obtained. The impending need to change a punishing destiny has urged the S.E.N. to venture in a desperate quest that will revolutionize human existence forever in ways they cannot imagine.

THE FISSURE

Antarctica · Secret Project AQUA-DE-VITA · Closing day.

H undreds of feet under the earth's surface, the research base conference room is full. Patrick Hanover, the *AQUA-DE-VITA* project leader, intervenes, trying to ignore the lump in his throat.

"Ladies and gentlemen—" he announces as he clears his throat with no success.

"It was always my deepest desire for this investigation to be our world's most important finding," he gasps, as he swallows viscid saliva.

"After six years of research, unfortunately, we will go back home empty-handed and with a grievous uncertainty about the future of Earth. The hope of a perishing planet was placed upon us! It is painful for me to say that our technology was not enough this time to discover a new source of potable water." Tears run down the cheeks of his wearied and saddened face.

"Today, we discover there is no such thing. All I have left to say is—it was an honor to work with all of you!"

Patrick Hanover's brief speech leaves everyone disheartened; he steps down from the podium and walks away. Each scientist, researcher, and team member goes back to their room to spend one last night at the base and start packing.

The robotic rovers are loaded and ready to take the excavation staff back to the surface the next morning at dawn.

Dr. Hanover and his assistants still have one more day before departing from the remote region. As well as a select group of gifted high school seniors and their teachers; who had the opportunity to be part of the expedition, to which carefree Henry Schulze belongs.

The next morning before sunrise, the research crew boards the android-operated rovers leaving the investigation site to never go back. Dr. Hanover, his team, and the high schoolers sit at the table to share their last breakfast together.

Henry approaches the table, late as usual, and greets them in his accustomed low voice.

"Good morning, Dr. Hanover. Good morning, Professor Mary G. Good morning, John. Good morning guys," he mutters while walking down the long table toward the vending machine.

"Morning, Henry—" a few of them answer spiritlessly in unison.

Young Schulze is obviously not one of their favorites; to most of them, he is just a spoiled boy with poor social skills. Not to mention, they are bothered that it was his wealthy mother's influence the main reason to make him part of the journey.

The boy grabs a thin metal tray from a pile and approaches the machine. The menu options offered by the robot achieve nothing more than a grimace of disgust on Henry's face.

"I don't even understand why it gives you options—everything is repulsive!" he complains while pressing the third button.

Food, even within the nations of the S.E.N., is no longer what it used to be, much less on the expedition where they had to feed hundreds of people. After three long minutes of waiting, the machine spits out a smoking silver wrapper. The smell coming from it makes the youngster so queasy, he looks forward to being back in his house's dining room promptly.

Students sitting at the long table try to occupy all available seats as Henry walks by so that he does not sit there. Unbothered by their childish reaction, the young man sits at a shorter table across from the head researchers.

Henry goes over what to say a thousand times in his head, before opening his mouth to speak to the expedition leader. The room is tiny; everyone will hear him, and he does not want to give any of them cause to belittle him. Henry knows they think him smug, way too emotional, weak, and a loser for randomly quoting things that are irrelevant when it comes to science. At least that is what the nicest of his peers would probably say about him.

"Ummm Dr.—last night I was thinking, and being frank, I don't want to leave this place before revisiting the excavation site. I understand there is nothing else to see. Still, I would like to take a last glimpse at the deepest point humanity has ever reached," says Henry sorrowfully. The other students look at him as a dud but lack the guts to say anything. Maybe they choose not to do it because, fortunately, by tomorrow, they will be out of there. They will never have to see such an insufferable guy again.

In Henry's eyes, even if it is meaningless to others, the site has a deep-felt significance, considering it is the first excavation he has ever witnessed. It is his genuine desire to become a field archeologist once out of high school—but none of that matters to the judgmental folks sitting at the cafeteria tables.

Dr. Hanover looks at the skinny boy with disappointment and sincere animosity, wipes the crumbs in his disgusting beard, and addresses the youngster.

"You have my permission to stay there for life if you want to—" to which the other teenagers laugh jeeringly.

Following lunch, young Schulze musters up everything he needs to go into the excavation area. Down there, the young man stands stunned to silence amid the irradiating heat and the extraordinary quietness emanating from the earth's core. He brings all the equipment to fully register the moment forever. Future archeologist, Henry Schulze, reaches the deepest point and turns on the halogen construction lights. The tunnel looks the same at first until he notes an odd fissure on the rock-solid wall.

Henry does not seem to remember seeing the crack before, and immediately peeks inside; it appears infinite. Pointing his flashlight into the gap, the beam of light gets lost in the dark. It is broad enough for the adolescent to crawl inside.

Excited by his new finding, young Henry decides to leave his belongings behind leaning against the wall and starts running back to the base to tell everybody. Sprinting as fast as he can, he gets on the elevator and pushes the up button.

Just at that moment, the earth begins to roar and shudder strongly. Layers of rock wobble side to side;

the young explorer loses balance and bangs his head against the elevator's hot rusty wall.

Waking up not knowing what happened, Henry looks at his holographic watch and realizes he has been unconscious for four hours. The site is so dark, the teen can't see the back of his hand inches away from his face. Patting his arms and legs to check for wounds, he finds the flashlight still hanging from his belt. He turns it on and discovers huge rocks sealing the elevator shaft. There is no other way out of the excavation site; he is trapped.

Having worked side by side with the researchers makes him aware of the conditions of the tunnel, nobody will be able to rescue him. Henry gets up and dusts off his pants as he wanders around the half-smashed elevator. For a few minutes, he tries to move the boulders but ends up sitting against the wall, where his frustration transforms into uncontrollable tears.

"I am going to die here, I will never see my mother again," cries Henry into the gloom of the empty tunnel.

Two hours go by before the teenager chooses to head back to the rock fracture at the end of the pit. He assumes he is going to die anyway, so there is not much left to lose. Seizing his backpack, the anxiety-driven youngster crawls into the fissure holding the flashlight in his mouth, hoping the crack will miraculously steer him back to the surface.

As he keeps going, the walls of the fracture get narrower, until the troubled boy can only slide his body like a worm moving through the soil. Wanting to give up and return to the tunnel, he points the flashlight forward, realizing something ahead looks like a subterranean vault. Henry slithers through the rift when a new thought comes to his mind; it fills him with fear. He realizes the slightest seismic activity would bury his hundred-twenty-pound body under tons of stone, and finish his pointless life.

The fissure is so snug that the rocks scrape his skin, while sweat makes the throbbing a hundred times worse. Henry continues to slide forward and reaches a broader space where he can crawl again.

An unlimited underground chamber appears before his tired amber eyes, and he can stand once more. Its ceiling seems to light up with an unusual fluorescence, somehow allowing him to see the surroundings.

Instead of finding a way out, the survivor appears to be on a new planet inside the globe. His thoughts of getting out vanish as he wanders about. An hour later, after walking around the endless cave, Henry realizes the chamber's ceiling might be roughly a mile from the floor.

Or at least that is what his eyes perceive after being filled with grit, tears, and sweat. Resigned to his luck, beyond dehydrated and exhausted, his body collapses against the rock floor.

Unexpectedly, Henry regains consciousness to face the fact that he has no strength whatsoever to get up. The lost boy is so weak he can hardly breathe, even though the air inside the cavern is surprisingly as fresh as the air on the surface.

His legs cramp because of the tiredness and lack of oxygen in his muscles. His spine aches from crawling through the narrow fissure. Young Schulze's body is as dejected as his soul.

Memories come to Henry's mind, his childhood passes before his eyes. Moments he and his mother spent together, added to the idea of a dying world, overwhelm him.

He feels his warm tears of dismay join the beads of sweat running down his face. It is so silent he can hear his weak heartbeat echo on the solid rock floor. The boy's fear of death evaporates along with his tears on the cavern's floor.

Henry's senses are weaker by the minute, and his tortured brain jumps to the conclusion that his life has been in vain. He has always wanted to be someone of worth, to his mother, and to the world.

However, the only thing he has ever accomplished is to be hated by anyone who has gotten to know him.

At least three days have gone by, and even something as simple as breathing is painful. The energy required to even think is considerable, and the teen doesn't have it. Henry feels his soul wanting to leave his body. He is unable to do anything except for remembering his mother's catchphrase, "Make your miracle happen!"

His heart keeps beating, yet clinging to the idea of survival three miles under the earth's surface is pure nonsense. He begins to embrace the thought of dying; the sooner, the better.

A faint sound reaches the young man's ears; it is very distant, but it is growing louder and clearer.

"What is that sound?" Henry whispers to himself with no strength to even open his eyes.

I hear it coming my way. No, it can't be, are those... footsteps?

His weak heart flutters.

...I must be hallucinating; it is common before

people die.

The sound of feet trudging toward him grows louder. *Yes, footsteps! They have to be footsteps.* He wants to yell. *Here! I am over here!*

But lacks the strength to scream. In an effort to be noticed and call for help, he surrenders to unconsciousness once more.

When he comes to, Henry finds himself resting in a room full of light, believing he is dead. He gazes at his surroundings and finds himself in a very cozy yet strange dwelling. Looking at his hands and feet, he wiggles his toes to make sure his spine is uninjured. All his gear dangles from a chair in the corner of the room.

I thought belongings only traveled to the afterlife with the Egyptian gods, and I am a 'nobody.' How come are they here? He wonders in amazement.

At that moment, a young-looking guy, remarkably tall, and of striking appearance, comes into the room. His dark blue, long, and dazzling hair, favors his intense cerulean eyes. He wears what seems to be a finely embroidered tunic. A belt with two angel wings on a silver buckle embellishes the stranger's attire. "Good morning," says the young-looking man.

Is he an angel?

The question automatically pops up in the back of Henry's mind. The youngster has never seen someone who looks like the stranger. The man's gaze is sincere. His blue eyes are kind yet unusually penetrating. While the boy stares stupefied, the first thing to come out of his lips is uttered in a fragile voice.

"Am I in heaven?"

"The complete opposite, my friend, you are way under the earth's surface!" answers the host, chuckling.

Nothing makes sense. Henry wants to ask a billion questions, but the first thing he does is thank the stranger for saving his life.

"By the way, my name is Ikhabot. What is your name?"

"My name is Henry, but you can call me Hen."

"Ok, Hen, I am glad I was there in time, and you are alive."

"In time for what? To save me? How did you know where I was?" Henry asks.

"I bet you're chock-full of questions. Answers will come in due time. For now, rest and get some food. Your body is still weak. When the moment comes, I will take you to tour the area," says the stranger. His voice is soothing and fills Henry with trust.

Without saying another word, the newcomer leans back against a pillow and starts to eat the delicious food, the kind stranger left beside his bed.

The food is not all unfamiliar to the teenager; the tray overflows with fruits and some sort of dinner rolls. He takes a bite, and it tastes so good, his soul begins to return to his body.

GHALABAN, LAND OF TENSHIA

The next morning, the blue-haired man enters Henry's room and gently wakes him up. He sets a sky-blue robe on the dresser, then drops a pair of lace-up sandals, similar to his, on the floor.

"Good morning, Hen, I hope you had a good night. Get dressed—someone is here to see you!" he utters before leaving the room and shutting the wood-carved door behind him.

Henry gets up and looks in the mirror. His big amber eyes look tired, and his rust-colored hair looks like it needs a trim. The last few days have taken a toll on the young survivor; he appears a little thinner and paler than usual.

However, his new robe suits him; he likes the way it looks. He grabs the sandals and laces them up, as he lets his acquaintance know he is ready. Ikhabot and an old man with short snow-white hair and serene eyes, dressed in a stunning silver tunic, come into the guest room.

"Hello, good morning!" the young visitor greets the two gentlemen timidly and receives a warm welcome in return.

"Hen! Look at you! Are you ready? A long but exhilarating journey awaits both of us. Allow me to introduce you to the wise Arwind, Ghalaban's great Satrap."

"Hello, my boy, I am very pleased to meet you. I am the spiritual guide in this city, and it is my duty to answer all your questions—do not worry. I know you are tremendously confused, and nothing you are experiencing makes much sense. I understand your skepticism; our world, our race, and everything else will be explained to you. However, allow me to tell you, you are not dreaming, nor are you dead. You have never been closer to the truth of this life than you are now, my young friend," says Arwind, helping the still weak boy out of the bedroom.

"Come on now—enjoy the view and pay close attention to all the information you are about to receive. I will catch up with you two later, I have somewhere else to be," states the old man in excitement. Henry is eager to see his new surroundings.

As they walk down the stairs into the main room, young Schulze cannot help feeling worried that everyone on the surface must be presuming him dead. Henry desperately needs to find a way to communicate with his mother and tell her he survived the earthquake.

Dr. Hanover could have already sent his mother an official notice about his accident, and her son's death will have unnerved her. Henry worries about his mother being upset and having no one to turn to. It is hard to have real friends in her financial situation and social status. Henry tries to hide his terrible anxiety and walks out of the elegant yet simply decorated house.

At the same time, Henry feels so welcomed; it is comforting to his soul. He somehow trusts he will be okay, and that these strange men will not hurt him in any way. They give him the impression that they genuinely intend to help him.

In a cavern so large it seems to have a horizon, young Henry is in awe as he listens to his new friend. The ceiling of the cavern is dark, yet fluorescent rocks shine like stars at dusk. All of them reflect beautifully on the vast and calm waters of the ocean bathing the city's coast. It is like another planet inside Earth.

Touring the city with Ikhabot, Henry realizes the

citizens have followed a line of development comparable to the surface. Its impeccable streets are adorned with impressive buildings flaunting a fascinating architecture, with finishes close to Arabesque patterns and Greek structures in a dazzling combination.

Roads and sidewalks, made out of the most elegant marble, make the city look a lot brighter than the dim environment offered by the cave.

However, unlike the large cities on the surface, people down there seem to build as they wish. No one lives very close to anyone else, or on top of each other. The intricately rock-sculpted houses shine like jewels amidst landscaped gardens.

The natural beauty of the place is beyond the imagination of any human from the surface; the young outlander can only marvel in absolute admiration. The teen lacks the language to describe the sheer simplicity of its splendor. The energy in the air is quite peculiar and different from the world he knows. It is as if every time he inhales, he receives a gust of pure energy.

Trees and plants, apart from their gorgeous colors, shine as if helping to illuminate the whole space with soft and welcoming light, in different nuances and shades. White, pink, red, green, yellow, and orange leaves are everywhere. Everything looks like a Christmas tree whose leaves work as shimmering light bulbs. A soft and refreshing breeze steadily blows, providing the city with a mild spring-like climate of about sixty-two degrees Fahrenheit.

Henry wants to ask Ikhabot why the plants have such a different appearance but decides to leave the question for another time. Besides, he thinks it is just logical to assume that the vegetation has adapted to the dim conditions of the cavern.

People walking around in the streets are wearing tunics similar to Ikhabot's, but each one seems to have a particular and unique design. They all have the same wing symbol on their belt buckles, from children to the elderly.

The inhabitants are all exceptionally beautiful and have honey-like skin tones, despite the lack of solar light. In Henry's opinion, they all look like they could be related to one another; there is no diversity, unlike on the surface.

"So, what do you think about Ghalaban and the land of Tenshia?" queries Ikhabot, interrupting the boy's solemn silence.

"It is... it is gorgeous. I have so many questions I would like to ask you about this place and your people that I don't know where to start. When can we visit other cities? I am so excited about all of this; I want to know everything."

"Everything? No human can learn everything

there is to know at once and not go completely crazy, my dear friend. I, at more than two-hundred years of age, still don't know a lot of things about this world, even though I am one of the guardians of this nether land. As for the other cities—Üversa, Alzamak, Olu, Gémeaux, and Burh—you have to wait, there will be time for that."

Henry cannot believe his ears and is filled with skepticism and more questions. He knows nobody can ever live more than a hundred years on planet Earth. He doubts that anyone in Tenshia can live longer, but as he believes the nature of this place is different, he avoids asking any further questions.

The two sit in Ghalaban's main square to chat. Ikhabot invites the boy to tell him about his parents, his school, and other minor details of his life on the surface. Henry, still shy with his new acquaintance, shares a little about his mother and his family while admiring the endless beauty of the city and its people.

As they talk, the boy delights in looking at the streets that uniformly align with the center of the square. In the middle of the park, there is an emerald fountain hovering about five feet from the ground. The incredibly clear water seems to have no source at all; it flows mysteriously out of nowhere.

"Hen, wait for me here, don't move! I'm going to bring something you're going to love!" says the guardian excited.

After five minutes, the Tenshian returns with two bronze mugs. He gives one to the teenager, who looks at the contents with a little distrust.

Ikhabot laughs, "Come on try it! You won't regret it!"

Young Schulze takes his nose to the edge of the glass and smells.

"What is it, Ikhabot?"

"It's a smoothie made with my favorite fruit. It accesses our taste buds' memories and then simulates the flavor of that which you enjoy the most, give it a try," he insists.

Henry brings the glass to his mouth and takes a sip of the milky, green liquid.

"This is the best thing I've had in my entire life," mumbles the boy taking another sip. Ikhabot snickers and chugs his cup as well.

When the mugs are empty, Ikhabot says it is time to return home, "Someone is expecting us."

When they arrive home, a muscular young-looking man is waiting by the door. His shoulder-length ash-blond hair and light brown eyes make his tanned skin stand out. Ikhabot greets him, "Hello, Atmix!"

Atmix does not seem excited to meet outlanders, and Henry wonders whether he could have offended him.

A girl that appears to be Henry's age stands next to Atmix and judging by her looks, it must be his sister. The sterling grey of her eyes hypnotizes the teenage boy immediately; she is a beautiful girl.

In that way, Henry meets Aurora, younger sister to Atmix, Ikhabot's companion.

Aurora and Henry have an instant connection, which he has never felt before with anyone on the surface. Although Atmix does not enjoy his sister's new friend, Aurora becomes Henry's partner in crime in this new land.

With Aurora by his side, the next few days, or cursus, as they call them in Tenshian language, go by as fast as a weather vane spinning during a hurricane. A cursus is never enough time to explore Ghalaban.

Aurora and Henry enjoy long conversations lying on the steep hills of luminescent grass. They spend hours looking at the rocks that light up the high ceiling of the vast underground cavern, finding patterns and shapes.

During these leisure days, Aurora teaches the foreign boy the basic techniques of meditation and self-contemplation. Henry never thought he had it in him, but he turns out to be a natural at visualizing his inner cosmos.

These techniques aid him in controlling the

anxiety of not knowing about his mother. The idea of not being in control of anything is disconcerting to him.

A few cursus later, relaxing in Arwind's finely furnished living room, the beautiful Aurora shows Henry how to play a Tenshian board game. Ikhabot joins them while Arwind, Ghalaban's Satrap, rearranges his bookshelves.

The surface teen has warmed up to his new friends and even laughs at Ikhabot's pathetic jokes. However, he is still filled with the same questions that he had when he first woke up in the guestroom at the blue-haired guardian's house. Without hesitation, he changes the topic and asks.

"How did you guys get down here?" He waits for an answer, attentive, and fascinated, not anticipating that he could receive so many different answers that he would feel like a waterfall was beating down on his head.

Aurora looks at him excitedly, while Arwind narrates a story that will change Henry's life forever.

"In the beginning," the old host says, "...when the physical world first came to be, there were two peculiar sons of Man on Earth called The Older

Sibling and The Younger Sibling. The latter died by the hands of The Older Sibling, according to the ancient book of Berit codes..."

Henry shakes his head, indicating he does not understand how that is related to his question. The wise Satrap abruptly stops his storytelling and reproves the boy.

"You need to learn many things before you can understand the answer to your question; a lot has to do with The Older Sibling!" Ikhabot tries to explain, but Arwind interrupts him.

"I see the worry in your eyes, your *sharah* seems disturbed. You see, every being in the universe generates an energy pulse called *sharah*, and some of us can sense it. It is about your mother, and the world running out of fresh water, am I right? Do not worry, child; she will be fine. And we must save your world too; it is our duty. Let us take a look at the surface; it will make you feel better."

A large image appears in the middle of the room. It looks like a multi-screen television without any structure to frame it. To Henry's surprise, the tenshian's technology is capable of receiving live broadcasts from the surface.

Arwind changes channels—as if looking for something specific. Various news channels, from different countries and in different languages, start coming up. The boy is frustrated to see that the expedition's failure did not make the news headlines. Instead, they are talking about

Henry going missing at a research camp, while omitting that he was part of the top-secret project, *AQUA-DE-VITA*. He sees his mother being interviewed; her face looks emaciated.

Right after watching this, young Schulze jumps to the conclusion that the Tenshians have been watching everyone, and starts questioning their character.

How long have they been doing this? No wonder why they are fluent in my language, too. If they are more advanced than the people above, does that mean they have been following our society closely? He thinks. *Why haven't they intervened in world crises? Do they have a way out of this cave to the surface?*

Panic takes control over his thoughts; he wonders if he will ever be able to leave this underground cavern.

He decides to break the silence once again and addresses Arwind with more questions.

The wise Satrap replies calmly, "Henry, my dear boy, for centuries we have been alert and followed what occurs on planet Earth. We were also aware of the excavation. We fractured the rock and created an entrance to our world. The time has come for the secrets of Tenshia to be revealed to the world. We ought to fulfill the purpose of this entire creation."

The old man continues, "...your arrival signals a change of era for this local universe. The shortage of water on the planet is just another sign. We have waited so long for this moment. The fact you were able to see the fissure on the rock and cross it, means that you are ready to start your training and become the Thakaiken from the surface."

Henry burns with disbelief while the Satrap goes on.

"Just as you went through the birth canal when you were born, you managed to come through the dangerous fissure in the rock to give birth to your inner spiritual self."

"A Thakai... what? Hold your horses, Mr. Arwind. I am truly sorry, but this sounds either like a fairytale or a terrible joke. I might not be an adult quite yet, but—I am not dumb. What do you mean by fulfilling my destiny? Why did Ikhabot say you were waiting for me? I do not have a clue about what is happening here. Are you trying to make fun of me?"

Henry loses his composure; it makes no sense whatsoever to him. *At first, everything seemed like a good dream, but now it is turning into a nightmare.*

Suddenly the teen's judgment gets clouded by uncertainty and terror of the unknown. He feels like daydreaming. Arwind clears his throat to focus

Henry's attention on what he is about to say.

"I understand your frustration, my young boy. A Thakaiken is a protector of creation, a bearer of the secrets of heaven. Please, allow me to explain to you in further detail what is happening. This way, you will have some time to meditate it all and accept your destiny," answers the old man placing a pile of books on the table and saunters to his armchair.

"My destiny? The only thing I want is to go back to the surface—to my normal life and see my mother. Ikhabot, I beg you. If you can take me back to the surface, please do so. I promise not to tell anyone about you, even if I did, who would believe me anyway. You can count on that," says the high school senior out of despair.

"Immediacy can never come before what is of real importance, Hen," whispers Ikhabot, responding to young Schulze's desperate comment. Arwind's gruff and deep voice proceeds to challenge the kid.

"How long do you think people on the surface will last without water? The available reserves of the S.E.N. are running out; two years at most, it's what you all have left! And what about the purgatories? They are becoming obliterated!" Arwind's voice becomes softer and full of sorrow as he continues to speak, "...drought and death are all people without lineage and wealth have left. People with power, the Elite, will only look over their shoulders when it comes to preserving poor people's lives on the planet. They plan to raid into the purgatories—kill as many men, women, and children as they see fit. They will take whatever bit of water they still own, and leave entire communities to perish."

The wise old man stands up from his armchair and starts pacing around the room. The blue-haired guardian can tell the Satrap is getting aggravated, notwithstanding his copious patience.

Ikhabot steps toward the man and escorts him back to his chair. Ghalaban's Satrap makes a pause, and closes his eyes, takes a few deep breaths and resumes.

"I assure you nothing happening outside the invisible walls of power comes up in the news, does it? I bet you are heedless about how people in the purgatories achingly manufacture all the goods your world takes for granted—textiles, houseware, devices! Do you really think your wealthy neighbors assemble your precious electronics? You don't even know there are communities with no water by now. Limited water reservoirs kept secret by small communities were taken away by their political leaders. Media doesn't talk much about the water shortage inside the affluent nations, am I right?"

Henry replays in his head the news he has seen on television and social media the last couple of months and comes to the conclusion Arwind might be right.

The Elite has been retaining a significant amount of information from the public. Thoughts that had never occurred to the teen come to his mind.

Ikhabot interrupts as if he could hear what the youngster is thinking.

"The future is not very promising, Hen—there is nothing else for you up there, my dear friend. Stay with us, learn and train, change the future of the common man," says Ikhabot, placing his hand on the boy's shoulder. Arwind smiles at Ikhabot's words and continues to explain.

"Every ruling government on this planet has intended for centuries to hold full domain over human existence. Should they succeed, creation will suffer a cataclysm like never before. Everything, absolutely every living thing, will be destroyed if we do not stop the Elite's ambition and hankering for control."

At this point, Henry's face is pale; young Schulze's frail faith is entirely shattered. Silence takes over the room, and Henry's hairs prickle on the back of his arms. He can tell everyone is looking at him, including his beautiful friend, Aurora.

"We must stop them before they bring this creation to a definite demise—" utters the Satrap, breaking the silence. "If the world leaders reach the level of control they seek, higher celestial powers will storm the heavens beyond the firmament. They will decree a cosmic war that could tear the entire universe apart."

"In all honesty—I couldn't care less if this is all true. What can I do anyway? I want to go back home," declares the youngster, both doubtful and enraged. Henry fills his lungs with a breath of courage and states, "Sorry, I am not like any of you guys. Please take me back to the surface now! I don't want to be here for another minute; I want to go back to my mother."

The disappointment in Arwind's eyes is evident—he looks at Ikhabot and whispers, "If that is what the boy wants, let us take him back as soon as possible, I don't want him to feel like he is a prisoner here."

"Fine!" the blue-haired Tenshian agrees.

Ikhabot stands and walks determinedly toward the boy and says, "Hold my hands—think hard about where it is that you want to go. Picture it in your mind."

"What do you mean? How is holding your hands and thinking of home, going to help me, Ikhabot?"

The blue-haired Tenshian rolls his eyes and smiles at the naive teen, "...you question everything, huh? You just don't know what to ask!"

Aurora giggles as Ikhabot clarifies, "...this is how we travel long distances. We can transport matter with our thoughts to almost any place in this world. Well, not just with a thought, but that is the basic idea. We call it ener-travel. Here, now visualize your house in your mind as clearly as you can," the guardian urges the teen, "...Concentrate!"

"If you can move so easily from one place to another—why is it that you have vehicles here in Tenshia?" queries Henry, trying to outsmart the two gentlemen.

"The fact that I can ener-travel does not mean every Tenshian can do it. And even if others could, we would not do it to go from one corner to the next one, or even to a different city. The energy spent on ener-traveling is massive," Ikhabot sighs at the boy, "I will do it with you because I can. Besides, it is the only way to get to the surface."

Henry finds himself speechless as Ikhabot's confidence and simplicity continue to surprise him. The guardian's ability to explain intricate concepts is fascinating. He looks only a few years older than Henry does, but he is as wise and patient as an elderly man.

The surface teen finally shuts his far-less-eloquent mouth and holds his Tenshian friend's hands while picturing his house in Zurich. The quantum of energy generated and the frequency of radiation are so intense, Henry loses consciousness and then vanishes.

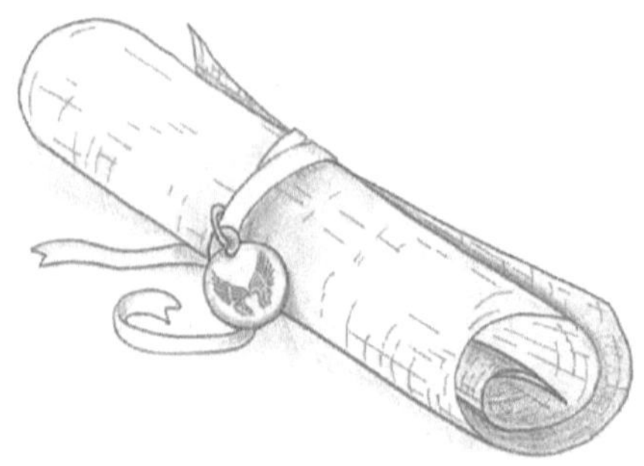

THE PETITIONS SCROLL

Henry opens his eyes to find himself back in his bedroom, lying on the bed. A sudden migraine strikes the teenager as he sits up, discombobulated, and utterly lost as to what happened and how long he has been sleeping. Young Schulze takes some time to stand; the urge to vomit is nearly unbearable. He wanders around, making sure he is alone in the room.

Was it a dream? Was the expedition part of the dream too? Yes! Yeah, that is what happened. Right? He says to himself, thinking about how his dream turned so quickly into a bizarre mystical nightmare.

The boy keeps on pondering.

I have to change the shows I watch before I go to bed! Last night's dream had me believing in a surreal underground world with weirdos all over! Where are these crazy ideas coming from?

Everything seems in place, but a look in the bathroom mirror is enough to bring the boy back to his bad dream. The overall he is wearing says AQUA-DE-VITA Project on the pouch to the left of the zipper.

Henry opens the waterfall faucet in his bathroom and splashes his face and hair with cold water. Resting his hands on the vanity, he begins to think about how the past events are even possible.

Maybe I passed out right here in my room before leaving for the expedition. Sure, that explains it all.

He convinces himself and takes off his coverall and underwear to shower and fully wake up. At that same moment, the boy's mother walks into the room to spend some time alone with her departed son's belongings.

When Mrs. Goldsmith sees her son's naked teenage body, she runs toward her kid to hug him instead of turning around or covering her eyes.

Henry panics and holds his breath, trying to hide his bare body with his hands. His mother's beautiful lips, saying his name and trembling with excitement, hush right before she gets to him. The woman faints and collapses to the ground.

"Mother! Mom, mom," Henry taps her cheeks to wake her up.

Did she pass out because she saw me naked? He

wonders. This is embarrassing. My mom hasn't seen me undressed since I was eight years old.

The kid places a pillow under his mother's head, and she starts to regain consciousness. He quickly reaches for a pair of pants and puts them on. He fears she could pass out again if he is still in the nude.

She opens her eyes slowly and whispers in her low sweet voice.

"Sweetheart, we thought you were dead."

All his fears return as fast as a snowball hitting his face. He refuses to believe that everything that happened is real.

Maybe part of it might be right, but not all of it. Henry thinks to himself. I went down the elevator to the excavation tunnel; there was an earthquake, I hit my head, and luckily, somebody rescued me. Maybe while unconscious, I had these bizarre visions.

All sorts of stories come to him while his mom hugs and kisses him with anguish.

Hold on; this is not logical, you blockhead. If that had been the case, my mother would know I was rescued. So—who brought me back? Was it this man called Ikhabot?

The half-naked teenager is shocked; he is suddenly able to remember his blue-haired friend's name. As well as recalling his angelic appearance, and his city called Ghalaban miles below the surface. Henry even remembers the face of a beautiful girl called Aurora. The memory of her silvery eyes does not leave his mind. Young Henry understands it is best for his mental health to look past these series of events. Now he is back home; he feels safe even though the expedition failed, and the world will still be running out of water in months.

The same day, the Schulze-Goldsmith residence overflows with reporters broadcasting the boy's miraculous return. They all have more questions than he could ever answer. Suddenly, Dr. Hanover and a group of investigators walk in, asking the press to leave.

In a matter of minutes, Henry sits with his mother on a divan, surrounded by men in suits with dark shades and wireless earpieces. In front of them, Hanover and other leaders of the expedition begin to ask the young man how he managed to escape the excavation site after the earthquake.

Henry claims he does not recall anything about what happened. Avoiding any details, clearly showing his uninterest in what they have to say, he apologizes, gets up, and climbs the stairs toward his bedroom.

"Please forgive my son! Henry is a good boy; he just needs more time!" says Mrs. Goldsmith, a split-second before Henry slams his bedroom door.

Two weeks after Henry's return, messages and phone calls from the press keep flooding Schulze-Goldsmith's voicemail. They beg young Henry to share his story on how he managed to survive. Henry, fed up with the whole situation, tells them there is no fantastic story to be shared, "...stop calling! Leave me alone!"

The media broadcasts the same thing about his miraculous and sudden return over and over.

S.E.N. spokesperson's only son, claims to have no recollection of how he escaped the collapsed excavation site in Antarctica. Is the boy telling the truth?

On the verge of boredom and annoyance, Henry opts to break the promise he made to Arwind and Ikhabot. Avoiding names and details, he vehemently tells Hanover's investigators the whole truth. The teenager describes the place and the people he met down there.

Every single one of them looks at young Schulze

like he is mental, and leaves the house's study in absolute disappointment.

Before exiting the Schulze-Goldsmith residence, the auditors make sure to suggest to his mother that the boy requires urgent professional help. They even dare to say Henry is experiencing post-traumatic stress, which could lead to a severe mental disorder.

The shock could be the reason he is making up stories as a defense mechanism, they say.

"Mrs. Goldsmith, these fantasies are a way of coping with the trauma following an awful experience—" explains one of the most arrogant researchers on the team on his way through the front door.

At least the real story is enough for them to leave the teen survivor alone for a while. Nobody would believe it, or go out there and find out if what Henry is saying is true, so he has nothing to worry about. Professor Hanover suggests it is best to stop asking the boy questions, "...it might encourage him to believe it, and end up in a deplorable mental state! The child has a whimsical imagination!" he laughs.

Henry has finally been enjoying some well-deserved peace for days until one of the housemaids knocks on his bedroom door.

"Mr. Schulze, sorry to disturb you, but I was about to take care of your clothes—and found this rare object in one of your pockets."

He opens the door. The maid holds a small silver cylinder in her hand. On the outside, there is a symbol that sends shivers down the teen's spine. "Two angel-like wings!" he shrieks before asking the maid to leave him alone right away and shuts the door. Henry is hesitant to open the little vial. He feels like getting rid of it, but curiosity overcomes his deepest fears. The teenage boy slowly turns the cap; his hands perspire and shake. Inside lies a small parchment scroll. The teen takes it out and starts reading it as his body continues to shiver.

Dear Henry,
He has no control over the tremor of his hands.

The transformation of life on the surface rests in your hands. Become a Thakaiken and protect the wellbeing of this universe. We are the only ones who can offer the world a chance for survival.

He feels a lump in his throat, and his feeble body

forces him to sit down on the edge of his bed.

P.S. Remember, the ocean that washes the shores of Tenshia is fresh water. We can help all of you.
Sincerely, Arwind

As Henry finishes reading, cold beads of sweat trickle down his forehead. His hands still hold the little piece of scroll despite the tremble racking his body. Henry is frightened; he cannot make sense of what it means to become a Thakaiken. The teen never thought of helping anyone; much less did he envision himself aiding to save the human race.

Acknowledging the alarming freshwater shortage, Henry realizes he does not have another choice. The young man understands he must return to Tenshia and at least bring some of that clean water back to the surface with him. Only now, there is no possible way to go back. The thin piece of paper contains no details on how to contact Ikhabot.

Wandering around his room, young Schulze blames himself for wasting the tremendous opportunity he had with the Tenshians. Henry hates himself for being so self-centered and closed-minded. He condemns himself for his lack of vision and determination, after understanding that he gave himself no time to learn anything about the underground civilization. In the long run, it is the Tenshians who seem to have the only solution to the drought the exterior world is facing.

A minute later, he ventures to gather his mind on communicating with Ikhabot.

Will he hear my call?

Wonders Henry knowing it is a very long shot. Ikhabot's mind is so powerful; he might notice the boy's loud call for help. Henry follows every step he practiced with Aurora about how to meditate.

Gradually and bit by bit, all of his thoughts wrap around his underground friend. But several minutes pass by, and nothing happens. Young Henry is about to have a mental breakdown because of the continuous stress; he desperately needs to establish contact with Ikhabot.

Henry keeps his eyes shut for endless minutes and pictures Ikhabot's face very clearly. Immersed in his mind, he loses track of time and gets startled by a deep and soothing voice he remembers well.

"Hi there, Henry, I am glad to see you again!"

The teenager rapidly opens his eyes, and standing there, is the man with dark blue hair and silver tunic. It is him, Ikhabot; he heard the boy. Henry rushes out of his trance and runs toward him, hugging him without uttering a single word.

"Are you alright, Hen? I heard you calling my

name all of a sudden. So—does this mean you are ready to come with me and start your training?" pumps Ikhabot in excitement to see his young friend again.

"I still don't know about that, Ikhabot! The only thing I am sure about is that I have to do something about the water. Humans on the surface do not deserve to die of thirst," explains Henry, admitting there is no other way to resolve the water crisis.

The youngster recognizes the urgent need to go back to Tenshia. Determined to leave, Henry realizes there is something that does not feel right. Ikhabot can tell he is hesitant about making a decision, so he asks the boy.

"What's wrong, Hen?"

"My mother! She is going to be very worried and upset if I disappear without telling her where I went. I know how much she suffered when she thought I was dead—I couldn't do that to her again. I can't just leave without telling her. Everybody would start looking for me again."

Ikhabot feels how anxious Henry is starting to get, so he sets his hands on his shoulders, and the boy regains peacefulness. After silently looking into Henry's eyes for seconds, the protector attempts to appease the boy's worries.

"You know very well you cannot tell her. You must keep Tenshia's existence a secret. We can provide the water, but no one can know about our civilization, at least for now. It is too dangerous."

"I get it, so what should I tell my mom? I don't want her to worry about me, start looking for me and not be able to focus on her job; her anxiety will devour her. My mom and I are very close; I want you to understand," says Henry.

"I understand more than you think Henry, but for now, you need to make a wise decision. Leave your mother a note, but avoid telling her where you are going."

Without doubting it another second, Henry grabs a pen and a piece of paper and writes his mom a note.

Dear Mother,

I have to leave you again, I am genuinely sorry, but don't worry this time. I will be safe. There is something I need to share with you but have no time to explain. When I come back, I hope to have fantastic news for everyone. You need to trust me, and please do not fear for me. I love you with all my heart.

Love,

Your son, Henry.

The teenager leaves the piece of paper next to the lamp on the nightstand. Looking around the room, he gets the cold feeling that is the last time he is going to be in his home.

Henry's eyes get watery as he holds his powerful

friend's warm hand. In seconds, the bedroom vanishes in front of his eyes, and his senses stop registering everything happening; the darkness shrouds him.

In the blink of an eye, they are back in Tenshia; they arrive in the same room Henry stayed at, the first time Ikhabot rescued him. The Tenshian protector goes straight to business and hustles Henry.

"There is no time to lose! We must go to the temple and meet with Arwind and the others. We need to discuss everything related to providing water to the surface from our ocean, and your training to become a Thakaiken."

"Wait a minute Ikhabot, I never said I wanted to become a freaking Thakai... nothing. I just told you I would come because I need to ensure the water supply humanity needs to survive."

"I think your cosmic compass points at much more than that, my dear friend," replies the Tenshian with a chuckle as he looks at the youngster with optimism and high expectations.

Henry does not know what Ikhabot believes him to be. Nobody has ever expected much from the kid before.

Why is this stranger expecting this from me? Muses Henry. *He barely knows me.*

They arrive at a place on top of a hill with luminescent trees, the kind of trees that decorate the charming streets of Ghalaban. The building looks like an ancestral temple. At its entrance, a label inscribed in stone reads *Aghora-Infinitus.*

From there, the boy stops and stares stupefied at the vast and pure freshwater ocean.

On the other side of Ghalaban's bay, faint figures with lights from other cities glare in the dim environment. There are also large boats sailing and crossing the ocean.

Inside the temple's main chamber, sits Arwind with two other young-looking men; they are calmly talking. Henry can tell they are being expected. The men also have the same angel wings engraving on their belt clasps.

He assumes it is some type of symbol of their civilization, but he has no clue of what it represents.

The Tenshians are, as usual, wearing very similar attires without losing their own individual style. He recognizes one of them, unfortunately for him, it is

Atmix.

The other guy sitting next to the blond guardian seems very quiet and serene. He has a noble-looking face, emerald green eyes, and bushy eyebrows. His hair is a peculiar—but very eye-catching lilac color.

The beautiful tunics of the Tenshian men amaze the kid. Simple, but artistically embroidered. Ikhabot's tunic is grey and silver, Atmix's is indigo and Silas's is pearl white. Arwind promptly interrupts Henry's contemplation by speaking aloud.

"Brethren, we are here today—" his loud voice stretches across the room, "because the time we have been waiting for is here. A son of the surface will help to bring the final amendment to our creation," he pauses and stares at Henry.

"It is necessary for a son of the surface to forsake the falsehood he has learned throughout life and accept the truth of creation. He must continue to live as a Tenshian and be completely restored according to the original model of Man. This individual needs to know in-depth, the secrets of the heavens, and how Man's true essence was originally intended."

The Tenshians next to Henry nod their heads and listen attentively.

"It is clear to us that the main issue is not about sharing our water—since we have plenty. We know about the real millennial conflict that lies behind the drought. Water is just the way for us to reveal ourselves to people on the surface. Declaring to the Muhalif their days are almost over is a priority."

Arwind's speech sounds demented to Henry. The teen feels like saying nothing. He believes it is best to play along and return to the surface with the water people are in desperate need of. However, a boy his age cannot evade curiosity.

"What the hell is a Muhalif—if I may ask?" inquires the boy, pretending to be interested.

"Listen carefully, Henry. Before we can share the freshwater ocean with your people, there are some demands the governments of the S.E.N. must agree with."

Arwind avoids answering Henry's question about the Muhalif, he shakes his hand, making it clear that it is not relevant at the moment.

"Only if these conditions are agreed upon, our water will reach the surface to be shared with the rest of humanity. There are no goods or services to be offered that we would like in return, but there are several things the governments ought to change."

Young Schulze's saliva gets thicker, and his palms begin to sweat. Then he whispers to his insides.

What do they want from us? Are we not suffering enough already?

"I am pretty sure you are aware of my mother's

influence in the government. I could talk to her—" suggests Henry with determination.

Arwind pulls a scroll from under his tunic and holds it out to the blue-haired guardian.

"Would you mind telling me what it is that you want? I mean—before taking the petitions to my mother?" says the naive boy.

"Absolutely, Ikhabot will kindly explain each one of our demands and the reason behind all of them," utters the ancient man reclining in his finely carved marble chair.

In that instant, Ikhabot clears his throat softly before asking the boy a simple question.

"How old are you, Henry?"

"Seventeen—turning eighteen in a few weeks," Henry answers with pride, without even asking himself about the purpose of the question.

"How old do you think I am, Hen?" replies Ikhabot.

"I don't have a clue! You mentioned you were over two-hundred, but it can't be, so... maybe, twenty, twenty-two at most? How old are you? I have wanted to ask that question since the moment I met you. You seem to know a lot, you are way too wise to be close to my age, though, you look so young. Tell me—"

"I don't know exactly how old I am," replies Ikhabot with a smirk.

"How is that possible, how can a person not know how old they are," Henry says confused before Ikhabot continues.

"In Tenshia, not everybody cares about how old they are—nobody needs to know. It is irrelevant. No one wants to control or limit anyone by knowing their age. No one will try to classify you or label you according to your age!"

Henry notices Atmix is staring at him, fierce and arrogant. The blond Tenshian always seems to be disapproving of Henry's presence among them. Ikhabot tries to be as transparent as he can for the kid to comprehend every detail.

"The only thing I can tell you—for you to be able to understand is that a Tenshian grows just like humans do until turning seven. That means, at seven years old, we look pretty much the same age. But on our seventh *birthday,* we welcome the second and sometimes the third portion of our soul into our bodies. This makes a huge difference as we start to develop and deteriorate ten times slower than any regular human. Man's average life span is seventy-eight years—a few people even live up to one hundred. That being said, if you do the math, a Tenshian might be able to live for more than a thousand years."

Listening to Ikhabot, even though it sounds bonkers, it somehow makes sense to the kid. The knowledge Ikhabot holds might be comparable to a three-hundred-year-old man. Henry is convinced no human in his twenties could have such a character, or uphold that much knowledge and wisdom.

"I don't want to overwhelm you with details. Listen, cautiously, I will now proceed to read the scroll,"

All human beings on Earth should immediately be informed of the finding of the freshwater ocean and should benefit from it.

Looking at Henry's eyes, Ikhabot makes a pause and makes sure the boy is listening carefully before continuing.

All registry of personal information of the citizens in the world must be deleted. Bank accounts, loans, lines of credit, and any type of debt; everything must be annulled. No one will owe the banks or the nation. The banks will assume all debt of those who cannot pay, as a loss.

Henry already knows this is going to be almost impossible to achieve. Even if his mother could convince some higher-ups in the government, it could mean the collapse of the whole system.

Ikhabot regards the teenager's angry reaction and

justifies the second condition.

"The Elite stores as much data as possible to control relationships, jobs, and level of education according to age and bloodline. They track every breath you take and watch over you. These men will say this was established to organize society, but those are nothing but lies. Identity is nothing but a cruel way for those in power to brand every single individual like cattle. Why do you think you have been given a family-name, Hen? It is one of the strongest control mechanisms in the world. This needs to change—it is merely a system to guarantee servitude and assure the Elite the right to rule, allowing them to remain in power."

Henry is thunderstruck after all the disturbing information. Ikhabot sounds mad. Henry refuses to bring his mother a scroll where one of the petitions is, nothing less but to delete all the data concerning the citizens.

Henry continues to think of this while Ikhabot carries on. *What type of unreasonable request is this?*

"I know you think it is ridiculous! Believe me when I tell you, the leaders of your world will understand what we intend by making these demands you consider extreme. We are confident they will accept all of our terms once your mother explains that we can provide the water for their survival. Without water, there is no life, they want to live and remain in power."

At this point, Henry can only look at the Tenshian's eyes and keep his thoughts to himself. There is no option but to keep on hearing what Ikhabot has to say, no matter how absurd it may sound. His face cannot hide the annoyance he feels.

"Let me ask you another question, Henry, haven't you noticed that everyone here in Tenshia lives under the same fair conditions? This brings us to the next petition—"

All resources should be redistributed for every person to own the necessary to have an abundant life. One's wealth should not represent another's poverty. The companies must be owned by the ones who work for them. There must be a redistribution of wealth to establish equality and equity of resources. Common individuals should be reeducated on the difference between abundance and excess squandering.

"Allow me to further explain this to you, Hen. Big financial and production institutions, which abuse the population, must make drastic changes in their remuneration policy. Everybody should benefit equally from the profit a company makes. We will take an active role in making the necessary modifications for the new system to be effective," clarifies Ikhabot.

Still, even a young person like Henry would know that it is impossible to attain.

This can never be achieved—corporations will not allow this to happen. They will never share their billions.

Young Schulze thinks as his frustration grows. Unable to keep his mouth shut any longer, the boy interrupts loudly, "One moment, *this* is far beyond ridiculous. Who will determine how much abundance is enough? Let me guess—you will?"

Atmix is starting to get aggravated with the kid's attitude. He stands up aggressively, but Arwind looks at him, and the grim-looking Tenshian immediately returns to his seat. Henry can perceive the tension he has created in all of them. Arwind notices it and addresses the boy in his hoarse voice.

"Be calm now, my boy, nobody needs to impose anything on anyone. Listen, Henry, the infinite wisdom we wish to share with Man on the surface will guide them on how to act. Once they learn, of course."

He sits down, and everyone takes a minute to allow the kid to calm down and center his thoughts. Ikhabot resumes reading the petitions scroll.

All political leaders and industry owners who control life on the surface shall surrender power immediately to the council of Tenshia, which will set the new path to follow. No one will rule the way it has been done, no one will need a ruler after some time. Every single man, woman, and child will learn to take responsibility for their actions.

The more Ikhabot reads, the more Henry's mind struggles.

This is absurd. Thinks the boy as Ikhabot talks. *The surface will never get the water this way. The Elite will never sacrifice that much for fresh water. They will use whatever means to obtain what they want, as they have done it several times. Even if it means bringing war and slaughter to Tenshia.*

"The following petition..."

Ikhabot makes a long pause and looks at Arwind, like what he is about to read is something transcendent, out of this world.

All conspiracies orchestrated by the Muhalif and the celestial princedoms to avoid the change of cosmic realms must be stopped. Humanity needs to be freed from astral mind control; they must be able to see the truth. Humans shall be given back their right to receive the secrets of Heaven. Otherwise, this world will be destroyed.

"We truly understand you cannot easily take in all this information, Henry." The old Satrap affirms with a subtle nod.

Ikhabot interrupts, "World leaders have always known their main objective is to unify the nations under one single way of thinking—political views, economics, and religious belief," explains the blue-haired guardian. "This way, the Muhalif harness all the energy they need from people's controlled minds—and become strong enough to attack the throne of Grand-Abbadi."

Henry's mind is a mess now; he spouts amid the tedious discussion.

"What the hell are you talking about, Ikhabot? Conspiracies, angels, celestial princedoms? Who is this Grand-Abbadi? What bunch of trash are you telling me?"

Losing composure, he stands up intending to leave the room. Ikhabot walks toward him and stands close. Maybe too close for the boy's state of mind, but the Tenshian protector's body irradiates serenity.

"You need to listen, open your heart, understand and accept the truth before you can go back to your mother. You need to realize the importance of becoming a Thakaiken. This conflict has never been about water alone; water is merely a natural resource. The real battle is for the human soul and the control of this universe. The conflict that started thousands of years ago is coming to an end. This will end, one way or another, and you are part of it, whether you like it or not."

Henry is somehow brought back to his senses by Ikhabot's words. He has never seen such a firm expression in the blue-haired Tenshian. Ikhabot takes another deep breath, then rolls the petition scroll, as he looks at the teenager.

"Mankind was deprived of its right to know the secrets of the universe and rule over the earth. The first man was tricked by an ancient, wicked being intending to rebuild his decayed world. At that moment, Man lost its place as a celestial being and is now a victim of astral entities," says Ikhabot.

"These entities are called Muhalif. Basically, they are ancient spirits inhabiting the planets and even some planetoids," explains Arwind.

Ikhabot continues, "And are the ones who reign over the material dimension wielding pain and suffering over the human race. They were created to serve Grand-Abbadi but instead joined NaHash in his rebellion, for they have envied humanity from the beginning of time!"

The Tenshian knows it is a lot of information for a boy like Henry. Nevertheless, he continues telling the youngster everything he needs to know.

"To make it worse, the first male had multiple sexual encounters with NaHash's feminine *self*, whose name I will not pronounce here. These abominable acts begot millions of unclean spirits known as Răȗ. These are the ones who restlessly, day and night, trouble humanity!"

Ikhabot makes a pause realizing the teen looks overwhelmed. The protector steps to an elegant marbled sideboard and grabs a tall mug from inside.

He pours some water from a bronze pitcher and gives it to Henry. Then, the blue-haired Tenshian sets a tray of fresh fruit on top of the center table and encourages the boy to take a snack.

"Hen, do you remember Arwind's tale about the siblings? Well, they represent two opposed human seeds in this world. The Older Sibling is NaHash's offspring, and the father to most people on the surface; The Younger Sibling is the father to all Tenshians. The Ruling Elite of your world are Muhalif half-breeds," he pauses, "allow me to explain this better. The Muhalif are celestial beings of great power and beauty not supposed to live among us. Millennia ago, they rebelled against their nature and became incarnate. NaHash has been altering this reality to achieve his goal of humanity's total enslavement. He has been controlling the solar system with cooperation from the fallen celestials. In a few words, my friend—NaHash, and the Muhalif are The Adversaries of the human race."

Ikhabot takes advantage of this golden opportunity to explain to Henry all the details about the eternal conflict.

"Every person on the surface is bound to an evil reality in which the only purpose is total control and destruction of the immortal soul. The Muhalif crave for human souls with no connection to Grand-Abbadi, who is the source of everything."

"...The supreme energy of Oneness!" Arwind interrupts abruptly in a loud voice, making sure Henry understands the importance of the eternal being.

Ikhabot continues, "...NaHash longs for being worshiped and governing as the absolute master of this world. To do his bidding, the Muhalif will decree an attack over Third Heaven, and defile all souls to feed on them, as vultures feed on carcasses. The Adversaries are aware that they are eternally banished from Grand-Abbadi's sanctuary. Therefore, they intend to remain on Earth and transform the human body into a vessel capable of hosting their wicked nature for eternity. By ending Grand-Abbadi's ineffable plan, they will deprive humans of their right to obtain an eternal, perfect state."

"In other words, my dear boy..." says the old Satrap, "They plan to reign here on Earth and overthrow the original Creator to guarantee no future opposition. If all humans become their vessels, Grand-Abbadi will be forced to destroy our planet. It would not be the first time something similar to this happens—it already occurred once, long before Earth, to NaHash's red planet called Maadin."

Henry's intellect crashes while trying to process the guardian's words. Everything is so new and hazy to him. The well-off boy never imagined this could happen in his world.

So much hate, so many wars; human misery is not entirely people's fault. He is unsure how to feel about it all and cannot reconcile with the idea that humans have been played with like puppets by these celestial beings. Moreover, people are not even aware of them.

Henry chokes back his sobs, trying to hide his frustration. He leans forward and lays his forehead on his hands.

Sorrow and anger flow through his veins before he realizes the young man sitting across the marble hall looks straight at him—it is Silas.

His penetrating green eyes irradiate peace. It is like he could ease the teenager's troubled mind just by smiling back at him. Silas turns back at Ikhabot before he carries on with the conversation.

"Time has come, Henry. The Muhalif are aware the temporal dimension is fading rapidly; the days are getting shorter since Grand-Abbadi's revelation draws near. The barrier keeping NaHash and his comrades away from Third Heaven has thinned. Every time they attack the barrier, they trigger a series of cataclysms on Earth." Ikhabot continues to explain, "Once Third Heaven reveals itself to humanity, destruction will fall upon anyone who's not ready for the change of era. Including The Adversaries—which is why they are trying to storm Third Heaven!"

The wise old man interrupts from his chair, "Our job, my boy, is to aid humanity in getting ready for the revelation before it is too late. Should we not succeed, many people will be destroyed. The only way to save humankind is by elevating their souls. To do so, we need the Thakaiken from the surface!"

"You see it now, Hen? We must stop the 'Muhalif' from gaining more control over people's minds, and attacking Third Heaven," says the blue-haired guardian.

"I see, but how is this important to me, Ikhabot," queries young Henry.

"The human race was created to rule over angels, Henry! It is how it was meant to be!" Ikhabot says, "The Thakaiken from the land of Tenshia must stop these wicked creatures and prevent humanity's destruction. Howbeit, the rebel celestial beings will fight to the death before they step down from the throne of planet Earth."

The teenager's mind has been blown away so many times in the past few minutes. He is no longer able to distinguish between what is supposed to be real and what is an illusion.

The young man remembers how insignificant his life felt when he thought he was going to die in the cavern. He feels he has not done anything worth a damn in seventeen years.

Yet there he is, being asked to join the dream team of *weirdos* and fight for humanity.

"Most humans on the surface are confused about the true purpose of their existence. Nobody knows what to live for anymore. People forget who they really are once they are born into flesh and blood. They choose to follow the path of darkness, surrendering themselves to corrupt actions—and then die without knowing the secrets of Heaven. Therefore, they cannot be reunited with the Oneness of Grand-Abbadi. Their tainted souls become food to NaHash, the Muhalif, and all the unclean spirits," explains the Tenshian. "You ought to learn the secrets of Heaven, Hen! Once you are ready, you will be able to access your timeless *self* and see the truth. You will understand why Man lost the place as the elevated entity it was intended to be and became a mindless *battery* to this corrupt system. You will be given a chance to become aware of the purpose for which mankind was initially created, and lament over the millions of souls that have been lost for centuries!" Ikhabot wraps up his speech by revealing the most critical piece of information yet.

"The Muhalif have used *ego* for humans to attack and diminish one another. It is *ego*, Henry, which has mankind immersed in a world of lies. For centuries, people have been given an overdose of *self-righteousness* and *self-entitlement*. Thus leaving their bodies and souls to rot—allowing the Muhalif to subdue humanity. They see the common man as servants without brains of their own; incapable of learning basic concepts about their own existence," affirms Ikhabot, to which Atmix revoltingly replies.

"You people are nothing but trash to these beings. You all are yet to realize you are mere marionettes playing their dirty game by only caring about yourselves. They achieved to swell you with hate, selfishness, apathy, and aversion toward life."

Hesitation takes over the youngster's mind and starts bombarding his own brain with questions.

I cannot believe any of this. Why would I believe this anyway? I met them not so long ago, and now I am supposed to be part of it? For all I know, they could be the 'evil beings' they are talking about. I don't trust them, but the fresh water they own is real, and we need it desperately.

The boy stops himself from giving his opinion. For the first time in the conversation, he must take things seriously. The water shortage is real.

"And according to you—what is it exactly that I should do? How do you expect me to believe all of this?" Henry demands in a haughty tone to which Ikhabot quickly replies.

"You will find answers and inner peace once your heart is ready to observe closely and handle the rest of the truth! Right now, your mind is still contaminated and imprisoned by everything you think you know; those are lies, Hen!"

Young Schulze is rendered speechless; his vocal cords entangle while he fidgets uncontrollably. His mind splits. He feels anger, fear, and absolute panic like never before. His brain comes to a pause; every neuronal connection has frozen. The look in Henry's face makes the Tenshians around him remain absolutely silent; the youngster is in shock!

What is happening to me?

MINERVA

A few days go by, and the young man tries to stay away from everything troubling his mind. Instead, he spends all of his time with the beautiful and exceptional Aurora.

The kindhearted young lady does an outstanding job of making the teen believe everything will be alright. Ikhabot does not approach Henry for a couple of days, to give the kid time to cope with his emotions and center himself.

Henry worries about Ikhabot being mad at him, so he decides to go and speak with his blue-haired friend. After all, he is the kid's favorite Tenshian.

"Ikhabot, if everything you and Arwind claim is true, then it means I have been living in an illusion my entire life. All people and I have been living a lie where there is no hope. Humanity's fate will totally rest in the Elite's hands in a few months. I never thought that being wealthy or poor, healthy or sick, hinged on a cosmic blueprint. Deep down, I always knew our world had things that were out of place. But I never imagined everything would be part of a celestial conspiracy as rotten as you described it," grumbles the boy as his wise friend nods.

Young Henry has been truly studying and meditating about a solution.

"I will bring my mom here to Tenshia, so she can listen to what you have to say. At this point, all I can do is show her this hidden land, and allow her to decide! I cannot force her to do anything. I cannot persuade her to present herself to the S.E.N. leaders with this scroll of petitions just because I say so—" states Henry while looking at Ikhabot with concern. "She will still have the power to decide whether she brings the scroll back to the surface or not. I am nobody to influence my mother's political views. And the last thing is, I don't think I want to become a Thakaiken, I am sorry, I am not up for any of this. Besides, I only really care about the water, I want no part in a celestial war with angels or demons. I stopped believing in fairytales a long time ago."

The tall Tenshian looks at Henry with kind eyes and chuckles.

"Cosmic timing is perfect, my dear friend—your

destiny will find you sooner than you think. If your wish is to bring your mother here, then so be it. We are willing to do whatever it takes to fulfill the purpose of creation."

Henry sees Ikhabot turning and glancing at Arwind with inevitable dismay. The teenager is not sure why but has a feeling it is because the wise Tenshian struggles with the idea of bringing someone else besides him to the mysterious and magical land.

The overwhelmed visitor spends the next cursus at Ikhabot's place as usual, where he learns more about Tenshian daily life. There is so much about Ghalaban itself that it would take Henry a lifetime to describe in detail how odd everything is done down there.

People's behavior, their vegetarian diet, their original buildings, their simple but elegant clothing, and their chipmunk-looking, meadow animals. Every single thing is so mind-blowing to Henry that he forgets about the real reason that brought him there. The teen prefers to think he will not be involved in any of the dire circumstances to come.

"A big cosmic and celestial conflict, how crazy does that sound? Me, Henry Schulze, saving the world? Nah! I have spent my entire life doing whatever I want, whenever I want it. My world is perfect, even though it is not for other people around me; I never worry about that. I know there is nothing I can do to change their situation, I believe they are not as lucky to have been born in a privileged family!" whispers the spoiled teenager to himself as he reclines in a marble lounger and cuddles the comfortable cushions.

The idea of having to do something for humanity is a little disturbing to me. I don't really care if other kids envy me and hate me. He thinks. *I want to go back to my wonderful life and have everything I need and want. I'll grow up to be a successful person like my mother!*

Leisure days in Tenshia are done when Ikhabot takes the youngster back to his mother. She reacts as if her son had just come back from the dead once again. The youngster's mother looks at him with eyes of worry as she snuggles him the way only she does.

The sophisticated woman has more than a million questions, but before she inquires, the boy asks her to come with him to the place where he has been for the last few days.

She must meet both the guy who saved her son and his leader, who requested to share some critical information with her.

There is only one condition, Mrs. Goldsmith is required to meet the Tenshians alone, Henry explains.

The security detail will not be allowed to accompany her. It is, of course, an unpleasant surprise to Henry's mother; she remembers how protected her son has always felt to have her security detail around.

Mrs. Goldsmith, fearful, gives the young man a look of insecurity for the first time in her life; she has always trusted him. Frustrated, she rebukes him.

"For heaven's sake, Henry, do you realize what you are asking? It is absurd, it is… absolutely insane. These people, all they want is to kidnap both of us. You are young and naive. Anyone can play with your mind and convince you to do stupid things, son. Dammit, Henry, it is a setup. Can't you see? We are in danger."

She stands up abruptly and rushes out of the kid's room to call Purm. Purm, if people could be dogs, he would be a Rottweiler. He is big, smelly, and makes part of the military guard that is always in the Schulze-Goldsmith's home.

Forever standing outside in the yard with two other tough guys, Purm has become a part of Henry's family—which is not an exaggeration because he never even leaves to see his own folks. The big guy has been around since Mr. Schulze passed.

He came to live with them permanently two years ago when a few remaining members from a fundamentalist group tried to murder Mrs.

Goldsmith. That, after she suggested free and mandatory vaccines in developing countries. *Wild extremists!* As spokeswoman Goldsmith would call them.

To this day, she still asks herself why they wanted her dead for something intended to benefit afflicted communities with no access to medication.

Henry tries to stop his mother before she talks to the bully, but it is too late.

"Purm, double the security, someone is trying to kidnap me!"

That same night, before going to bed, Henry plans to go into his mother's room in a desperate attempt to convince her to meet the Tenshians.

He is hesitant since he cannot tell her much about the underground civilization. The distinguished woman will think her son has gone mad and will send him to treatment immediately. The lady is a hypochondriac when it comes to her son.

The boy paces back and forth in the corridor, thinking about how to convince his mother to visit Tenshia. If he hands her the petitions scroll, she will take it as a prank. The kid has no other choice but to tell her that the people requesting her presence, possess a source of fresh water that could save the planet.

He hopes his mother does not believe he has lost his mind.

"Listen, mom, there is no easy way to say this, but—I found an underground freshwater ocean; there is where I have been while I've been gone! I want to take you down there, without security, just you and I. Once we come back, we can share the news with the world. This is what the guardians of the ocean are demanding that we do. Don't you see it? We need to do as they say and trust them if we want the water, it is the only way."

Henry's mother remains silent while delicately cleaning her makeup in front of the mirror. Undaunted, she tilts her head, like a dog would tilt his, trying to comprehend. Not yet persuaded, she turns around and responds.

"You have found a freshwater what—?" she yelps in surprise, "No! No! No! If what you say is true, then tell me where this ocean is. We will go accompanied by a diplomatic delegation and security. Under the ice of the Antarctic, is that right? Where you almost died?"

"Mom, the truth is that I have no idea how to get there. I have been traveling to that place in a very unconventional way, like teleporting or something—"

His mother looks at him as if he was a harebrained, "he has finally gone bonkers," she thinks. The worst part is, no matter what the adolescent says, the more he tells her about this place, the crazier his words sound.

"Mother, I have never lied to you in my life. Please come with me, it is the only way to get the water."

She appears nervous on the spur of the moment as if the information the boy is giving her, brings back a memory. She seems to have heard something about it in the past. Little by little, her facial expression changes from looking nervous to being full of curiosity and excitement. She looks at Henry with so much love, and with a deep sigh, she hugs the young fantasizer as tight as she can, whispering in his ear.

"Okay, son, take me there—and make your miracle happen! Let us use your alternative transportation."

Henry, puzzled, but thrilled at the same time, lets his mother know it means everything to him; to the boy, there is no love like hers.

They have no time to lose. The young man closes his eyes and welcomes the power coming from deep inside his mind. He calls Ikhabot as loudly as he can with his mental voice.

Then he opens his eyes and warns his mother that somebody will be appearing out of thin air in the room in a few minutes, just like magic.

"Please don't scream, okay? He is my friend, and he will take us to the land with the freshwater ocean."

As soon as Henry finishes saying these words, Ikhabot turns up out of nowhere just a few feet from them. Henry's mother, shocked, falls to the left side of her bed.

She has to cover her mouth to avoid screeching. Her eyes are transfixed; she is not able to look at anything else but him.

It seems like the Tenshian reminds her of a particular life event, a painful one. She looks like she has just seen a ghost, but his body is right there and is as real as hers.

Ikhabot introduces himself and mumbles, "We have no time to spare!"

The three of them hold hands and vanish from the bedroom while Mrs. Goldsmith remains in bewilderment. Young Schulze cannot help thinking to himself that his mother reacted as she had seen Ikhabot before.

The refined spokeswoman of the S.E.N. was raised in a prominent family. Her ancestors have been in the ruling class for centuries.

To date, the Goldsmiths remain to be part of the pecking order, which controls the crowds with religion, money, and legislation.

Henry's mother's life is nothing but a script of how life as an aristocrat should be. Everything around her is always meant to be perfect, except for the fact that Henry has no clue Mr. Schulze is not his biological father. That is something no one mentions in their family.

The missing piece of information, in a complicated puzzle of lies, would ruin the impeccable reputation of the Goldsmiths.

Sparks of energy on one of Ghalaban's hills indicate the travelers have arrived. In front of them stands Arwind, the great Satrap.

Henry's mother is no longer surprised; moreover, she seems pleased with what she sees, as if she had been waiting her whole life to see it, like a dream come true. Arwind welcomes them with a warm smile.

The next morning, Mrs. Goldsmith and her son are ready to leave Ikhabot's house. Silas is standing outside, waiting for them. During *three* cursus, all they do is walk with Silas around the impeccable streets of Ghalaban.

He tells the new visitor that there are six cities around the freshwater ocean. The six cities are what they call Tenshia. Henry's mom is charmed by the surroundings; she is astonished. She learns a lot more about Tenshians, and so does her beloved son.

Tenshians do not only dress, but also eat, live, and

breathe differently; they are much more than an advanced civilization in the spokeswoman's eyes. Not only do they have an elevated consciousness, but remarkable humbleness as well.

The most impressive of it all to the S.E.N. official is the technique the Tenshians use to transform the earth's energy into a nutritional supplement for their bodies, minds, and souls.

Given they do not consume food daily as an average human, the process of cellular oxidation hardly occurs. The harshness of time does not take a toll on their bodies the same way as for ordinary humans.

On the morning of the fourth *cursus* in Ghalaban, Arwind turns up at Ikhabot's house to discuss the terms with Henry's mom. The Satrap walks them to the Aghora as he explains their willingness to share the fresh water with mankind.

He also highlights all the conditions defined in the petitions scroll. The S.E.N. and world leaders will have to agree to their terms if they want a share of the precious natural resource.

However, Arwind does not explain the whys and wherefores as he has previously done with the boy.

After listening thoroughly to Ghalaban's Satrap, the spokeswoman is somewhat disappointed and puzzled by the kind of demands the people of Tenshia are making. Something tells her that the leaders of the S.E.N. will not agree to this document; the board will never accept such terms. Henry's mother knows something most people on the surface ignore, something that just a few members of the Elite know about the system.

Henry recognizes by his mother's body language that she knows who the Tenshians are. It is quite hard for her to believe they actually exist. Arwind hands the woman the petitions scroll after explaining every detail and kindly escorts them back to Ikhabot's home.

Mrs. Goldsmith walks by her son's side disheartened; he feels guilty, for there is nothing he could possibly do to comfort her.

Finally alone, at Ikhabot's house, she walks into the guest room and looks at Henry.

"I need to tell you something important."

The boy knows she has a lot on her plate and would like to be alone. However, he decides to sit on something similar to a dresser to the right of the bed. Henry gets ready to listen to what she has to say.

"Hen, it is time to talk about something that happened a long time ago—"

Her voice starts to break and breathes deeply after swallowing a bitter gulp of saliva.

"It is time to talk about your real father."

The teenager's eyes open wide like a full moon,

and his heart rate increases when those words reach his ears.

"Real father?" yelps the boy, "Why today, why here?

We are miles under the surface of the earth, and suddenly want to talk about this stuff? For heaven's sake, mother!" burbles Henry in anger, trying not to be heard by Ikhabot.

"You are right, son, but you need to hear me out. I am completely sure that your father was one of them!" says the woman as tears fall from her eyes.

Covering her face with her hands, embarrassed and at the same time frightened by what she just said, Henry falls paralyzed against the wall behind him. His weak body does not move. His mouth, now open, cannot produce even the slightest sound, and the blood running through his veins threatens to stop.

"What do you mean, *one of them*? A Tenshian? How mom, how is that possible—why are you telling me this now?"

She continues to whisper as tears run down her face, "I met your father when I was sixteen years old, he was young as well, and very handsome. His hair was—blue! Deep blue, just like your friend's hair. Even worse, he looks just like him! He was the Bentley's foster child. They lived around the corner from your grandparent's house. He was a brilliant boy as well, many of the boys our age were jealous and afraid at the same time because of the things he came up with. I fell deeply in love with him. He would always say he came from another world. A world under the surface of the earth. I believed he was messing with me or trying to impress me. He said things no one our age could even fathom. He was always talking about crazy spiritual-and-cosmic stuff beyond anybody's understanding." She explains to her child. "He promised he would take me to his birthplace once he finished his mission on Earth. We were so in love. My parents did not approve of our relationship, so we ran away. When my father's men found us, I was already five months pregnant!"

She sobs, then she says in deep grief, "I believe they got rid of him! It is so cruel. I know they did, I never saw him again. Your grandparents did not want this young man to claim paternity on the baby I was expecting, that could not happen, not in my family. The Goldsmiths have never had descendants out of particular bloodlines. It is forbidden; it is a deathly sin to even mention it."

Mrs. Goldsmith does not stop shedding tears as she tells young Henry her story. He never thought his mother could keep all those secrets without crumbling down.

"Your grandparents did not make me have an abortion because I was in the second trimester, and it could have been fatal. Their main concern was the other families in our social circle. They wondered what would happen if they decided to make a scandal that could lead to an investigation. They allowed me to give birth to you with the condition of never talking about who your father was. They chose who your father was going to be, and they made up a story that everyone would believe. I kept it to myself all this time to protect you, son. I was afraid that if I ever mentioned anything to you about your father, you would want answers that I could never give you."

The boy's mother stands up from the bed and walks near him to give him a hug. She weeps inconsolably on her son's shoulder for several minutes. He holds her by the shoulders and whispers in her ear.

"I somehow knew Bruce Schulze was not my real father, I loved him as such until the day of his passing, but I never imagined you were keeping this big of a secret."

The new information makes the kid's spirit agonize and twist like a caterpillar close to a furious flame. Just when he thought things could not get any worse, his mom comes up with a shocking turn of events.

What a piece of crap. I would have never imagined my mother was keeping this from me. This could explain the reason Ikhabot told me they were expecting my arrival in Tenshia, and the reason why I was able to crawl through the fissure in the tunnel. Henry thinks while his mother lays her head on his lap and cries silently.

He can feel her tears falling on his tunic. The heartache she feels remembering everything she had to go through is abysmal.

"Henry, I also need to tell you that the minute I take the petitions scrolls to the S.E.N. council, they are going to ask who wrote it or who sent it. I'm afraid the Tenshians will have to attend a private hearing with the world leaders and discuss the demands written on the scroll,"

"Please, do not worry about a thing mother; everything will be alright, you'll see—" Henry reassures.

The boy kisses his mother's forehead and tells her he will be right back, runs to the door and leaves the house.

"I need to find Ikhabot, I need to hear more about my father. I want to know who he was—and why he was on the surface. I cannot wait another minute to learn more. There is so much my heart is trying to understand, I wonder where I fit in this cosmic puzzle. Did I just say cosmic?" He talks to himself while walking around, looking for his blue-haired friend.

"Oh! Ikhabot! There you are. My mother just told me the truth about who my real father is. You knew it all this time, too, and mentioned nothing to me?"

Ikhabot chuckles at the kid's reproach. "Would you have believed me if I had told you?"

Henry lowers his head, knowing his friend is right. The guardian starts telling him about his father. He mentions how close they were, and holds sadness in his eyes as he speaks. Henry notices how nostalgic the guardian feels as he remembers him.

"Khazios, your father, went to the surface because he was the first Tenshian who wanted to restore creation. He fervently wanted to bring down the corrupt celestial princedoms."

The boy takes his time to ask a lot more questions, some of which he believes Ikhabot would know the answers to, but the Tenshian refrains himself from getting into details. They walk for several minutes to one of the most beautiful hills of Ghalaban.

Lying on the velvety grass, they look at the crystals in the distant ceiling of the cave. Ikhabot talks non-stop, and Henry listens attentively to everything regarding the adventures his father and Ikhabot shared growing up.

The boy was never so happy and confused at the same time. However, there was nothing more important than, at last, knowing everything about his biological father. Ikhabot, hoping to gain the boy's trust, only tells Henry what he believes the kid needs to know.

Back on the surface, Mrs. Goldsmith presents the Tenshian parchment to the S.E.N. council. Just as she predicted, they demand to know who these beings are and request to be taken immediately to the land called Tenshia.

"Who do they think they are, to send you, Mrs. Goldsmith, with this ridiculous scroll of requests, it is daring and insulting to the functioning governments of this world!"

At least a dozen of them stand at once, all in protest. The prestigious leaders insist the refined spokeswoman must reveal where the freshwater ocean is, with the sole purpose of establishing direct communication with this civilization called Tenshia.

But Henry's mother reminds the supreme board members the Tenshians have demanded she must be the one and only to negotiate with them as an ambassador to both sides.

As Henry and his mother feared, the reaction of the leaders is drastic, and no scroll or further considerations are welcome. They are willing to apply extreme measures to obtain the freshwater ocean and act against the mysterious individuals with ruthless military action if necessary.

Mrs. Goldsmith and her son travel back to Tenshia to inform Arwind and the others what the members of the S.E.N. higher-ups had to say about the scroll. She also warns them of what the leaders might be thinking of doing to take possession of the fresh water. Henry's mother goes into Arwind's house to speak with the old satrap. Ikhabot and Henry wait in the front garden.

"The supreme board of the S.E.N. demands a private hearing with Tenshia's leaders. You need to come before the board in less than a week, to substantiate the conditions on your scroll."

The woman stands silently and immodest after finishing her conversation with the old man. She does not agree with most of the petitions anyway. Being born in the Goldsmith's family means that she has spent her life as an aristocrat sitting on top of the economic pyramid.

The only sympathy she feels for these strangers is linked to the memory of Henry's real father. The boy knows his mother is mostly doing it for him, out of the purest motherly love.

She believes in the not-too-crazy idea of taking half of the fresh water by force, before the Tenshians attempt to modify and manipulate the way the Elite does things on the surface.

"With your permission, Mrs. Goldsmith—" intervenes Arwind after listening to the woman's argument, "We apologize for putting you in such an uncomfortable situation with your colleagues. I recognize these are also extreme changes for you to understand and agree with; it is undeniable that you fiercely believe in the system you are running up there! Nevertheless, I am afraid the conflict between both sides goes deeper than the freshwater ocean itself—" sighs Arwind, "Very well! We have no issue in revealing ourselves to the S.E.N. council; in fact, we will be there tomorrow. Go back now and tell them to be prepared to listen to our requests directly from us. The world will hear about the land of Tenshia tomorrow morning."

After leaving the old wise man's house, Henry is forced by his mom to leave Ghalaban in a rush; he had no time at all to see his beloved friend, Aurora.

Back home, the fine woman starts making phone calls and the necessary arrangements for the hearing. The meeting is to be done in secret due to S.E.N.'s high officials not wanting the public to learn about the situation.

Even a few members of the supreme board are to be kept in the dark.

Morning sunlight hits the panels covering the meeting room windows of the European S.E.N. headquarters, and everyone in the room sits awaiting the mysterious *visitors*—as they call them. Minutes go by; it is almost ten-fifteen, and there is still no sign of Henry's Tenshian friends. The meeting is set for ten eighteen.

The high members are at a huge rectangular table, all sitting on one side, full of skepticism, some of them whispering about the visitors not showing up. Henry sits on a small chair in the back of the room. To the teen's right, tall and mighty—rises the S.E.N. flag.

When the hands of the clock point exactly at ten eighteen, the doors open. Dressed as they usually do, Arwind, Ikhabot, Atmix, and Silas walk into the meeting room.

As they walk inside, a solemn quietness permeates the room. Awestruck, the surface leaders, stare at the intimidating visitors. They look at their tunics, their astonishing appearances, their firm but humble posture.

None of them dare to speak a word until Mrs. Goldsmith breaks the silence and welcomes the Tenshian men. After introducing them to the council, she invites the four men to sit down. One by one, the suited member of the S.E.N. start presenting themselves.

Immediately after the last one says his name and position in government, Arwind takes the petition scroll and starts reading each request making a pause in between sentences.

He reads slowly, to assure every aspect is as clear as it can be and leaves no room for confusion. Faces of disgust and disavowal to these words start to be the majority in the hall. Eyes of rage and hate glance at the angelic visitors.

If some of the members were given a chance, they would end the Tenshians' lives right there. Henry's mother forewarned Arwind there would be no agreement to those terms; it is impossible, but the Satrap agreed to the hearing anyway.

"What type of ridiculous requests are these? This must be a ruthless sham!" Mr. McArthur, the secretary-general of the S.E.N., stands aggressively.

"A plot of fallen angels? Please! Who do you think we are gentlemen?" He adds, losing his temper.

Mrs. Goldsmith clears her throat uncomfortably,

then clarifies, "Excuse me, sir, but I believe they are taking this very seriously—"

"Oh! Are they?"

Mr. McArthur sits back down disapprovingly. Looks to both his sides at his colleagues and states,

"Well, I suppose there is nothing else to talk about, gentlemen. Obviously, we will not reach an agreement under those ridiculous terms. Actually—I am ordering your immediate arrest under the charges of conspiracy and political extremism. In addition, you will answer everything we need to know about the freshwater ocean immediately. Gentlemen, you are under S.E.N. custody indefinitely for threatening mankind's survival. Consider you have committed a crime against humanity!"

The secretary-general could spit fire at this point if it were up to him. He finds it frustrating that the visitors remain calm after hearing they were under arrest.

"I expected nothing better from you, Mr. Secretary General. We knew we could not expect any different from The Older Sibling's descendants, especially after breeding with the Muhalif. Your *kind* has wanted to overthrow Grand-Abbadi and take total possession of the physical universe from the very beginning. The will to destroy everything enlightening and true, runs through your veins," Arwind says from his seat.

Every man in the room is speechless. The way the older man addresses the chairman is unacceptable. The leaders, talking indistinctly, discuss among themselves what the white-haired gentleman claims. Mr. McArthur and his nearest colleagues stare at each other, acknowledging Arwind's declaration is truthful.

"Gentlemen, before we leave—I would like to tell you who we are. That way, you might understand trying to hold us up, is useless," utters Arwind in a passive voice still seated. The sage purposefully ignores the security agents and the androids surrounding and pointing straight at them with menacing weapons. He knows they are ready to shoot should any of them make any movement, "The Younger Sibling is the father of our nation—the father of Tenshia. I assume you know what this means!"

The room is dead silent for a minute before Arwind starts his final intervention.

"Our history is not registered in the books you all have on the surface. The Older Sibling was the only one who knew the truth and took it to his grave; it was not meant to be known. As a result, his lineage populated the earth. The ones carrying The Older Sibling's seed, along with the Muhalif, have remained in power for too long. You deceive humankind about life, and about the Creator himself. You deny the true knowledge and purpose of the secrets of the universe—" explains the old satrap as all eyes in the room look at him, "...The Older Sibling not only ended The Younger Sibling's life; he aimed to destroy all his descendants who still lived on the surface. It was then, when some of Grand-Abbadi's angels came to Earth and took our mother Sophia, pregnant with triplets, to what we know as the land of Tenshia today. They protected her by command of the Creator and nourished her soul with heaven's deepest secrets. The three children were raised strong. Their minds and bodies were meant for greatness; their task—to eventually heal the world under the will and mercy of Grand-Abbadi. Rulers of the surface, the time has come! Your world's prince is due for judgment."

With these words, a force field appears around the Tenshians. The guards and the Androids open fire. Bullets torrent ablaze over the visitors but stop suspended in the air inches from their bodies, like flies trapped in a spider-web.

All four Tenshians disappear before the council's men and women. Their eyes mirror anger and despair while the scroll's pages fall with the same serenity a leaf plummets from a tree in autumn.

"Arrest Mrs. Goldsmith—and get her kid out of here immediately!" yells the secretary-general.

Henry sits in the corner of the room overwhelmed by the gunshots, but when he hears these words coming out of some suited guy's mouth, his heart stiffens. One of the security guards restraints and cuffs his mother, causing her discomfort. The boy stands from the ground and losing his temper jumps on the bully's back wanting to break every bone in his miserable body. Henry feels something slamming his neck bones, and his eyesight gets cloudy. The teenager drops to the floor while his body writhes until the pain causes him to faint.

Henry Schulze wakes up in his room, not knowing how long he has been unconscious. The family doctor, Hank Schaffhauser, sits on the ottoman next to the bed. He seems worried.

"Mother! Where is my mother? What happened to her?" young Henry squeals.

"Calm down, kid, you are still awfully weak—" murmurs the doctor.

"Where is she? What did those miserable army bastards do to her?"

"Unfortunately, Henry, your mother is now in the hands of government intelligence agencies. She is being interrogated in a maximum-security facility," Hank explains, trying to calm the boy down.

"She is being treated like a criminal. We cannot allow that; she was just trying to help," yells Henry sitting up in the bed and starts sobbing out of desperation. The doctor tries to comfort the boy. Hank Schaffhauser has been close to Henry since he was born, so he recognizes the kid is scared.

"Henry, I know that something is going on, and that you do not wish to talk about it, but I have a feeling everything will be okay. Your mom will be back very soon, calm down. I am sure it is a misunderstanding."

"You do not get it, doctor, they will kill her! I need to get out of here and save her!"

Young Schulze jumps out of bed with determination, puts on whatever he can find in the dresser.

The doctor keeps trying to soothe him down, but his voice is no more than a faint sound to the enraged boy's ears.

The only things Henry can pay attention to right now are to his brain and heart, telling him, *you need to get your mother out of wherever she is!*

Leaving the room with the spirit he has left, he notices that there are security agents all around the house.

I bet the meeting with the Tenshians yesterday has

them on the verge of madness and are making this a priority. The boy thinks seconds before being noticed by one of the agents.

"Mr. Schulze! Where do you think you are going?"

A deep unfriendly voice calls him from the other side of the hallway. The suited man's tone is more aggressive with each syllable.

"I need to go, I am in danger as well," grunts Henry running toward the stairs, but out of nowhere, one of the agents tackles the skinny teen and brings him down.

Damn it! He got me! As if that was very hard to do! His huge body is suffocating me, my bones feel so weak. He is going to break my spine beyond repair.

Thinks Henry, not knowing what to do; every cell in his body feels humiliated.

Shortly, his own life stings; he hurts for his mother; he grieves for the world. Bitter tears stream silently down his cheeks, branding his face as they fall.

The agents drag him back to the bedroom and force Doctor Schaffhauser to give the kid a strong sedative. Everything goes dark once the needle punctures

Henry's skin and the clear fluid is flushed down the syringe into his bloodstream combining with his blood.

"Good afternoon Mr. Schulze—" hears Henry waking up to more men standing in his room.

"What did you poison me with? Is this even legal?" inquires Henry, just looking at them. Then closes his eyes, and his mind begins to sway inside his subconscious. Deep inside, the boy tries to find the purpose in all of what is happening. He thinks about his mother and the happy moments they recently shared in Ghalaban. It is frustrating to him how it all crumbles in the blink of an eye.

I need help to get out of here, I tried to do it alone but it was impossible. I need Ikhabot to get me out of this place.

The boy tries hard to focus and starts calling for his Tenshian friend with his thoughts as he has done before.

He will help me rescue my mom and go to Tenshia. Yes! There is where we need to hide from our new enemies. Thinks Henry as he concentrates and continues to repeat Ikhabot's name, but nothing happens.

...Is he not listening?

Wonders the youngster as he is forced out from

his meditation when he hears one of the guards outside the bedroom door.

"It is the teeny's turn to be interrogated!"

Henry's heart aches to think Ikhabot and the others left him and his mother behind, "They could have taken us with them when they disappeared in the middle of the meeting. But they did not! Why?" the boy cries in his bed, feeling betrayed.

Young Henry is angry, but the feeling of fire burning in his chest goes away when the bullies drag him out of bed like a stray animal from his right leg, blindfolded and tossed into a van.

Two hours later, Henry sits in a disgusting little room. Dimmed lights surround the teenager tied to a rusty chair, like in a horror movie. The precinct has a sickening stench of kerosene. The boy's mother is strapped to the chair facing his. She looks emaciated, exhausted, and helpless. She is wounded on her face, and who knows where else.

These bastards!

"Mom, Mommy, I am here! They brought me here to interrogate me as well!" he whispers.

"I told them you know nothing, I told them you do not know how to get to the freshwater ocean either.

They told me that if I do not tell them, then you will! They don't believe me, son, and just keep beating me up for information I don't own. I am going to die here, Hen. I am truly sorry for everything!" murmurs Mrs. Goldsmith fighting to speak; she is even struggling to breathe. The former government official has been brutally hit; she has been physically and mentally abused.

"No, mother, Ikhabot will come to help us, he has to. He was the one to get us both entangled in this. I know it! I have tried to reach him with my thoughts like I did last time. Remember? Something must be interfering with my thoughts. I will keep trying, he will come, you will see. It is his responsibility, dammit!"

Two oversized men with big torsos and beer-bellies walk through the door. One of them pulls the woman's head back and forces her to look at her son. The other one stands behind her child.

"Don't hurt him! Please—I beg you! He doesn't know anything, I have told you what we know already. Do not touch him, please!"

The one standing behind Henry leans over and speaks close to his ear. The boy's mother shudders, trying desperately to loosen the ropes that hold her tightly against the rusty chair.

"Okay, pretty boy! Do not take this personally,

but the government is waiting impatiently for some answers. I assume you are a smart kid, so this conversation will be short. Just tell me where these freaks are hiding the water, and you and your beautiful mother can return home safely," whispers one of the bullies.

"I do not know—no one knows. They are the only ones who know the location. There is no in or out. You do not have the technology to find them either," Henry stutters.

"You have a remarkable sense of humor—" he snorts, "and an admirable imagination kid; however, it is not the time for jokes," the bully threatens the terrified adolescent.

"You need to believe me, no one knows, please let us go."

"I am sorry, kid, but I cannot trust what you say. Let's find something to motivate you—a little incentive for you to share with us the information we need."

He walks to a corroded table next to the filthy wall. Grabs a small pistol-looking gadget and walks back to the table slowly, with a grin on his face. He places the device against the boy's neck and injects him with a thin needle.

"AHHHHHHHHH!" Henry screams as hard as his lungs allow him to. The fluid burns every inch of Henry's neck and runs up to his head.

"AHHHHH! PLEASE MAKE IT STOP!"

Young Henry's restrained legs start shaking beyond control, as he loses feeling in his hands. He cannot move.   "What is happening?" squeals the kid's mother, "Leave him alone, please! Leave him alone, you rat!"

She shouts uncontrollably, drowning in her own screams and tears. Henry hates to see his mother cry. Even though the teen is in agony, the bully grabs another syringe—this one with an amber liquid.

He injects the other side of Henry's neck, and the kid loses control over his mind. He is still awake, somehow present, but has no control over his muscles.

The serum makes Henry answer to everything the bully asks without hesitation, words just come out of his mouth readily.

With no control whatsoever over his body and remaining lucidity, the boy tries to focus and contact Ikhabot one more time; yet nothing, it is hopeless.

In the furthest gap of his subconscious, he spots Aurora's face, looking at him.

Maybe she can help; perhaps she will be able to hear me.

He believes it is stupid to even try, but right now, the boy's reasoning is not at its best. He listens to his heart and impulses himself to do it.

...it can't hurt. Let me give it a try!

Henry focuses and sees the Tenshian girl's sweet and beautiful face appear bright in the middle of the darkness; she shines like a sun on a clear winter's day. Henry sends a cry for help, from inside his mind like a ray of light falling on the girl's head. Encouraged, the boy wishes to be heard.

With the remaining energy left in the teenager's body, he lifts his head, and out of the corner of his eye, looks at the back wall of the room.

There, on the very edge of that dirty room, a shadow starts to take the shape of a person. Henry sees a man landing a finger on his lips, asking him to be still and quiet.

After a few minutes, the two bulldog-looking guys realize there is someone else in the room.

They get close, maybe too close.

The almost invisible energy is too fast for them to stand a chance. The bullies are lifted from the ground and smashed against the walls and the floor.

"Game over bastards!" Henry whispers.

The silhouette is Ikhabot. He takes Mrs. Goldsmith's beaten body in his arms and picks the kid up from the collar of his shirt. Henry gives him a look of hope, unable to speak due to the serum.

His body is weakened after being injected twice with who knows what. Without a moment's hesitation, Ikhabot and the two victims vanish.

Several hours go by before the effect of the narcotics clears from young Henry's bloodstream. Henry and his mother are back in Ghalaban. He gets out of bed and sees his mother on a bed next to his, still unconscious.

Her wounds have been taken care of, bandaged, and cleaned. Not wanting to wake her up, Henry leaves the room quietly and goes looking for Ikhabot.

The Tenshian is downstairs with Henry's least favorite person in the entire world; Atmix. The blond guardian notifies Ikhabot about a private matter and seems more agitated than usual. Looking at the boy with disappointment, Atmix says nothing once Henry walks downstairs.

Henry feels uncomfortable around the arrogant Tenshian. He is positive Atmix believes he is not worth it, and that his opinion in this matter is irrelevant.

"I am sorry for everything you are going through, Hen. I want you to know that you have all of our support. Not only you and your mother but those in the purgatories as well—"

"Thank you, Ikhabot, I really appreciate it," mumbles the boy.

Atmix leaves shortly after, he cannot stand being in the same room as Henry. Sitting in the living room with Ikhabot, Henry tells his wise friend, sorrowfully, everything about what happened after they disappeared from the meeting room at the S.E.N.'s headquarters.

While waiting for Mrs. Goldsmith to wake up, the boy comments, "...being patient is not something I consider I am good at, should we go check on her?"

"Give her body some time to recover, Hen. Besides, Arwind is on his way; I am sure he will be able to heal her,"

Ikhabot comforts the teenager.

Full of uncertainty, both men wonder which will be the government's next move. The leaders' rage and hunger for power will, for sure, bring suffering upon the least fortunate.

The kid's mother is not awake yet. He decides to go upstairs to the room. Henry comes close to his mother, but her diaphragm is not moving.

She is not breathing.

Placing his finger under her nose, he realizes there is no air flowing in or out. Henry's pulse starts to rise, fear consumes the young man.

He quickly rests his head on her chest and faces his worst nightmare, her heart is not beating. Her face is lifeless, already without color, her hair has lost all its shine, her skin is cold as a winter's night. Henry screams as he loses his mind.

"Mother! Mom, please! Come back to me, mommy, I am begging you, do not leave me here, all alone," the teen sobs and yelps devastated. Ikhabot hears him and runs out of his room; there is nothing he can do. He stands close by and stares at the kid's mother's dead body. Nothing on the surface, nor under, could bring Mrs. Goldsmith back to life. There is no such power, not even in Tenshia. Ikhabot hugs his young friend tightly to his chest.

"Let it all out," Ikhabot consoles his young friend.

"Everything that I have worked for ends today; my mother is gone. I am nothing..." sobs the boy while a thousand feelings flood his body and soul.

"There is nothing else to be done; everything is gone to hell. There will be no agreement, the people on the surface will eventually die of thirst, and the S.E.N.'s army will destroy countless lives just to find Tenshia. By this time, I must be the 'most wanted' person in the entire universe."

The ache in his chest is nearly unbearable. All the goodness in him escapes, as rage starts to nestle in his heart.

Who is responsible for all of this?

Henry thinks clouded by anger. His insides shift, and a taste of bile rises to his mouth, leaving a bitter metallic taste.

"This is your fault! I am done, I do not want to know anything about you ever again. I do not care about the fresh water, nor about Tenshia. I do not give a damn about life anymore. My mother is dead because of you! Because you are cowards; you are hiding underground like rats, selfish idiots, neglecting to share what you have and what you know! If we are so wrong on the surface, why have you not gone up there to help us, huh? Did you abandon us to our fate? Lies, everything is a lie. My mother is dead because of your lies and your stupid water. Why do you even exist dammit?" yells Henry wanting to be out of that place and never go back. "I do not want to see you again, meeting you was the worst thing that ever happened to us. You took everything from me. If I had the power, I would finish all of you right now."

Ikhabot looks at his pal silently while he continues to spout all the hate and anger he is feeling, polluting Ghalaban with his toxic discourse and hunger for revenge.

After three *cursus*, and against Henry's will, the Tenshians bury his mother. They warn the teen should he go back to the surface without being careful, his destiny would not be much different from hers.

Minerva Goldsmith will forever rest inside a little cave in Ghalaban's hills, surrounded by beautiful violet and white everlasting fluorescent flowers.

Ikhabot, Arwind, the lovely Aurora, and her brother are standing next to the sobbing teenager. Some of Ikhabot's friends are there too.

offers to say a prayer, Henry accepts. The kindhearted Tenshian starts to utter some words in the gorgeous but intricate Tenshian language.

Henry has only heard Tenshia's unique dialect a few times before.

The boy has no full understanding of the words, but as Silas speaks, each word seems to bring relief to his aching soul. They all look so calm, except for Henry.

Obviously, they are not the ones to lose it all; the unfortunate boy is the one in a bottomless pit where there is only misery and anger. He hates them as he hates himself.

I despise the world. I could do nothing to protect or save my mother. I would sell my soul to the devil just to have the strength to avenge my mother right away

WANTED

"**I** believe there is nothing else for you up there, pal. Only death awaits you if you go back. Should you choose to stay, you will become a Thakaiken just as Atmix, Silas, and I, to defend this creation by our side. I understand you are hurting, but there is no other way. Whatever is meant to happen; could have never happened any different."

The minute Henry hears this, his reckless answer does not make itself wait.

"I want nothing to do with any of this. I wish I could evaporate. I want to know nothing about the surface, or about you, or about anyone. Leave me alone, I hate you—I hate all of you."

Regardless of his words, Ikhabot interrupts the furious boy with a firm voice.

"You need to know that once you go back to the surface, you will not have our protection any longer. You will be on your own, and your pursuers will find you and kill you if they must; there will be nowhere to run. Come to terms with your destiny and embrace what you are meant to be. Do not risk your life by letting anyone know of your true identity, you are important, Henry."

"Important? I do not believe anything you say anymore, but if you say so, then so be it. I do not want to be alive anyway."

The firmness in his voice challenges Ikhabot's conviction.

"You are my blood, Henry; I am not going to allow my brother's child to waste his life. You are not going anywhere. You are staying here, you will grow and become the Thakaiken that the world needs! You have no idea how important you are in all this."

This time Ikhabot's voice is no longer filled with kindness; he is not joking. Henry has never seen Ikhabot upset, even if it is just a jiff.

Hold on! Did he just say 'brother's child'? Is Ikhabot my uncle? He thinks in dark bitterness. This has to be the cherry on top. Could my situation be any more miserable?

He quickly understands why his mother mentioned Ikhabot's incredible resemblance to his father. They were brothers. Henry feels uncomfortably puzzled.

What could be worse than this right now, huh?

Young Henry looks straight at the Tenshian disapprovingly.

"Good-Bye, Ikhabot. I cannot stay and pretend to be one of you, much less a Thakaiken. I have never been one of you and never will. If you were so worried about us, why did you not look for me when I was a child? Why not bring me back here and raise me like a Tenshian? But now, my mother is dead because of you! Now you say you need me! I have no idea why you need me, are you going to force me to become one of you? Forget it! I am leaving right now. I refuse, and it is a shame that my mother's remains will stay in this place," snaps Henry, walking around seeking to calm himself down. Takes a deep breath and continues.

"I need to find the answers in my world. I need to see up there if everything you told me is true, and when I do, my heart will tell me which path to take. Something I am certain about, I will never become one of you!"

Arwind approaches the blue-haired Tenshian and pats his back, whispering to his ear, "Ikhabot, let the boy go. We have no choice but to let him be. He must be on his own. Take him back now. Please! Do not delay his own correction any longer. If he dies, let him die, if he lives, he will be back. It is Grand-Abbadi's will. He has already chosen the right path, but it is not the right time. Besides, you and I must rush to the purgatories. The S.E.N. has decided to start reducing the population by big numbers, and that is something we are not to allow."

Henry notices the great satrap's worry as he says these words. He gently taps Ikhabot's shoulder as he finishes his speech. Ikhabot looks at his nephew with resignation and great sadness.

He extends his hand toward the boy, and in a muffled, sad voice, he tells him to visualize wherever he would like to go.

Minutes later, Henry walks in a peculiar driveway in Switzerland, not too far from Zurich. There he is, standing overlooking a Victorian-looking house, the home of his mother's best friend. The boy walks to the back of the house, looking for the spare keys hiding in the same spot they have always been since he was way younger.

The famous musician and songwriter, Frank Waltz, was there for Henry growing up.

He might be able to protect me.

The teen is lost in thought as he yanks off the

Tenshian tunic.

Smart, caring, and philanthropist of high reputation, Frank is open-minded enough to comprehend everything the teen has to tell him. All of his life, the musician has been a rebel without a cause.

Or at least, it is what Henry remembers his grandfather used to say about Mr. Waltz. The man has, several times, spoken publicly against the aristocracy in which he was born. He loves Henry's mother as no other man does, and Henry is like the son they never had.

Minerva's son lies down on the guest bedroom's daybed, looking at the hills outside through the thick glass window.

Everything is so silent, so much peace and time to think. It gets dark, who knows how long he has been staring out the window. Assuming he is still alone, he walks downstairs to the kitchen around nine. He is starving.

Henry opens the refrigerator, and it is full of fancy food. He takes all of what he needs to satisfy his voracious appetite and steps out to the terrace across from the kitchen.

The tired teenager sits and rests his body in a comfortable chair. His eyes get lost in the beauty of the hills around him, they stand beautifully lit by the lights of the houses nearby.

Old Victorian-looking houses, stone facades, and large windows. Beautiful courtyards behind each house, one of them with a small pool where the lights inside of it make the water sparkle on a dark night, with no stars.

Gorgeous landscaping decorates the peaceful valley. There is even a vineyard on one of the hills on the horizon.

Everything looks untouched by the water crisis.

"Why do all these trees and plants get to live and the ones outside the walls do not? How is it possible that I am looking at a pool when many people will die of thirst?" says the teenager.

A sports car rushes into the underground garage, and the roar of the six hundred horsepower engine shatters the perfect silence.

Frank must be home.

Henry decides to wait for him upstairs, eyes wide open looking at the garage stairway, ready to run toward the dark hills in case it is someone different.

Young Schulze sees a shadow walking up the steps, lights are off, so all the boy sees is a silhouette. The man enters the kitchen as Henry looks silently from the terrace.

"Frank! You scared the living hell out of me!" yells the boy rushing back inside and starts apologizing for breaking into his house like a burglar, "I had nowhere else to go."

"Hen!" howls the musician dropping his car keys to the ground and jumps.

He runs toward Henry and hugs him tightly, squeezing the air out of the boy's lungs. Henry does not recall Frank being so affectionate.

"My boy! Henry! Are you okay? I have been watching the news this past week, you and Minerva missing, you are wanted by the authorities for conspiring against the S.E.N. and for global terrorism threats. Talk to me! What is this about? What is happening? It does not make any sense. I have been trying to reach both of you unsuccessfully. Every phone call is being redirected to the department of security."

A gulp of vile rises to the teen's mouth. Henry wants to tell him everything, but his voice begins to break, and ears fall from his eyes beyond control.

"My mother is dead, Frankie!"

The look on Mr. Waltz's face changes drastically. They both cry inconsolably for a few minutes, standing in the middle of the room. Minerva's best friend cannot believe the woman he loved all his life is now gone.

Sitting on the couch, the boy tells him everything from the very beginning; ever since the earthquake back in the tunnel where he fainted, for the first time after hitting his head. The teenager tells him about Tenshia, what the Tenshians said in the meeting, and everything that happened right after.

It is past three in the morning, and the famous musician is still listening to the youngster with the same attention a toddler listens to a bedtime story. With every detail, more tears run down Henry's cheeks. With nothing else to say, Frank stands quietly, hugs the kid, and walks him back to the guest bedroom.

"You will be safe here Hen, I am a lonely man; no one ever visits. You are aware that I have no relationship with my family whatsoever. I believe that there are many things about this world that I have been blind about, I do not know how it works exactly, but here is what I can tell you. First of all, the ones in power have never been interested in the common man. They work for themselves and themselves alone. They only seek their self-benefit and their own profit. I no longer talk to my family because I do not want to pursue the same ruthless ambitions. I refuse to be part of the disguised slavery they have been embracing and enjoying for centuries," says Frank, not agreeing with their ancestry convictions and their entitlement to rule.

Then placing his hand on Henry's head, more tears

of anger and frustration slide down his fair face.

"Besides that, I am afraid I cannot help you any further. You will have to find the answers to your questions, on your own, Hen. All I can do for you is keep you hidden and support you financially. But for now, you must stay here, you cannot go out, at least while I find you a new identity. It could take up to two weeks, or one if we offer a large amount of money. Surveillance can be easily fooled since they feel overconfident about their machines. Once you banter the S.E.N.'s security, I suggest that you leave the territories of the S.E.N. immediately, and visit the world beyond the invisible walls. You must travel and look for answers in every corner. The information out there is way more legitimate than the one you can find here, where every piece of it has been manipulated. The minute you think you have the information you need and the answers you are looking for, decide what it is that you want to do. Either be the same old Henry in a corrupt society or follow your real father's footsteps."

"The world, Frankie? Do you mean beyond S.E.N. controlled territories?" asks the boy.

"Absolutely, Hen, there are many other places beyond the invisible walls of this surveilled world you and I are allowed to live in. You will find valuable information that will help you discover the answers you need. You will have a unique experience in the purgatories."

Frankie looks at Henry with compassion; he understands how much the boy ignores. Before he can say anything else, Henry decides to ask the composer a question he does not want to know the answer to, but it is one of those things he needs to find out.

"Did you know my real father?"

"Oh, yes! I did. He was a bizarre lad, not unlike you actually, but with a knowledge that no one else around him possessed. He saw things from a very different perspective, a bit dangerous to our political system," replies Frank.

"Why did you hide that from me?"

"For the same reason, your mother hid it from you; to protect you! Now, I think that the answer to your problem is past knowing about your father. Go and look for the truth Hen, untie all the knots, and maybe you will realize how the hatred that you now feel toward your father's people will disappear for good. We humans fear and hate everything we do not understand."

"But without my mother I am nothing, I want to do nothing, I just want to die as well," murmurs the kid talking to himself as he takes a step away from Frankie.

"Then you will allow your mother's death to be in

vain, my sweet boy. Get some rest, answers will come in due time. Have a good night," laments the musician getting a throw from the closet and leaves the room after kissing the kid's forehead. Henry lays in bed and closes his eyes. In the darkness of his saddened mind, he thinks that he could never allow his mother's death to be in vain.

I will take Frankie's advice.

It is morning, Henry wakes up and lays in bed thinking about his next move.

I am going to travel the purgatories looking for pieces to this puzzle, looking for evidence about the real situation of this planet...

Not entirely understanding what he is getting into "...I need to try for the memory of my mother. I think I need to leave the countries of the S.E.N., I need to find the way out. I will do whatever it takes to find the darkest secrets the S.E.N. leaders are hiding. I need to see beyond the invisible walls that separate us from a suffering world," whispers the teenager as he looks out the window.

Henry walks down to the kitchen and turns on the television to watch the news while fixing himself some breakfast. According to the media, Minerva and

Henry are fugitives, who have been missing for days.

The American and European armies have joined forces. They are collaborating on the search for the unknown visitors with their most advanced technology. The headlines are what surprise Henry the most.

ALIENS FINALLY REVEAL THEMSELVES TO HUMANS AND DO NOT COME IN PEACE.

Every important channel around the world, no matter the language, has similar headers. They show Ikhabot's picture using his power to protect himself and the others while getting shot.

But in these photographs, it is not evident they were trying to defend themselves instead of attacking. Also, a deceiving video message is being sent to every streaming device:

This image was captured days ago when an extraterrestrial terrorist group attacked some high-rank officials, to overthrow the government of the S.E.N. These visitors possess compelling power and could strike again at any moment. Any information valuable for the immediate capture of these criminals, or their accomplices Henry Schulze and Minerva Goldsmith, will be generously rewarded.

"Extraterrestrial terrorists? Criminals? Accomplices?" Henry scorns.

The media knows very well how to manipulate

information. They are fully aware of what fear does to people.

Some of Frankie's words come back to the kid; the reporter mentions nothing about the abusive—probably illegal—interrogation, and his mother's death.

They still have not said anything about the freshwater ocean. Media only poison people with fear and hatred against the Tenshians.

Frankie walks in the kitchen from the terrace after his morning run. Turning his heart rate monitor off, not wanting to interrupt, sits next to Henry at the breakfast bar.

"Good morning Frankie, did you sleep okay?"

"Hen! Good morning, my boy—not really. I could barely close my eyes. I cannot stop thinking about everything that you are going through and how much I will miss your mother now that she is gone. I am deeply sorry that this happened to her."

His tone gets aggressive, and he starts cursing in German. All Henry does is stare. He has never seen the talented musician lose his temper.

"These bastards from the government, if they just cared about people, but no! No one is worth a damn to them. We are mere pawns in their gigantic game of chess. They are nothing but puppeteers, sons of ..." stops and takes a deep breath followed by a never-ending silence.

"I am so sorry, Henry, I do not wish to burden you with my emotions. Grudge never brings anything good. Were you able to get some sleep, at least?" The musician asks his godson.

"Surprisingly, right after talking to you, I feel relieved and supported. I know I am not alone, thanks for that, Frankie. I slept like a baby for the first time in weeks," Henry answers humbly.

Tell me something, Hen. You have been through a lot and truth walloped you, what do you think about the world you live in now?"

"Honestly, Frankie, everything matters now. Even the tiniest of details can't go unnoticed. Everything I saw in Tenshia, and everything that has happened since then, showed me that the world leaders can be as cruel as Ikhabot claims they are. They have absolute domain over the whole thing with their stinking wealth."

"Hen! Why do you think money was created? Which is the real purpose?" Frankie questions the teenager. To which the boy responds, still with a bite of food in his mouth.

"I would say that it was the easiest way to exchange for goods and services, but now I notice that there are a few people with a lot of money and a lot of people with little or no money at all. So the larger group, the poor, has no money or nothing to exchange," explains the boy proud of himself.

"You know, money was invented so commerce would become more manageable. But in no time, the ones who created money, whose primary ability and resource was mining, created the need for using *money* for every product transaction. This way, these tricky merchants had access to the products they could not obtain on their own. The only thing they had was gold and silver. These pieces of exchange were lent to people at a high-interest rate, so to speak. This way, when the debtors no longer had the means to pay, they lost all the assets they owned. Everything, absolutely everything, ended up in the hands of the creditors. This has been going on for hundreds and hundreds of years. In other words, Hen, money was created to strip people of all their hard-earned resources—" sighs Frank, then continues, "Once those resources entirely belong to a select group of people, money will no longer matter, and people will become consenting slaves to fulfill their bare necessities. This is the ultimate objective."

Henry believes Frank's hypothesis is not so crazy after all, it makes sense to the teen's ears. It somehow sounds like part of the domain plan the Tenshians were talking about.

"Now, just a few people inside the invisible walls suspect or know about the water crisis. I assure you that people outside the advantaged world have no idea about the *AQUA-DE-VITA* project, and will never find out. The Elite will not share the water with the purgatories once they find it. I do not think those bastards care about anyone outside the S.E.N.—" Frank says, "Thousands will starve to death, as drought and thirst scourge the countries outside these walls. After the water runs out, everything will fall into chaos even in the wealthy nations, and money will be put out of circulation. Only then, will people understand the only thing they really had was an account with imaginary digits stored in a database."

Frankie still talks about how money is nothing more than signed pieces of paper and has no real worth when a flash reaches Henry's mind showing him a clearer picture.

The famous musician was born and raised in an affluent family but hates what his relatives support, and condemns the suppressive mentality they promote.

Henry quickly realizes his eyes have been blinded by privilege all his life. But now that he sees the world for what it really is, he decides to go deeper down the rabbit hole.

"How long have you been thinking this, Frankie?"

Curiosity is now Henry's guide; the hunger for truth is now his motivation.

"Well, I started to suspect things were not fine in this world since I was a child, this is why I have always had issues with my family. I am not a violent man, so they see no threat in me when I say what I think. I must admit that everything became clearer when I heard your father, Khazios, talk about the stuff he used to."

Henry begins to believe there should be a different way for human existence—a freer life for all humans. Both remain in silence for a few minutes. Frankie gets some pistachios from the cabinet and sits down before he cracks the first one open. He offers Henry some, and even though the boy is not fond of pistachios, he gets a handful.

"You never know if this will be the last time I get to eat one!" says Henry, throwing one in his mouth.

The only sound in the room is that of pistachio shells being pulled apart. The musician and his godson sit next to each other, looking at the hills through the window.

"Frankie, I need to find the truth about our world. I need to leave this afternoon. There is so much I want to learn. Can you give me any ideas on where to find the answers I am looking for?"

"Of course, my boy, but we need to wait for your new documents to arrive, we cannot risk you being followed. We should focus on that first, then I will contact a trusted pilot so you can use my private jet; that way, you will be safe. Get ready, Hen, you need to tour the world in less than eighty days, and beat Jules Verne's Phileas Fogg—" he laughs hysterically, "I would love to join you in your quest, but I imagine they will soon send someone to watch me! I will be here having my boring days as usual. Everyone thinks I am still in Germany, which is good. But it will not be long before they find out I am back home, and they will come to interrogate me. They might even assign me a surveillance detail with some of those androids—" grunts Frank, "Once we receive your new documents, you need to be ready to leave the same day. In the meantime, get some rest and focus on all the harsh facts you will come across. I will make a list of the places you should visit. We cannot tell anyone, or contact anyone, as of right now everyone is an enemy, everyone we know will turn you in, and I believe you know that!"

After a brief pause, he adds, "You need to do this on your own."

Meanwhile, the surface leaders send troops to the purgatories. They are using the search for the Tenshians as an excuse to justify their violent interventions.

The world's Elite's biggest fear right now is the high power of the Tenshian ambassadors. They do not know if all of Tenshia's population has this mystical and supernatural power.

In that case, three guardians will not be an enemy to be handled with conventional weapons or any man-made armament. The influential leaders of the S.E.N. are aware it could become a war of epic proportions, unlike any other war the earth has seen before.

As the sun sets peacefully and the grass waves with the wind inside the enclosed territories, the international intelligence agency signs a contract with the government to guarantee the population reduction in the purgatories.

Through a visual wave emitted through all kinds of screens, no matter how small, they will influence individuals living in the purgatories, to commit suicide or murder each other.

The operation will start Sunday morning, and will not stop until the last inhabitant of the purgatories has been eliminated. Entire families—fathers, mothers, grandparents, and children, everyone close to a screen will be dead.

No human is immune to that kind of visual wave; no one will suspect the optical surge is responsible for the genocide.

Sunday arrives, and the first victims are found dead; panic downpours through the wretched cities. None of them are aware of what is happening, fear and uncertainty take over the purgatories. Each hour the death toll increases.

Homicidal madness flows through the streets and homes like lava sliding downhill, destroying everything in its path. Confused and stunned, the commoners look for answers in social media and news channels, ignoring that a simple glance at the screens brings the same punishing fate upon them.

S.E.N. agents and soldiers of the army arrive at the purgatories in their flying vessels. They pretend to be there to help with the crisis, but in reality, they come to clean up their mess. Soldiers pile up lifeless bodies as if they were dead animals, then load them in cargo ships that disappear seconds after taking off.

Chaos hits the streets; screaming, crying, shooting, agony, and hopelessness, is all these vile communities have left. In some cities, the few who discovered the danger was coming from a visual wave, destroyed the screens and are still alive in hiding, but not for long.

The military is relentless, and missile launchers are

ready to deliver upon the cities their deadliest loads.

Multiple blasts announce the end of hundreds of purgatories; the flames are so high they can be seen from miles away. The sky quickly fills with ashes accompanied by a reddish glow.

From miles under the Earth's surface, the three Tenshian guardians rush to the least affected areas. They believe they can still find people alive, but time is running out. Ikhabot and Silas are heading to South America, while Atmix flashes as a lightning bolt to Southeast Asia.

The guardians know the military has to be more careful in these areas. They cannot risk damaging the food supplies, silos, and crops located in the still-fertile purgatories.

In the southern hemisphere, Ikhabot tracks the aircraft hovering over a small city in Northern Brazil. These aircraft are still aiming their missiles at their targets, waiting for orders to strike. He knows what needs to be done to stop the attack.

In a split-second, three of the silent aircraft turn into war machines. Bursts of bullets and projectiles fly across the sky and yellow and red flashes of light fall over the city.

As one of the lethal missiles is launched from the aircraft, Ikhabot closes his eyes, places his hands close to his chest, with interlaced fingers. Then, he opens his eyes with a determined look, and full of supremacy, Ikhabot screams with his powerful voice.

"MaHott!"

Everything in seven square miles stays still, suspended in time, encased by a wave of magnetic energy. From the tiniest dust molecule to the largest aircraft in the army are left almost motionless. Ikhabot is the only one able to soar freely through the thin stationary air.

At an impressive speed, he gets all the pilots out of the flying vehicles and takes them to open space far from the range of the explosion. At that moment, Ikhabot, with incredible strength, hits the projectile breaking it into a thousand pieces that start floating in the air as if gravity did not exist.

The scene, seen from the ground, is as fascinating as it is terrifying. The sky suddenly lights up like a mosaic of colors, fire, and smoke. A single man furrows the heavens, and with his own hands, crushes and destroys every single one of the attack planes into pieces.

In less than two minutes, all the war crafts are reduced to smoldering debris. Pilots and soldiers stare perplexed at their flying machines reduced to ashes. They have a nameless fear of the young man, who, like a destroying angel, humiliated everything they believed invincible.

Thirteen miles west, Silas locates incoming troops. Six thousand men with tanks and rovers riding down the road with the sole purpose of terminating every human being in the remaining towns.

The humble Tenshian strolls following the line on the old hot pavement road.

In the distance, he can see the dust kicked up by the military convoy driving toward him. The tanks stop a few yards from where Silas is standing. One of the dudes in uniform jumps off of one of the jeeps and warns him not to make a move and identify himself.

Silas replies, "My name is not relevant, and you should consider going back the same way you came!"

The man does not take Silas's words too well; without hesitation, orders his men to open fire. These men are trained to follow orders and be hostile.

Terror seizes all those present when the bullets simply dodge the strange individual who approaches the convoy as if fleeing from his presence.

The aggressive men are now devoured by fear, which increases the number of bullets flying through the air. Hundreds of rounds per minute. Some of them run toward Silas with sharp knives.

He observes static, analyzing, and prepares for his next move. Right before they can reach him, he takes a deep breath and whispers to the heavens.

"Power of Gaivur!"

The soldiers running to attack him, and those standing by the rovers, are left as if they had no mind. Docile as puppets of flesh and blood without a puppeteer to handle them. Ready to receive and execute any order. Silas looks at them with pity, feeling somehow guilty of having to do such a thing. With no choice, Silas thinks of the best way to finish this.

"Go! Take all your weapons and artillery and get out of here. Destroy the military base you came from and give up your military lives forever."

Without a peep, the battalion turns the tanks and trucks around and disappears on the horizon without leaving a trace of blood. The S.E.N.'s mission in South America is over. Their plan to massacre all humans in the purgatories and claim the right over the remaining drinking water is completed.

Halfway around the planet, Atmix does what necessary to get the survivors out of the conflict zone and make sure the troops stop the attack, which he accomplishes with brutal efficiency. Atmix is a fighter gifted with an indomitable spirit and tremendous physical power.

Minutes after the three guardians manage to frustrate the S.E.N.'s attacks on the purgatories, they come together and decide to take the survivors to Tenshia, where they will be safe for the time being.

Back at the S.E.N.'s headquarters, the tactical leaders are furious and exasperated after receiving a report about the Tenshians' intervention in South America and Southeast Asia.

"The world can never know about the latest events involving these strange aliens. They exceed the power of our most advanced weaponry. They make hundreds of years of war technology development seem like a waste of time," fumes one of the higher-ups.

"Yes, Minister, we need to do something about it. Secretary-General, any thoughts on this matter?"

The secretary-general, taking into account the visitors' outrageous power, decides to secretly contact a shady and plutocrat individual who calls himself The Prince.

For the majority of mankind, he is just a legend. But according to those who know him, he has saved the earth from several crises throughout history.

The common man has never heard of him before; most even think that mentioning his existence is the most ridiculous speculation. The rumors heard about this being sound as if coming out of a fiction novel.

Only a select group of people know who he truly

is, and the secretary-general is one of them. Mr. McArthur, the Minister of Defense, and another one of the top executives leave the meeting room, followed by two of their bodyguards. They climb to the rooftop and get into an HMX-1 helicopter.

Hours later, Steve McArthur and his companions chat in the presidential suite of a luxurious resort located on an island not registered on any map. Sitting before their eyes is The Prince, accompanied by a gorgeous young woman, and standing behind them, a few goons. They all have beautiful countenance and notable appearances.

"Greetings, Steve, to what do I owe your unexpected visit? I hope it is something I am unaware of. You very well know that 'time' is coming to an end. My time is considered a high-value commodity."

The Prince's mauve eyes rest with high expectations on the secretary general's face, who has a shiny bead of sweat trickling down his temple.

"The motive I come before you today is due to a group of angelical looking beings we have encountered. We have no clue of where they dwell, but their powers immensely surpass human capability. I witnessed their supremacy when the council refused to sign a ridiculous scroll of petitions they presented in exchange for the fresh water they possess. They have extraordinary abilities, and we do not have the resources to match their greatness. Less than forty-eight hours ago, only three of these individuals managed to frustrate the decimating of the population, by displaying hulking skill and determination. I'm afraid this is an enemy with whom we cannot fight militarily, they are beyond our league. It might be time for you to take charge of the situation," mutters the secretary.

Sitting still, with his eyes fixed on McArthur's face, The Prince takes several seconds to answer.

"I am already fully informed of everything that is happening on Earth. Have you forgotten that I find pleasure in overseeing and obtaining every piece of information available? There is nothing you can tell me that I do not already know. You were not even capable of finding out where they come from, unavailing as usual. But now that you are here and have the audacity to waste my time with information that is not new to me, allow me to ask my daughter to kiss you goodbye."

The young and astonishing woman stands and walks toward McArthur in a ravishing red dress. Leaning over him, she gently kisses his lips, sucking the life out of his body in seconds, leaving his mummified body sitting on a velvet chair.

The secretary's companions lie stupefied in their seats, governed by the deepest of terrors. The imposing mauve-eyed man stares piercingly at the secretary general's companions who are both pale and petrified.

With a grin and his eyes locked on them, he addresses his goons after taking a sip of liquor.

"Phillip! Dracco! Arrange the search for the boy that knows the visitors, do not hurt him, just bring him to my city. We will treat him well and get all the information I desire. Look for him over land and sea, I need him alive, and I need him now! Understood?"

Meanwhile, back at Frank Waltz's house, Henry waits for his false identity documents to arrive. Eight days have passed, and the boy has done everything he can possibly do to remain sane.

Frankie comes into the room and tells him the new passport is ready, "you need to leave right away!"

The musician drives fast to a private airport in the middle of nowhere, considerable miles away from his house. Entering a top-notch hangar,

Henry sees the beautiful private jet. Frank introduces the kid to the pilot, retired Sgt. Conner, and tells the boy he would trust the guy with his own life. Mr. Waltz hands Conner a small briefcase and turns around to give Hen a tight loving hug.

With tears in his eyes, he wishes the boy good luck and gives him a piece of paper with the places he should visit.

"Son, remember to be open-minded. Observe, examine, contemplate everything, and most importantly, as your mother used to say, Make your miracle happen! Conner will keep you safe. He knows the secret routes and is an expert landing in extreme conditions," reassures Frankie.

Henry hugs his friend once more before stepping into the Eclipse that will take him and Conner around the world. The inside of the jet is ridiculous in the boy's eyes—taupe interior, a minibar, and a 65-inch screen.

He sits on one of the reclining seats and fastens his seatbelt. He looks out the window at the Swiss Alps while the jet takes off.

An hour after departure, Hen seats in the cockpit chatting with Conner. They talk about school, girls and other frivolous things.

Then, teared up, Henry tells the pilot about his mother's death. Suddenly, Conner receives a signal from one of the two Italian aircraft flying behind them.

"Questo è Alpha-Charlie-Romeo cinque due nove, ora sei nello spazio aereo italiano e devi atterrare immediatamente. Tutti i passeggeri devono avere i loro documenti di identità pronti. Ripeto, questo è Alpha-Charlie-Romeo cinque due nove, ora sei nello spazio aereo italiano e devi atterrare immediatamente. Tutti i passeggeri devono avere i documenti di identità pronti."

"What the heck?" spouts Henry.

"Fasten your seatbelt, we need to land immediately!" rushes Conner.

Conner begins to descend escorted by the two military aircraft. Once they land in Milan, Conner opens the door, and three agents come on board. The teenager hands them his passport and stands in silence, waiting for his documents to be verified.

A blend of fear, adrenaline, and anxiety are ironically keeping the kid calm. At the same time, Conner talks to them with a peacefulness challenging to imitate.

The retired pilot gives the agents the information they want to hear and tells them the boy is his nephew. The military patrol agents offer sincere apologies and let the two men return to the aircraft and continue with their journey.

The same thing happens several times before

leaving the countries of the S.E.N.

Several hours later, exhausted due to the lack of sleep, fear, and stress, Henry and Sgt. Conner, manage to cross the invisible walls.

They leave the affluent territories of the S.E.N., and finally land in the desert a couple of miles from Henry's first destination, Egypt.

Conner and young Schulze climb off the jet and hop on an empty old jeep waiting for them on top of a sand dune. Cruising through the pale sand at about fifty miles per hour, Henry starts to see the city of Cairo a few miles ahead. He notices how the entire region has been brutally ravaged by the S.E.N. army.

The soldiers must have trashed the place looking for the Tenshians.

In fact, the army destroyed everything wherever they went, and apparently turned the city of Cairo into a ghost town; there is not much left to see. What Frank Waltz thought the boy could find in that place might no longer exist.

"I do not think anyone back home knows the situation has taken this destructive path. It was a terrible idea to visit the purgatories," mumbles Henry.

Everything has been completely desolated. Henry has a feeling he could also be exposed out there. Some of those areas might still be heavily surveilled by the S.E.N. It makes sense to the kid to assume that every territory outside the invisible walls has also been destroyed. Risking his life to continue with the journey is pointless.

Conner turns the jeep around and heads back to the jet. The teen spots a sandstorm approaching from the east. They need to hurry before it gets too close.

Jumping off the jeep, they rush into the jet, but it is too late to take off. They barely make it inside the plane to take shelter from the tons of sand and strong winds.

Henry sees the jeep disappear in the sand while the carbon fiber walls of the aircraft shudder; everything outside gets darker. The wind is so intense and abrupt, the jet starts shaking, and the frontal landing gear begins to bounce off the runway.

"This is not a regular sand storm, the wind should not have such power," Conner yells.

The boy panics and tries to hold on tight to one of the panels dividing the cabin from the cockpit, his weak body cannot move.

"I cannot believe that I am about to die again," howls the teenager.

The high winds tilt the aircraft, and the left and front wheels are lifted off the ground. All of a sudden, Frankie's jet is no longer touching the runway.

Henry manages to reach one of the seats while the plane is beaten by the wind and sand. He clings to it using all his strength, stretches the seatbelt, and fastens it tightly around his waist.

Everything is whipped. Abruptly, the expensive plane is flipped upside down and begins to spin in circles. There is no use in shouting. They are going to die.

Conner attempts to level the jet, but he does not succeed and screams again, "hold on tight, kid!"

Unexpectedly, the airplane enters a strange type of non-gravity zone, and the wind seems to ease, stabilizing the aircraft. Hovering still in the middle of the storm, Henry looks out the window and sees sand still twirling around the private jet.

The experienced pilot does not understand how that is possible; neither does the kid. The flying vessel is pushed down by an unknown force and begins to free fall vertically, but the speed decreases instead of increasing until they land in a beautiful garden in the middle of the desert. Someone is evidently controlling the aircraft from the outside.

Could it be Ikhabot saving my life again?

MIZRAIM

Henry's mind searches for a logical explanation. Coherent situations seem improbable following his first encounter with the Tenshians.

Is it even reasonable to explain to my brain what my eyes have seen in the past month?

He thinks overwhelmed, and befuddled. The garden is the prettiest garden both men have ever seen in their lives. Two men wait for the pilot and the boy at the end of a shiny ivory path. Both are blond and tall and wear black designer suits and thin black ties; they welcome Henry.

What shocks the teenager the most about the entire situation, is their pets; two leopards with glistening white gold leashes sitting alongside each one of the men. Henry has not seen many live animals.

He has only seen very few cats and dogs owned by

the wealthiest and most influential people, besides a few wild animals kept in the sanctuaries. Having a pet is more than a luxury in the world he knows.

"Welcome, gentlemen! The Prince appreciates your visit."

The Prince? Who is this guy living in a sumptuous oasis in the heart of the Sahara? Besides being able to control the airplane and bring us here? Wonders young Schulze. *Perhaps he is even able to control the sand storms?*

"Where are we?" inquires Conner.

"We are not authorized to disclose any information. We have orders to take you safely to his Majesty, The Prince."

"If we deny going with this Prince, what would happen to us?" replies Conner with haughtiness learned after years of service in the air force.

"Why would you reject The Prince? He will be deeply offended, and to be honest, I do not recommend flustering his Majesty. He is not a tranquil individual, much less when his guests refuse his invitation. Besides, how are you planning to go back? I believe your aircraft is in no condition to fly."

They turn and smirk at each other, like two kids plotting a prank. Henry notices they do not have a choice but to go with the two men.

One of them slowly opens a limo door inviting the

kid and the sergeant in with a grin on his pale face. Conner and Henry have no choice but to get in and find out who *His Majesty* is.

As they ride in the lavish limousine, the boy cannot help to notice the massive pyramid in the center of the oasis. It must be as tall as a two hundred story-high building.

The masterpiece seems to be the city itself. It has roads on the inside, and some can be seen from the outside. The limousine enters the structure through a big granite arch. People on the streets dressed in spectacular thawbs stare at the limo as it drives by.

The architecture of this place is captivating; both Henry and Conner stare astounded. Various granite pillars hold the edifice together, so tall, they are almost impossible to track. Water flowing from white granite fountains, amid gorgeous gardens, make beautiful rainbows when hit by the shining sun rays.

The place is unimaginable. Each lantern along the avenues is plated in gold.

Street market stands, with the most beautiful fruits, adorn the alleys, as well as workshops with fine silks, linens, and jewelry showcases. The parks are decorated with statues in granite; everything is impeccable. The lawn seems to be greener; the flowers are prettier than anywhere else on the surface.

Men and women walk through the markets in

their thobes, finely sewn with gold thread. The pyramid city is as ostentatious as it is spectacular. The monument spreads for at least ten square miles.

After driving for thirty minutes, they arrive at a mansion on the last level of the pyramid city. A beautiful park with a flawlessly mowed lawn and a small lake can be seen from the mansion's terrace.

Tall palm trees and immaculate landscaping decorate the boulevard. The front yard is full of winged humanoid monuments that the boy had never seen before.

Everything is built of white granite and gold. Statues of chimeras align along the sidewalks, and at the center of the park, an enormous dragon-looking sculpture coiled around a six-story-high column rises to the top of the desert city.

Entering the mansion, the pilot and the teenager walk to a great hall where they are being expected by a peculiar gentleman.

A very handsome man with shiny navy hair and big mauve eyes looks at the boy from his chair. Henry finds that the man is hard to look at and cannot explain the strange feeling.

His appearance, even though striking, is weird and extremely intimidating. The energy coming from him is cold and somewhat dark, despite his looks.

Henry cannot stop looking at the mesmerizing

individual. The handsome stranger stands and welcomes the visitors.

"Come in, gentlemen. Welcome to my home, the little city of Mizraim is happy to host you. Get comfortable, it is an honor to have you two as my guests. You will find this city so charming that you will never want to leave—" squints and smiles gently, "Do you know why you were brought here?"

"No, we have no idea; in fact, we thought we were going to die in the sand storm," the boy answers fast, awaiting an explanation.

"Ah! The sandstorm, of course. Truth is, have I not intervened, you would be dead. Tartuross relishes pranks; bad, bad pranks," snickers as he slowly stirs the drink he has been holding since Henry and Conner walked into the great hall.

Henry is clueless about who this Tartuross guy is, but it all points at him being responsible for the sand storm. Conner looks at the kid.

The retired pilot has never been so terrified in his life. Henry, on the other hand, is not very surprised. Not after meeting the Tenshians.

There are beings with incredible power among people. Henry thinks. *The kind of power that overcomes the laws of nature.*

The air force sergeant fears for his life. The pink on his cheeks is gone, along with his peace, and his mind. The teenager remembers the feeling when he first started to hear about supernatural humans; he could hardly believe it.

Henry feels sorry and can only imagine what is going through Conner's head right now.

The pilot's mind is just coming to terms with the idea of being alive after the sandstorm. He will need more time to understand that the wind and the aircraft were being controlled by a man called Tartuross.

The Tsar of Mizraim notes the air force pilot is overwhelmed and addresses him once more after taking another sip of his exclusive liquor.

"It is not my intention to pester you right now; please allow one of my servants to escort you to your chambers. There, you can rest and get cleaned up. You are more than welcome to join me for dinner later tonight. That way, we can get to know each other better."

Conner stares at the boy dubiously as they both walk down the hallway to the guest bedroom. The major-domo opens the doors to the room, and they step inside. He shuts the door behind them.

The suite, quite like the rest of the place, does not skimp on luxuries and comfort. The pilot appears to have a lot of questions, but they both fall asleep the minute their bodies touch the huge mattress embedded in the floor of the opulent chamber.

Henry wakes up before Conner, he saunters to the vanity and stares at his face losing track of time. His hair is a mess, there is sand on it still. The dark circles under his eyes make the boy's face look paler than the day before. He has lost more weight since his mother died.

Looking withered and miserable, he opens the gold faucet in the ceramic tub and lets the water run until it gets warm.

The sun coming in through the window brightens the white and gold tiles on the bathroom floor. The teen stands in front of a large mirror on the wall and pulls his shirt off.

The reflection of the light makes his torso seem thinner than he is used to. Obviously, the nerdy kid has never been an athletic guy but has not once seen his ribs and collarbone wanting to pierce out of his fair skin.

The young man gets in the tub and soaks his body in the warm water.

I am, once again, thankful to be alive.

At sunset, one of the butlers knocks. Conner opens the doors. The kind man hands him a pile of fresh white tunics and courteously addresses the pilot.

"The Prince awaits; dinner will be served shortly."

Entering the dining hall, Henry notices they were not the only ones invited to the feast. There are ten spots at a long table, and all of them are filled except the ones reserved for Conner and him. Somewhat timid, Henry pulls out the chair next to Conner's, as The Prince gestures to them to sit. The pilot seems to be less tense as if comfortably sedated.

Looking at the expensive chandelier hanging from the ceiling, young Schulze gets the feeling of being watched by someone across the table, to the left of his Majesty. The teenager lifts his chin slowly to see who this person is as he intends to sit.

Good heavens!

The boy's eyes are fixed on her. Time slows down. Everything around the young woman becomes blurry, and the voices around him muffled. She is the most spectacular human being that Henry has ever seen in his short life. She is perfect.

Celestial. Stunning. Breathtaking.

A girl has never made him feel a rush of heat, he feels his skinny body burning on the inside. He is consumed by her beauty.

Abruptly, the face of Aurora pops in Henry's mind but is outshined hastily by this woman's splendor.

The teenager begins to sweat as the stunning lady leers at him. Her liquid gold-colored eyes are stuck looking straight at the boy's eyes. The nervy boy tries to find the seat beneath him, but it appears that the world underneath his body has disappeared.

Clumsily, he sits down and presses his sweaty hands tightly between his knees, trying to hide the uncomfortable, yet exhilarating feeling.

I want to know everything about her, I want to get lost in her gorgeous eyes.

Henry thinks as adrenaline pumps through his veins, and he can hardly contain his accelerated breath.

"Henry," The Prince calls the boy's name, forcing him out of his daydream, "...allow me to introduce you to my daughter. Cristabella, this is Henry, our visitor. He got here almost by accident."

The Prince just called me by my real name. How can this be? Henry thinks. *This guy has more information than I can imagine. Am I in danger?*

"Almost? You know there are no accidents, Dad!" she tells him without taking her eyes off of the shy teenage boy as he tries to catch his breath before speaking and make a fool of himself.

"I—I am pleased...pleased to meet you," stutters Henry.

"The pleasure is mine, Hen. May I call you that?" answers Cristabella, chuckling, and snapping Henry out of his worries for the time being.

"Absolutely, that is how my mother used to call me!" Henry giggles trying to hide his grief.

Why would I say that? That is how my mother

used to call me. Why would she need to know that? I am an imbecile. Now she is going to think me a momma's boy, which I probably am anyway.

Henry ponders as he blushes.

After hearing the people talk at the table and Conner interacting with the gentleman sitting next to him, Henry gets more comfortable. The Swiss boy and the retired pilot enjoy the moment.

Everything is splendid, top restaurant food choices, silver cutlery, and the most exquisite porcelain china.

The fear Conner and young Schulze had when they first met The Prince, has dissipated. The more both eat and drink, the more relaxed they feel.

At the end of the feast, Conner and Henry feel among friends overlooking the danger they really might be in. The air around the ballroom is loaded with comfort, vogue, and luxury.

It is just like the parties the boy used to go to with his mother, but way more extravagant.

"Bella, would you like to show our dear Hen around? Take'im around the city and show him how to have fun with some of your friends," The Prince entreats his gorgeous daughter as he wipes his lips tenderly with a thousand-thread linen napkin.

"Absolutely Daddy, I'd be pleased. I promise you he will have the time of his life."

"Marvelous! If you are so pleased, I assume it would be no problem for you to be Henry's personal hostess, and show him around Mizraim. Please, take him everywhere with you for as long as he decides to stay," crows the fine gentleman.

"Sure, Dad! Leave everything to me."

Shortly after everyone finished eating dessert, and The Tsar orders the servants to clear the table, Cristabella stands up and walks toward the teenage boy in her short burgundy dress. She grabs Hen by the wrist, almost lifting him off his chair, bringing her bright lips to the boy's ear and whispers.

"It is time to go and have some real fun."

The boy has no choice but to go with her, not that he would not enjoy going with her anyway. The teenager takes a tour around Mizraim in Cristabella's sports car.

The city is a splurge of wealth. Henry wonders who this family with such power is.

Who is this Prince? He has a perfect society in the middle of the desert.

Henry ponders as the girl drives. Thinking about his mother, Ikhabot, and the water crisis, the boy can hardly believe what his eyes are seeing. The city itself is a miracle.

Cristabella and Henry arrive at the central park.

It is huge. Henry remembers the old magazines he

found in his mother's closet several years ago. The park reminds him of a panoramic view of New York City's Central Park he saw in one of the articles.

Bella and Hen walk around the beautiful gardens talking about the city. She tells him pretty much everything entertaining about their society; it is all fascinating to the boy.

The gorgeous woman shows Hen the statues in the park and explains to him the meaning of most of the street art. He is just hypnotized by her, totally bedazzled; everything Bella says is so exciting, and her voice alone is charming.

Shortly, the thoughts about his mother fade away, and Henry gets trapped by Mizraim's nightlife vibe. All the questions the teen had are gone, the feelings he had were replaced by glee, yearning, and curiosity.

Henry enjoys Bella's company, and her friends seem to be kind to him too. She makes the boy feel a combination of delight and desire, making him feel relaxed.

Never being surrounded by this many people his age, Henry realizes they seem to be enjoying his company too.

I actually feel welcomed and popular. This is the first time I have a beautiful girl wanting to do anything I want. I never thought a girl like Cristabella, with her astonishing looks and big circle of friends, would take an interest in me.

No one besides his mother has made him feel so important. "This is paradise!" The boy's heart and soul wrap around the inexplicable joyfulness, spread by all those around him. The young group party, dance, and laugh.

"Cheers to Mizraim! This is the best night of my life," shouts the boy raising his glass.

Driving back to the mansion, Hen looks out the window at the desert sky and the city lights, totally forgetting the purpose of his journey. Why leave? All he wants is to enjoy the place. The city and its people make young Henry feel plenitude.

I am sure, now that I have been from one place to another, Mizraim has the best artists, top professionals, finest chefs, and the smartest professors. The Prince has gathered the world's best and brought them here to have them at his service. Everyone seems comfortable, happy, and entirely satisfied in every aspect.

Back at The Tsar's contemporary palace, he looks at Cristabella, not wanting the night to end. She holds his hand as they both walk down the hall. Henry can tell she feels very comfortable with him.

She takes him upstairs and opens a double door to her bedroom. The place is massive and gallantly decorated. The young man stands in the middle of the room and takes a few seconds to look around.

The living area has a stylish leather sofa with cedar armrests, the coffee table is a cut trunk of an ancient tree, he can tell by the number of rings in it. The centerpiece catches the boy's attention.

It looks like some horned creature Henry does not recognize, but decides to ignore its creepiness and turns his gaze back to Cristabella.

She is delicately taking her high heels off, sitting on one of the stools at the bar.

Bella pulls out a champagne bottle and pours herself a glass. She then walks toward the couch and invites him over.

With one clap, the lights dim in a soft scarlet hue.

Right after, she says something in a language unknown to the boy, and soft music starts playing in the background. Henry sits on a comfortable sofa, not too close to the alluring young woman.

Then, young Schulze notices how she stares at him with her ochroid, sublime-looking eyes.

"So Hen, what do you think about everything you have seen today?"

"Everything is wonderful, I am spellbound by the town and every person you introduced me to tonight. The places we toured are amazing, the park, even the view from your room is unbelievable. I wonder if all the city is like what I saw today and if every person living here has similar living conditions."

"Most live as comfortably as possible, almost everybody has the same living standard. Here, everyone is happy; people only worry about pleasing themselves. They all worship The Prince, just because of the joy of being a Mizraim citizen. They can have whatever they wish for, without limits, guilt, or regrets, becoming addicted to instant gratification. They are so used to the comfort my dad provides, that they would kill or die for this place."

"But, it becomes a problem when everyone fancies the same thing, I guess!"

"Not really. My dad makes sure everyone gets exactly what they want, whenever they want it, the way they want it. The only restriction is meaning to rule, and no one really craves for that. My dad does it exquisitely, so nobody inside Mizraim wants his place," explains the young woman.

"I still do not understand how everyone would get even their slightest wish fulfilled," queries Henry.

"There is nothing my dad cannot bring to Mizraim. You will see for yourself soon. But enough of him, I want to know more about you. What do you think of me?" she chortles at her new friend as she asks the piercing question.

The blood streaming through Henry's veins rushes, and the warm sensation returns. Henry has never been in a similar situation with a girl. So he chooses to be honest with her.

"I am very attracted to you, but out of curiosity, how old are you?" mumbles nervously.

"Old enough to be holding a glass of Champagne." The girl teases him.

"You want to kiss me, right?" she taunts.

Henry's hands start sweating. He is not sure what to say.

I do want to kiss her, but what is she going to think if I tell her so. What if she feels uncomfortable? What if I deny it instead, will I lose my chance?

The abashed teen debates, trying to encourage himself to tell her how he truly feels.

"That is all I have wanted to do since I first saw you."

Cristabella grabs her glass of champagne, almost empty already, and takes her last sip. She then stands up from the other side of the sectional sofa and walks toward the visitor.

Henry rubs his hands against the linen tunic, seeking to dry his wet palms. His heart is pumping, and he struggles to control his breath.

The charming girl sits next to him and slides her fingers behind his neck. Shivers go down the boy's spine as she gently pulls his hair.

Before Henry is even able to get his thoughts

together, she leans against him, and her lips find his.

"You know, Hen, you can stay here with me if you wish."

Cristabella winks at him, gets up and walks away to a lounge behind a granite chimney. He follows her crazy in love.

Henry lies in bed and closes his eyes; burning sweat drips down his face. He feels like there is no time, there is no space, and his body floats in the infinite cosmos.

With one faint clap, Cristabella commands the double doors to her room to lock themselves and then lies down next to him.

Henry sees the sun rising behind the dunes of Mizraim. Cristabella, resting next to the young man, looks at him with her dreamy eyes as she rubs his hair.

"I am in a perfect house, in a perfect city, with a perfect girl. How did I get so lucky all of a sudden?" he whispers.

Her warm breath on his neck and her delicate face against his skin is now his most cherished feeling. Closing his eyes, he unfolds into her arms again, and they both fall asleep.

Henry wakes up, it is dark outside. He looks at the

time and realizes it is past midnight as he walks to the bathroom in the dim room.

The teen splashes cold water on his face before seeing his reflection in the mirror.

Instantly he realizes he has lost count of how many days they have been locked in the girl's boudoir. He does not remember eating anything, yet his body seems well-nourished and toned.

I do not understand. How is this possible?

Cristabella walks into the bathroom and hugs him from behind. She kisses the boy's left shoulder as he looks at her reflection in the mirror.

"Hey, handsome! How does it feel to not leave a room for four days?" laughs the girl.

Four days! This is insane, I have not eaten in four days, and I still have this rush of energy rushing through my body?

The teenager thinks turning around and holding his new girlfriend in between his arms. She makes him feel romantic—in love, crazy for her.

Nothing else matters to the boy right now, he just wants her to kiss him over and over again.

In Mizraim, life is perfect. There is nothing to fear. His Majesty provides everything the citizens want and need.

Nothing is too much, nothing is an excess. No one judges what they wish for, people just receive it, no questions asked.

People have nothing to worry about in Mizraim, they will never lack anything and will have endless joy. It is like being in an elevated mindset where they just need to wish for something to obtain it.

A few days later, Henry meets with The Tsar of Mizraim again. The incredibly handsome individual talks to the teenager in such a natural way.

He does not seem to know his daughter has been locked in her bedroom with the boy for days—or at least he pretends not to know.

"Good morning, Henry, have you been having fun? Is Cristabella treating you well?"

Henry timidly answers to his Majesty's question. He tries to sound casual, acting as if nothing extraordinary is happening.

"Everything has been great, sir. Thank you for asking. I actually wanted to know if there is a way for me to become a citizen of Mizraim. I would like to stay here permanently."

"You are a wise boy. Fine, consider it done! You are most welcome here. All you need is to tell me how you can contribute to this great civilization, and we will make it official."

Even though he smiles and looks peaceful, Henry notices each one of his words comes out with a thoughtful purpose.

"Conner, your pilot, has been asking me about you. I told him you were a bit busy with my Cristabella. He requested to stay in Mizraim as well—" comments The Prince, arching his right eyebrow when mentioning his daughter.

He chuckles and continues, "Certain procedures need to be followed before you can become a citizen Henry. These are essential to keep our paradise running. But before going into detail, I am interested in some information I know you possess. So I wanted to ask just out of curiosity. Where is this great freshwater ocean? Who guards this magnificent place? It is an intriguing story, I find it fascinating, and I would like to meet their guardians someday."

Henry's heart drops to the bottom of his ribcage. The teen cannot believe The Tsar knows about the freshwater ocean and his connection to Tenshia.

Is this why I am here? Could this be the real reason why our plane was brought to Mizraim?

He thinks, trying to remain calm.

The dread he has had for weeks swiftly comes back to his body.

I am going to be handed back to the S.E.N. He thinks, striving to hide his fear. *I am going to die*

"Sorry to tell you, sir, but I do not know much about them. I do not even remember the name of the place."

The Prince knows the boy is not telling him the truth.

"Do not worry, kid, you will remember at the right moment. In the meantime, continue to enjoy your time here in my city."

Several days go by, and Henry cannot keep his mind off Cristabella, she is the boy's new hobby. Even though he wishes they could spend more time alone, she takes him out for a stroll through the pyramid city.

With time, young Henry forgets about the uncomfortable moment with The Prince.

He goes back to being sedated by the luxurious metropolis. People on the streets look happy; no one seems stressed or troubled about anything. People can use their time freely unless summoned by his Majesty. They tend to him with a smile on their faces. In return, people get long lives, freedom, and infinite joy.

The pyramid city is beyond many people's wildest dreams. There is no need for a god to pray to; no evil, no accidents, no adverse consequences, or shadow of death. Fear is an unfamiliar feeling to any of Mizraim's citizens.

Walking around the higher levels of the city, Henry is taken aback by meeting celebrities and scientists who no longer live in the world he knows. Society believes they are all dead.

Some of them are even in history books and have memorials in their honor. Still, they are right there, in the beautiful city in the middle of ever-changing dunes in the Saharan desert.

Most of them enjoy unnatural longevity, easily surpassing eight hundred years of age. The teen starts to feel alarmed about the peculiar situation.

The famous people Henry presumed dead, make him hark back to his endeared mother. Young Schulze keeps Minerva in his thoughts until they go back to the mansion.

Once in Cristabella's bedroom, the boy cannot help to feel discontented; if his mother was still alive, he could have brought her to Mizraim. Yet she lived such a short life, and it is all his fault.

Cristabella notices the young guy's thoughts are off. "What's wrong handsome?" she asks him

Henry tells her what happened and omits every detail regarding the Tenshians. Young Henry asks his girlfriend how come the people they saw today are still alive, but she eludes talking about it.

"I don't know, you should go see my father!"

Two days later, Henry has the opportunity to speak with his Majesty about his worries. He believes it is unfair his mother had to die, and yet some people in Mizraim live for centuries. So Henry chooses to ask The Prince.

"I see that you are a smart young man, Henry. You noticed some celebrities walking around Mizraim after they decided to disappear from the world's spotlight. You are probably asking yourself, how some of them are still alive after many centuries," the Tsar replies tittering.

"Yes! How is that possible?" Henry's answer comes out a little aggressive, maybe as a result of the pain and jealousy for they are alive and his mother is not.

"You see, Henry, the response to your problem is a lot more complicated than it seems. But I will try my best to put it into words you can understand. After all, I already consider you part of the family."

The teenager's face reddens assuming Mizraim's Tsar knows what he and Cristabella have been up to all these days.

"Any human being has the capability of generating sufficient energy to transform anything and everything in this realm. The important fact here, my dear Henry, is that most humans do not know this. It would be dangerous for a select group of individuals, including myself if the average man were to learn this piece of information. We have accomplished to transform the majority of mankind into a massive negative-energy generator. This energy, we harvest and absorb. In other words, this energy is what we use to stay alive…"

Henry has come face to face with surreal situations recently. But soon, his mind will be blown away beyond his imagination

"Allow me to explain that a little bit better—all the vitality needed in Mizraim is obtained in different ways. The biggest percentage is a product of the negative emotions people experience daily outside of these walls. The emotion we harvest the most energy from is fear. The best part, Henry, is that everybody fears—" the Tsar chuckles and continues, "Our other source—is the misuse of a man's seed. The incorrect use of sexuality is key, and sincerely, it is our preferred form of energy! Last but not least, all the dead whose souls do not return to the source of light, are ours to feast on."

Henry promptly recalls his mother's death; he wonders if that was her soul's destiny.

He aches to ask The Prince about his mother's soul, but frightened decides it is best not to know. Instead, the boy asks something else he finds intriguing.

"Sir, what do you mean by misused seed?"

"Do not worry about that now. It is not my purpose to overwhelm you with information. I surely have more answers than you have questions. I just want you to understand how lucky you are to be here with us now," The Prince's delicate robe waves with the breeze as he walks to a carved ivory desk. He sits down and stirs a cup of tea just poured by one of his maids.

"Let me tell you something to wrap up our conversation. The more chaos we cause in the outside world, the greater the amount of energy we harvest. As long as the common man continues to ignore their true purpose, their lives are nothing more than a carousel of rage, hatred, fear, sorrow, murders, wars, marriage, romance, and sexual immorality. The best of it all is, the most barbarous chaos can be, sometimes, mistaken as harmony," he explains as he sips his tea, "At the end of the ride, they lose their souls to us. And this, my boy, is why we will continue to harvest, transform, and utilize this energy. Mankind will remain subdued and give us what we need to be invincible, at least until we shift this creation into exactly what we intend it to be."

The look on his pale face, as saying those words, is ghastly. It all seems like a horror movie that Henry desperately needs to get out of.

A revolting fluid swirls in the pit of his stomach. Abruptly, all the pleasure he has felt so far becomes a burden.

The boy's eyes had been blinded by desire, but he wakes up from the inexplicable numbness. Henry's mind takes him back to the last memories of his mother; her dead body lying on a bed at Ikhabot's place, and her burial in Tenshia.

Shaking his head, he tries to get rid of these dark and unwelcome thoughts.

"Are you alright, Henry? I understand how hard it must be for a young man like you to accept this truth, but you will get used to it once you understand your new nature. I will show you how to train your soul to receive and enjoy these benefits, despite the gruesome consequences for others. It will take some time to dispose of that feeling of guilt. Meanwhile, breathe some freedom and appreciate what you have right now."

His spirit is at war.

What should I do?

There is no safe place for his heart to entrench amid his fight. Even though Henry wishes to make a new life in Mizraim, the idea of people having to live a miserable existence for his own benefit sounds disgusting.

Henry suddenly remembers the hope in Frankie's eyes before he left on his quest.

I cannot grow part of The Prince's evil society.

He reflects before addressing the Tsar.

I am sorry your highness, but I must decline your offer. I am leaving right now! And I am not leaving alone, I am taking Cristabella with me."

A slight grin saturated with cynicism pops on The Tsar's perfect face before reacting to the boy's pathetic attempt to leave.

"Unfortunately, my dear guest, the only one who can get you out of here is me. And as I mentioned previously, you are now part of my family, and I never let go of my family. Allow me to say that Cristabella would never leave this place either. I have spent a long time away from my father, and I could not stand my daughter doing the same. So I am afraid that your departure is not possible. The quicker you accept it, the more pleasant your life will be here in Mizraim. You are the one to decide whether you make this a living hell or a paradise if any of those two exist! What if I make you a deal so ridiculous, it will erase all doubt from your mind?"

Young Henry has no idea what The Prince is going to propose.

"Would you consider changing your mind, if I were to bring your mother back from the dead to live here in Mizraim?"

Checkmate! The powerful man reclines back on

his chair with open arms and a convincing evil grin on his face. Henry's brain freezes. Time and space disappear from his senses, just like before when he traveled with Ikhabot.

Still, and remaining in the same spot, his heartbeat echoes in his ears from the sudden excitement and rush of adrenaline. The boy forgets any feeling of compassion for the commoners in seconds. He would sacrifice as many lives as necessary to hug his sweet mother again.

"Yes! Yes! Please, your highness, do it now if possible!" He pleads, falling on his knees under the mighty Prince's nose. The teen begs with his eyes filled with tears and quickly goes from demanding to leave to imploring to stay. Henry loses all ability to think objectively.

"I was certain you would change your mind and feel better. Give yourself to me Henry, give me your body and soul, let me be the one who controls your life, let me live within you. Allow my very essence to consume you. You and I will have the power to bring your mother back to this world!"

An overpowering emotion takes over the kid's nature; he sees things from a vastly different perspective now. He does not feel any fear or guilt; he is willing to do anything.

The boy does not care if he has to condemn half

the world's population to see his mother again. He only fancies the moment when he is in his mom's arms once more.

"Now, young man, we must have a little patience. It is not something that can be accomplished in one night. The first step is to get your mother's remains. You must take me to her tomb, take your time, and let me know when you are ready to go get them."

"Sure, your highness—I will do whatever it takes."

Willing to loot his mother's grave, Henry would do anything to have her back.

Getting her body means infiltrating Tenshia without being caught. But I will do it, nothing else matters to me right now. I love my life in this place, all I have to do to obtain everything I want is stick to this sweet reality and follow his Majesty's orders. I cannot wait for my mother to be here enjoying this with me.

Henry decides he will reveal the name of the city where the Tenshians buried his mother.

No one could ever get the boy out of Mizraim now. The pleasure and delight he experiences when he is with Cristabella are infinite. Henry's life could not be any better. At almost eighteen, the young man has all he could wish for. Romance, richness, glamour, unlimited pleasure, and good health.

I am popular and accepted, and the best of it all,

Henry ponders. *Is that Cristabella is by my side.*

One more thing Henry would never have to worry about again would be death. He believes he will live for hundreds of years if he stays in Mizraim. He totally forgets the Tenshians told him about the fading of the temporal dimension.

"I will decide when to leave this world. I will live every day to the fullest, my life is here and now. I feel powerful, I feel invincible," says to himself, looking in a tall mirror. Now the only thing he is concerned about is if his Majesty will, in fact, be able to bring Minerva back to life. Everything has a price, and to save his beloved mother, he has to sacrifice the secrecy of the hidden underground world.

Days before going back to Tenshia for Minerva Goldsmith's remains, Mizraim's Tsar invites young Henry to a small private temple located at the top of the dragon pillar.

The hidden room can only be accessed by the powerful man. No stairs or elevator can reach it. The only way in and out is with The Prince himself.

"Why did you bring me here?" Henry asks, confused but curious at the same time.

"I want to share with you part of our secret to rule

over the earth. You see, way before the creation of Man, my family and I were already on the third planet."

These words instantly echo in the boy's mind as he recalls Ikhabot's speech about The Adversaries. Henry wonders if The Prince and his family are part of this group of intruders planning to overthrow the sempiternal source of energy called Grand-Abbadi.

Both men walk down a long and dark corridor toward two tall gold doors. Carved in these doors, is some kind of solar system with scriptures in a weird language the kid does not recognize. The doors open automatically once his Majesty lays his fingers in one of the letters.

They enter a dark chamber, everything seems atypical to the boy; the walls have writings in the same language as the ones on the door. The lamps on the wall are made out of gold; they shine charmingly with the reflection of the pillar candles they have inside.

The floor is made of gold, as well. Henry had never witnessed such an amount of the precious metal in his life; the room alone must be worth billions.

Astonished, he remains silently walking behind the mighty Tsar to the center of the place where there is a circular opening on the floor, about six feet in diameter, with a floating hologram underneath.

Henry stands on the crystalline surface and looks

at the captivating dome below. Mizraim's Tsar looks at the boy as he beholds the hologram's beauty.

The tall, handsome man asks "Do you know what it is?"

It looks like a map of the earth, but I am not sure why it is not a globe, and the continents seem to be shaped differently. Thinks Henry. *The surface is flat, and the clear dome covering it has clouds, so I assume it is the sky.*

But frightened to be mistaken, he tells the mauve-eyed man he is not sure.

"It is planet Earth, Henry! But it is not quite a planet."

"Not quite a planet? But, wait—I thought the earth was a sphere."

"It has never been Hen, this is its real shape. Everything you know about Earth has been manipulated by us since the dawn of time to build confusion among Man. We cannot allow humankind to explore the universe's foundations and its secrets. Only a handful of my people are worthy of creating, ruling, remaining perfect, and being worshiped," he teaches the boy.

The dome below gets closer to where the boy is standing. He can clearly see the earth's surface surrounded by an immense wall of ice. The floor in the middle of this hall is made out of a transparent material as clear as water. Henry feels like walking on it as he sees the sky and all the stars under his feet.

Everything on the map can be zoomed in or out with simple voice commands. Mizraim's Tsar sees every corner of the Earth through the sophisticated hologram; nothing is hidden to his eye. It is most definitely the best surveillance system ever created.

Genuinely flabbergasted by the things The Prince is showing him, the kid is sure it is barely the tip of the iceberg of what the cunning man can do from this room.

The intimidating Tsar saunters toward the boy, his penetrating lavender eyes are staring right into the youngster.

"Every single empire on Earth has worshipped us for centuries without knowing it. Absolutely all of them have devoted their lives to my siblings and me through the religions we have created. It has been us since the beginning. We are what humans call god! We made this world into what you know. We have created politics, religion, cultures, art, and poetry. Everything you see, it has been us. Each kingdom of Earth has been designed and shaped to our liking.

Since the beginning, our purpose is to get the people to work for the resources needed here in Mizraim. The common man is not to find out about this place, or that their lives and even their souls are the fuel that keeps our idyllic land running. Our only law is personal satisfaction. Soon, there will be more cities like this one around the world, when we carry out the entirety of our plan. Human lives belong to me!" unfeelingly explains the stoning man.

After a long pause and only his steps echoing in the room, he continues.

"We will continue to recruit individuals who represent a threat to our system and bring them here. The rest will continue to live in ignorance and be our slaves without even knowing it. Once I extend my reign to the rest of the world, I can complete the last phase of my plan—." He pauses; his awkward silence accompanied by a soft smile, then continues. "We will extend our domains to heaven itself!"

Henry quickly lowers his gaze and sees things clearly. The young man remembers Arwind and Ikhabot's words and realizes the Tenshians are not wrong after all.

The kid's dendrites begin their synapsis—he starts to understand who the guy is. A chill runs down his head and gives him goosebumps all over his arms. He falls in grave doubt.

The boy questions himself before asking the Tsar something more to hide his bewilderment.

"So, all the people's suffering is due to your comfort and delight?"

"Yes! Most of that suffering is because of the things we do to obtain our energy. But if you can live with that, you will be able to stay here and live for centuries with all that you desire. Wealth, pleasure, power, and your mother. If you do not learn to live without guilt, you will be miserable because there is nothing you can do now to get out of this place!"

Judging the way the mighty Tsar speaks, the teen comprehends that even if he wishes to decline his Majesty's offer, there is no way out.

I am just a little bird imprisoned in a gold cage.

Concludes the boy while feeling hopelessly trapped. At the same time, he finds himself wanting to stick to the plan and recover his mother's body. Henry's rational mind screams to get out, but his heart longs for holding his mom again.

A part of him does not give a damn about the people that need to die; what Henry desires most is to have Minerva back. The dark monarch, walking by young Schulze's side, intuits the teen's sentiment and shoots a lethal question.

"So, Henry, should we go and retrieve your mother's remains?"

THE CELESTIAL GENERALS

Ikhabot, Atmix, and Silas are ready to become Thakaiken. They meet daily to train and learn at the Aghora in Üversa, another beautiful city in Tenshia. Their main challenge is to find the safest way to reach the surface without being spotted by the authorities.

The three young guardians explain their plan to the Satraps of the six Tenshian cities.

Arwind, sitting at the end of the table, is leading the meeting. What they all ignore is that Mizraim's Tsar is already fixated on capturing the powerful Tenshians; his men are standing by for his orders.

Leaving Tenshia and getting to the surface without being noticed will not be an easy task. The guardians will have to circumvent all of S.E.N.'s security to reach their destinations. Their technology is very advanced, so they will most likely be able to trace the outlaws. And if they do, Ikhabot, Silas, and the strong Atmix will have to deal with soldiers and androids once more.

The old man warns the soon-to-be Thakaiken that their enemy might not be only the military. The old man suspects that after their last encounter with the army, the world is well aware of their powers, and the Elite's leaders must have informed the Muhalif about the Tenshians. As the meeting goes on, Ikhabot cannot keep his mind off of his nephew.

Is he alive? Is he dead? Where could he be?

The situation fills him with uncertainty and succeeds to unbalance his inner peace. Ikhabot's feeling becomes harsh, knowing that he does not have the option to leave Tenshia, and travel the world trying to find the boy.

The wise Satrap from Üversa stands and tells Arwind and the others, "We are running out of time, and so are the people on the surface! Arwind, proceed!"

"Brethren, you ought to leave immediately and finish your training! This creation needs you. The window to achieve change in the stellar regime is about to open. Henry's arrival in Ghalaban is an unmistakable sign, written all over the stars."

In the meantime, the leaders of the S.E.N. and their teams are pushing their limits to find Tenshia.

They firmly believe that if they find it, they will be able to take the freshwater ocean by force. People in Tenshia, concerned and restless, await knowing dark and difficult days are coming.

Ikhabot and the other two guardians fear not being present to protect their people and the refugees, should an unexpected calamity befall the hidden land.

The blue-haired guardian and his peers are overwhelmed by the situation; however, Ikhabot seems more distracted than usual. Atmix realizes that his best friend is bearing a heavier weight on his shoulders.

"Hey, pal! What is it that is troubling you? I have noticed that you have been quieter and more unfocused than usual. I know you, blue-head, something preoccupies you. Your mind seems to wander in another dimension these days."

"You are right, my dear friend. As a matter of fact, it is because of Henry. I have lost track of his *sharah.*—I know he is not dead, but I feel as if he has been taken to someplace outside of this realm, where my soul cannot access yet."

"Well, if you ask me, it is best if he never comes back. I do not trust that arrogant ninny from the surface. My gut tells me that he will betray us at some point, I am sure of it, Ikhabot. He will sell us out to save his own neck. When the moment comes for him to make a choice, he will pick The Older Sibling's side, the path of the wicked, you will see—"

Atmix gets agitated. Henry has never been his favorite person, much less since he became friends with his younger sister.

"And I want him as far from Aurora as possible!"

"Do not be so harsh, Atmix. Henry might be confused. He is just a boy who is barely beginning to know how the world works. It is absolutely normal to be frightened and make stupid choices," says Silas, leaning on the wall contemplating the jewels on the cavern's roof. He cannot help to get into his friends' conversation.

As always, his compassion is more prominent than anyone else's. However, Atmix quickly replies, mocking him with a slightly mischievous smile on his face.

"Oh my sweet Silas, you are always looking for the silver lightning in every situation. Be cautious, for your mercy for others could bring death upon you before time. If so, we will be completely lost."

Ikhabot takes a deep breath trying to filter Atmix's sharp sense of humor, then closes his eyes and journeys deep inside his soul. His mind travels at the speed of light jumping from neuron to neuron, frantically trying to understand the situation from a different perspective.

"It will not come to that, my beloved friends. We must trust and have faith," he pledges.

Silas places his hand on Ikhabot's shoulder and gives Atmix a look of disappointment.

"Ikhabot, how about we finish taking the remaining refugees to the other cities and get them settled. That way, we will be able to leave and finish our training as soon as possible."

Concurrently, back in the strange temple in Mizraim, Henry strains to get rid of the ordeal of judging right and wrong. Unenthusiastically, the boy decides to reveal his mother's remains whereabouts. He demands The Tsar for the journey to Tenshia to be made for that purpose alone.

"Before I say anything, I want you to promise me everything will be done in secret, and the place and its people will be left unharmed. Once there, I will give you the exact location of my mother's grave, so we can avoid any unpleasant misunderstandings."

"We have an agreement then, I assure you I have no problem keeping that promise. So—where exactly is this place?" ambitiously inquires The Tsar.

"Well, you will find it hard to believe—" the boy underestimates the desert Tsar, "It is hidden underneath the earth's surface. It can't be reached with any machinery you possess here in Mizraim. It is called the land of Tenshia!"

"I can solve that problem, Henry. I know the name of the place now. After all, a mere name holds a ton of information. There is so much I can do with just a name," smirks The Prince looking at the boy's eyes. "Is this land of Tenshia, where the freshwater ocean is located?"

"Yeah!"

"Good! How about we bring some of that water to the surface, Hen? In the end, the world is about to die of thirst. Don't you think it is just fair?" Mizraim's Tsar has cruel intentions but shares very few, or none, with young Henry.

Ikhabot and the other two Tenshians decide to begin the last phase of training to be granted the power to become Thakaiken. They will soon receive the ultimate energy they require to confront what is coming upon them.

The three young-looking guardians know the change of era is close at hand; the temporal dimension is vanishing minute after minute. The stability of the material universe is at stake, and the astral bodies know it is the right time to increase the strength of their Specters.

NaHash will attempt, accompanied by his celestial generals, to crumble the barrier which hides Third Heaven. They will strive to stop the Thakaiken from sharing the secrets of creation with humanity to mend the earth.

They dread to be banished from the planet's throne forever; therefore, they will seek to gain control over Third Heaven at all costs before being purified and transformed.

Without further ado, the encouraged Tenshian men are ready to travel beyond the limits of the known world. They will journey to the ice wall, toward the south, to complete their preparation and fulfill their destinies.

Atmix and Silas rest on a hill of Ghalaban, looking at the immense sea of freshwater. Ikhabot comes walking toward them, observing as the tender air that continuously flows inside the cavern makes the luminescent grass wave.

The three guardians sitting on the hill, chat about what shortly awaits them. Atmix, always ready for new challenges, tells his friends.

"Do not feel bad when I'm the one who finishes the training first," he laughs. Ikhabot and Silas cannot help but laugh too. All three know how dreadful the next few days will be, but a sense of humor and a friendly attitude, in addition to great wisdom, is what keeps the future Thakaiken strong-willed.

"What you have of muscle—you lack in brains," Silas mocks him, and Ikhabot cannot disguise a burst of big laughter. Both make fun of their friend, Atmix, for several minutes until tears come out of their eyes.

"I think I've never told you, but you two are the best friend's life has given me—" says Ikhabot with some melancholy in his voice, "However, Atmix, needless to say, I will be cheering for you from the finish line."

The blond-haired Tenshian takes a handful of grass and throws it in Ikhabot's face. The young protectors stroll toward the Aghora, talking about their future adventures, where Arwind awaits to give them some final instructions.

At the ancient temple, the old Satrap welcomes his beloved apprentices and asks them to sit at the table.

"It is time, my dear friends, you will soon become the Thakaiken that this planet needs. Remember that once you pass the ice wall, you will not be able to ener-travel," the old man says with some concern in his eyes. "Be very careful, there are still thousands of men looking for you on the surface."

The wise Satrap looks at Silas and gets up from his chair. He creeps behind the chair of each of his apprentices and puts his hand on each one's shoulder, wishing them success.

He leaves the Aghora with a rekindled spirit and saunters back to his house. Silas, who has a keen ability to problem-solve, superior to his peers, tells them his strategy, so they may reach the ice wall without being spotted. A blue hologram appears in the middle of the table.

"We will ener-travel together to Southern Africa. Once we arrive and secure the perimeter, then we will separate to avoid being followed. I have found three islands not registered in any of the maps of the S.E.N. There, we will be safe, and each one of us can stop to meditate and rest. We cannot stay more than seven hours on these islands, so make sure to use your time wisely before heading for the ice wall."

The hologram expands, showing three flags in the South Atlantic Ocean. The young-looking protectors stand and walk toward the entrance of the Aghora. They look toward the horizon of the cavern where the crystals and the freshwater ocean meet, forming the most beautiful glow. They grab each other's hands and disappear.

The three Tenshian guardians are once again on the surface of the earth. They speak for the last time before saying goodbye. Ignoring entirely that The Prince has pinpointed their location, Silas emphasizes in his words the importance of traveling as fast as possible to the limits of the ice wall.

The trip must be kept a secret if they do not want to jeopardize the quest. Everything seems to be quiet and safe, but they do not anticipate four formidable Specters are already on their way to eliminate them. The Tenshian protectors cannot sense the cold and ruthless beings stalking them.

Starting from South Africa, the Tenshians commence their journey in different directions. Atmix decides to hide in the crater of Mont Ross, in the Kerguelen Islands.

Not too long ago, they were called the Desolation Islands, but the French colony nowadays is nothing more than the mouth of the volcano.

It is the only thing that remains exposed to the Kerguelen Plateau.

The lilac-haired Tenshian takes refuge in a beautiful ice cavern in the South Orkney Islands.

The icy wind does not seem to bother Silas, who meditates sitting on the ice with barely one layer of fabric covering his honey-colored skin. To the northwest of the cavern where Silas rests, about two thousand miles away in Tristan de Cuhna, stands Ikhabot.

The Tenshian guardian cannot help thinking about his nephew; however, he understands that the success of his training is crucial to ending NaHash's princedom. He settles on the edge of a cliff on a lovely island facing the Atlantic Ocean and closes his eyes.

They will meet in solitude the severity of the trials to obtain the power of a Thakaiken. The purpose is to find the true essence of their souls; they must discover their genuine identity in eternity to receive the ultimate knowledge.

Only then, they will be capable of attaining the secrets to influencing and modifying the universe.

Atmix, squatting by the edge of the crater, meditates into the cosmos, and dives in as far as his mind allows him to go. He still has a few hours before having to cross the ice wall. Suddenly, he perceives someone is watching him; a dim, powerful, and mysterious *sharah*.

"Who's there? There's no way you can hide from me. I cannot see you, but I feel you, alright! Let me see you," he speaks to the blowing wind with an abrasive and direct attitude.

"Are you sure you want to see me?" answers a voice in the cold wind.

Atmix is confused. He looks everywhere, fearlessly, as it is common in him.

"Who are you?" asks the Tenshian.

Suddenly the Antarctic air begins to take shape around a figure dressed in black. The individual has a tunic with a hood covering his entire face. He is of intimidating stature even for a Tenshian.

"I'm Tartuross, may I know, where are you headed?" the stranger asks without hesitation.

"Why do you want to know where I'm going, do you even know who I am?"

"I do not know, but I suspect you are not from around here, I presume you are with those outlanders who attended the meeting with the S.E.N. leaders. I have been made aware of your guardianship over a freshwater ocean."

Atmix understands his life is in danger. Although he only sees the colossal man a stone's throw away, the dark power he senses coming from him means things could get ugly.

"Yes, I'm one of them, my name is Atmix, son of Amadin! I'm one of Tenshia's ambassadors, and now if you'll excuse me, I must go."

"I see, but I cannot let you go, I came here to kill you!"

Atmix turns his face to the defiant entity and tells him what comes to mind, laughing, "Do you think you scare me because I can't see your face?"

"I see that you do not fear death, but before I finish you, you will beg for your life," mutters the wicked Specter.

"Stop saying nonsense, you have a big mouth, try

to kill me if you can!"

The Specter drops his hood along with his tunic to reveal an athletic figure. He is a man with bold red hair and reddish eyes, dressed in an onyx armor made out of dragon scales; tailored to his mesmerizing torso.

He wears black boots with a peculiar metallic shin guard, and his muscular arms are decorated with black armbands on his wrists and thick biceps.

Tartuross, known for his extraordinary strength, casts energy spears out of the palms of his hands to attack his enemies.

Atmix tries to escape, but before he can run, a wild fist lands in his abdomen. He gasps instantly, as his face hits the snow.

"I'll make you eat all the ice in this place," Tartuross taunts.

"You can go to hell from where you came from, I know who you are—one of the six celestial generals that have rebelled against Grand-Abbadi." The Tenshian spits when a drop of blood drips down his lower lip.

Tartuross, disapproving of the young protector's answer, launches himself on the blond man to finish him once and for all. Atmix, seeing the speed of the Specter, realizes he must flee as quickly as possible, or he will perish.

The young-looking Tenshian cannot do much for

himself. It is not the kind of battle in which a Tenshian has the upper-hand. Without thinking twice, he puts his feet on the Specter's chest and pushes him up in the air with compelling strength. The warrior runs back to hit him, but in a fraction of a second, before Tartuross's fist touches his face, Atmix yells.

"OHRRRRRR!"

The crater of Mont Ross fills with incandescent, blinding light. Tartuross is stunned. Atmix slowly stands up while the Specter searches for him like a madman, unable to see anything.

When the glow fades, the Muhalif warrior regains sight. Atmix is sitting on the ground about ten yards away.

"...You still here?" Tartuross laughs, "Not only are you weak—but also stupid—you should have fled when you had the chance, this will be your end!"

The red-haired Specter, standing in the mouth of the crater, closes his eyes, and his body starts to show an ominous aura. Atmix notices he is accumulating a large amount of energy in his body. Tartuross opens his eyes and starts running with the strength of a train toward Atmix, then throws a powerful kick with all his might.

Atmix does not blink; he does not even protect himself, and the Specter's boot misses his target as if kicking the air.

The surprised Specter does not hide his frustration and howls, "What's wrong? My attacks cannot reach you!"

The blond-haired protector stares at him and smiles with mockery. Tartuross attacks him with his energy spears, while the Tenshian serenely sits on the edge of the crater. His futile attempts do nothing but generate wild gusts of wind.

"You can never reach me, I'm far away from you now."

"What do you mean, coward?"

"Allow me to break it down to you. Even though you can see my body, it is already in another realm. I recognize that you are a formidable enemy, and I have no choice but to flee at this moment, but I warn you, hellish monster! Soon, I will come back, and tear you apart, you will not be a worthy opponent."

Atmix brags at the Specter, who is desperate to shred him to pieces. Tartuross, enraged, roars at the young guardian.

"How dare you threaten me? Damn you, insolent scum! I'm going to blow up this dimension and the other one until I find you, and kill you. No one threatens the great Tartuross!"

The Specter's husky voice resonates throughout the Mont Ross volcano. All the stones around the intimidating entity shatter due to his energy. Atmix, as if in an unbreakable bubble, looks closely at the vulgar display of power.

"What a great power you have, but unfortunately, I cannot keep wasting my time with you. I have to go now, but keep in mind that when I see you again, I will give you what you deserve. Sayonara!

The ruthless warrior feels how the blond Tenshian's words pierce his ego. Tartuross explodes in frustration and implacable anger, however, he realizes there is nothing he can do about it. The celestial general leaves the volcanic island at a fantastic speed, fleetingly in search of the other two Tenshians who must be close in some different latitude over the robust wall of ice.

Not too far from Tartuross, two of the other celestial generals are already on the lookout for their victims. They savor the moment of attacking and tearing apart their young opponents.

Tiamat and Merodak, are standing in two of the few icebergs still floating in the ocean littered with decades of plastic waste. Both look toward the horizon, waiting for the Tenshians.

Seals and penguins that once lived in Antarctica

are extinct; seagulls are no longer seen lurking fish in the icy ocean, nor are the sea wolves howling. Instead, an overwhelming silence surrounds the Specters who wait for a big kill.

Tiamat wears a long, dark sarong up to the ankles made of metal grids. His hair is ginger, and his full thin eyebrows highlight his deep blue eyes. He is also of incomparable physical beauty.

His boots reach almost below his knees, shining like the most lustrous leather. Both Specters also wear sumptuous bracelets that cover their wrists and biceps. Their upper armors, made with the most potent ancient dragon scales, protect their sculpted bodies.

The implacable Muhalif, Merodak, is standing about a hundred feet away from Tiamat. Unlike the ginger general, his armor covers his entire body except for his arms and admirable pectorals.

They stand out as proof they are much stronger than any element in the world. The Specter's thin but impenetrable outfit forged with gold-bathed scales of the mighty flying reptile. The muscular man's hair is a cascade of chestnut curls held at the top by a bun. His face is hidden by a ghastly golden mask.

After several minutes, they finally notice the air blowing over them becomes agitated. At a remarkable speed, Silas runs past them at a pace that causes thunder.

Immediately, the two ruthless warriors start their aggressive pursuit. Shocked, they realize that Silas is too fast, and they have no choice but to attack him from afar.

The ginger Specter shoots darts of fire he summons with his hands. The fiery missiles hunt the Tenshian down the snowy ground. Silas dodges them with incredible agility one after another but keeps running for his life. The vengeful Specter fails to hit his target.

Merodak condenses his energy, forming hot smoke. With strange movements of his muscular arms, generates enough friction to form plasma beams.

The golden-masked warrior launches his attack. The energy bursts a couple of inches from the protector. Silas jumps side to side, dodging the flares; Merodak's attacks are unsuccessful too.

Deadly energy blasts scorch the air, making it impossible for the young-looking guardian to escape. Swiftly, one of the plasma beams hits him on his left leg. He starts losing speed; he is no longer able to jump or run.

The humble Tenshian is falling on his face, not being able to control his body about to hit the hard ice layer of the iceberg.

Silas's leg burns; tears appear in the corners of his eyes and trickle down his cheeks, while the Specters come closer. Rushing at high speed toward the downed youthful man, Merodak reaches out to grab his tunic, but it is too late.

The lilac-haired guardian disappears before the eyes of the hungry hunters. They collide violently with an invisible force field severely injuring their ribs beneath the armor that covers their muscular bodies.

Almost unconscious, they collapse, and their bodies hit the dry ice. Panting and gasping, Merodak speaks to his companion, who lies on his right a few yards to the right.

"Damn, Tiamat! This fellow has escaped. Who knows where that bastard is now?"

"Our only option is to hunt the last one of 'em, he hath not yet reached the ice wall. We canst not appear before his Majesty empty-handed. It could be a mistake that could cost the life of any of us."

"Let's go; there's no time to lose, I sense the other guy is a couple thousand miles west of here!"

The wicked generals, still injured, rush to reach the third guardian and ambush him along with Kharas, another one of the Specters seeking to hunt the Tenshian travelers. Ikhabot ener-travels to the farthest point he can reach before passing the ice wall.

He stops on a small island covered in snow. The ice wall is already very close. Calm as always, the youthful protector stands fearless.

Everything is silent, but his instinct tells him there is something suspicious about the place. The atmosphere is dense and heavy, full of sadness and violence at the same time. Ikhabot immediately perceives a dark *sharah*. From above, a chilling greeting is heard.

"Hello, warrior!"

The blue-haired Tenshian looks around for the source of the voice calling his name. He tries to stay calm and looks up. About twenty yards in the air, a man is sitting on a lead-colored cloud. His emerald hair matches the color of his piercing eyes. The Muhalif warrior is skinnier than his comrades. Yet, the tight suit disguising his entire skin does not hide the perfectly toned torso despite the absence of bulgy muscles.

"Yes, it's me who calls you. Where are you going?" The Specter asks him. He laughs and answers to himself, "Apparently nowhere since you have run into me. You see—in the past—none of the enemies I've faced has survived to tell the tale."

Ikhabot remains silent. He only looks at him a moment and analyzes his options, then peacefully answers.

"Why do you call me a warrior and an enemy? I'm just a traveler somewhat lost in the confines of our planet."

"I'm calling you a warrior because whether you want to or not, now you'll have to fight for your life."

Ikhabot looks down again without a response to the menacing words. The Specter addresses him with disdain, "are you afraid? Or, are you shy?"

Ikhabot, silent, closes his eyes and sharpens his senses. He is alert, for the Specter can attack him at any time. Kharas, impatient and tired of being ignored, sends a jet of gas that, when mixed with humidity, corrodes everything in its path.

The humble Tenshian, stops the deadly gas blast covering his chest and face with his strong arms. The impact pushes the guardian several feet back, leaving a trail in the snow, but no burn on his clothes or on his skin. Ikhabot, with his feet firmly grounded in the snow, is the only one of the three Tenshians who does not contemplate fleeing as an immediate option.

Unlike his two friends, Ikhabot seems intrigued by his opponent, although he knows that Kharas has a peculiar power. Trusting everything will be fine, the protector is convinced he will reach his destination.

He approaches the adverse situation with serenity as if he had enough power to defeat his opponent with the snap of his fingers.

The fearsome Specter's reaction to his attitude is precisely what Ikhabot had in mind.

With the deepest of wraths, the celestial general

lets out his rage in a single loud outcry, "I'm going to crush you, insolent worm!"

Enraged, the Specter starts spraying the ground with his unforgiving gas. The snow melts quickly; everything is corroding. The soil, a few feet under the snow, is consumed by lethal gas; even the large rocks begin to disintegrate. The Specter's destructive power leaves nothing in its way.

A gas that destroys everything containing any humidity can still feast on a planet that is running out of water. Ikhabot walks forward with difficulty, among the debris that continues to crumble around him, seeking to stand under the lead-colored cloud. A hint of surprise and anger gleams in the Specter's eyes as he sees Ikhabot unscathed by the deadly attack.

The strong-minded Tenshian stands underneath the cloud and viciously jumps. Kharas, still sitting on the water vapor cluster twenty yards above the ground, freezes in surprise. His body cannot react before Ikhabot crashes his fulminating right fist in his face.

The Specter falls from the cloud, and in less than a second, his stunned body hits the dirt abruptly. The Muhalif warrior was not expecting an attack, so fast, so decisive. A few pieces that fell off the Specter's steel armor stand out in the remaining snow.

The young guardian waits for Kharas to recover from the swat; he understands running away is not promising if the Specter is still conscious. He knows the strike did not cause any significant damage.

Ikhabot stares at the Specter, who sits on the ground, trying to recover. Suddenly, the Tenshian protector's chest flinches with an unpleasing hunch; he looks up at the horizon, and in the distance, the silhouettes of the Muhalif, who come from pursuing Silas, come into sight. From the east, to exacerbate the circumstances, someone baleful is also approaching.

Ikhabot is about to be ambushed.

"It's not going to be easy to get away from this," he hears himself gasp with concern. A second later, Kharas draws near him with a wicked grin.

There is no time to think, it is time to act.

Ikhabot looks up and sees Tartuross approaching him from less than a mile away. Tiamat and Merodak run with astonishing velocity, so fast, that their feet seem not to touch the icy water of the pole.

By the time the guardian decides to step back, he finds himself already surrounded by the other three Specters.

Tartuross's spears are suspended in the air next to his spiky red hair. Tiamat plays with his fiery darts that sparkle over his palms and Merodak stands by, but is prepared to strike the Tenshian.

Like three hungry wolves whose appetites and egos have not been satiated, they fiddle with their powers, trying to intimidate Ikhabot. Their armors stand out scandalously in the immaculate snow of the austral landscape.

Ikhabot reduces his heart rate significantly, causing his perception of time to be altered. He takes a few seconds to meditate,

I can't feel my friends' sharah. There are only two options; either my pals are already dead, or providentially, they are now beyond the ice wall.

Whatever happens, the Tenshian convinces himself he has to cross the frozen barrier and get to his training spot.

Encouraged by his unbreaking will, Ikhabot decides to speak.

"You must be four of the six Specters, right? If so, you all have come here to kill me. This means that my brothers and I no longer have time to complete our training! However, since all four of you stand before me, it must be because you have already killed my brothers," says the young-looking guardian.

Tartuross interrupts instantly.

"I see that you do not miss a single detail, young Tenshian. What a powerful intuition. It really surprises me!"

Merodak laughs and speaks to the protector, daring him.

"Yes, we crushed those two like insects. But they

were lucky compared to what I'm going to do to you. We will not give you a quick death, my dear friend."

Ikhabot analyzes the masked warrior's words with great care. He thoroughly scans everything happening around him and adds.

"...you finished them? How strange," whispers the Tenshian.

"What's strange? You moron, you're going to die too!" growls Merodak.

"I'm sorry, sometimes I forget that you do not know it all about the universe. Let me enlighten you, gentlemen. Every time someone takes an innocent person's life, the soul of this individual leaves an indelible mark on the murderer's soul, as a sign of their transgression. I wonder why it is that you do not have such a mark if you claim to have assassinated my pals. You are lying!" Ikhabot pauses, and continues smiling, "...Given the situation—I am going to render you some piece of information," the guardian states convinced.

"If you did not manage to capture my friends, the four of you together will never be able to catch me!"

Ikhabot understands that at the moment, he cannot battle the four wicked warriors, but he knows he can play with their minds.

The protector suspects that the only way to escape is to run. He is aware Tenshians are not strong enough to fight the celestial generals. He just needs to have faith and believe he will soon cross the wall.

Tartuross, with no warning at all, is the first to attack Ikhabot. Dodging the energy spears, the Tenshian harnesses all his power in his legs and jumps.

As fast as a rifle bullet, the guardian rushes to the ice wall.

Tiamat sprints behind him, shooting his flaming darts at the guardian with no mercy, with the sole purpose of killing him.

Even though Ikhabot's speed and agility to dodge the attacks are mesmerizing, he is still not as fast as the Specters usually are. Nevertheless, Ikhabot outruns them as he has conditioned them mentally and made them significantly slower than him, without them realizing it.

The other two Muhalif stand by believing their comrades will get the job done, but they stay close in case they need support.

Tiamat and Tartuross continue to strike.

Ikhabot anticipates each attack without receiving a single impact, but he knows he will not last much longer.

Bursts of ice and snow rise high behind the running guardian, the Specters seem to lose sight of him. The blue-haired Tenshian needs to go past the limit of the ice wall soon before the Muhalif warriors realize they are on a mental blockade.

Merodak and Kharas still watch the fight from afar; they study the Tenshian's strengths and possible weaknesses. Merodak recognizes Ikhabot is stronger than the other two guardians.

If the other two morons escaped. He stops to consider. *This one might do it too!*

The creature in the grotesque mask turns to his comrade and says, "Kharas, we cannot allow this man to escape. Should we fail, you can only imagine the punishment that awaits us. Tiamat and Tartuross are failing to strike him down; they have been trying for a while now."

"You are right," growls Kharas.

"It is now, or never. We need to come up with a lethal blow. Our loyalty is not with Tartuross or Tiamat, but with The Prince," adds Merodak.

"This does not look good, and I have a feeling that if we do not act now, we will regret it. We will be left empty-handed. We must hit at the same time," thunders Kharas.

Combining Khara's toxic gas with Merodak's plasma beams, the two Muhalif generate a fulminating attack. Not caring about their comrades, they strike producing a blinding light and an explosion of immense proportions.

Ice, dirt, rock, and fire are everywhere, the earth

shudders for a few seconds. Several minutes pass before the smoke disperses in the air, and the absolute silence returns. The two Specters pursuing the guardian are now severely injured on the floor.

A stunned and light-headed Kharas walks through the wrecked ground looking for the Tenshian's corpse. Merodak also searches the surroundings, fearful and distressed.

"Darn it, where could this idiot be?" screams anxiously. "The Prince is going to kill us, Kharas, what are we going to do?"

The evil celestials know the moment Tiamat and Tartuross get up and recover, they will seek revenge and try to kill them.

"Hurry, Merodak, let's find the guy and get out of here! They'll wake up in no time," his comrade says. The injured warriors will use their energy to heal quickly.

"We should make a decision now, what do you think if we kill them and blame the Tenshian?" Kharas stammers. Merodak answers anguished.

"But how can we explain to the cruel Tsar that we failed; to make it worse, we will also have to explain he lost two of his warriors!"

Kharas cannot stand the frustration and squeals.

"Damn it, damn it, damn it! Do you know what's going to happen now? We will be skinned alive if his

Majesty finds out. Tiamat and Tartuross will try and destroy us for attacking them; our only option is to run away! We should kill them right now," he panics.

"It's a possibility, Kharas, but we can't lose our minds. Not right now. Let's go with The Prince and explain everything. Maybe he might understand what happened and that there was nothing we could do."

"It seems you don't know him at all, he is not the understanding and forgiving type, Merodak, don't be naive!"

"So you think it's a brilliant idea to run away, Kharas? Where would we go? He will find us and burn us alive!" Kharas looks at him with doubt, however, at the same time, he knows there is no other option, it is impossible to flee or hide from the powerful Prince.

Merodak comes close and begs his comrade, "...listen to me, the best thing we can do is go back to Mizraim right now. The Prince needs us."

"Okay, let's get going before these two come to. Let's hope they do not freeze to death," he says with concern.

BEYOND THE ICE WALL

I n the middle of a beautiful forest lies Ikhabot. His body is hurt, and his clothes a little torn. The branches of the trees fan the Tenshian with the rhythm of the wind that blows warmly.

The sound of the leaves awakens the young guardian. He sits up confused, the last thing he remembers is running as fast as he could and a blast coming from behind. The young guardian stands up and turns around, analyzing his surroundings.

How did I get here?

All of a sudden, he feels an ethereal being approaching from his right. Ikhabot turns his head slowly and discovers a bright glow coming toward him through the beautiful green trees, about two hundred feet from where he is standing.

The bright light resembles a person, yet dressed in

a cloak made of blue light. The being has dark black hair, but incredibly shiny at the same time. Ikhabot approaches cautiously. The brightness makes it hard for the Tenshian to fully open his eyes. He had never seen such splendor.

"Come closer! Doth not fear."

Ikhabot hears a warm and soft voice coming from the silhouette, now only a few steps away from him.

"I can't, the light is too bright," replies the Tenshian. "Who are you, or what are you?"

"My name is Maikeru."

"Maikeru?" the guardian stutters, "The—the celestial Chief?" Ikhabot seems to be speechless. Happy, but somewhat shy, he asks,

"You...you saved me from the Specters?"

"I did not save thee from aught. Thou hath reached beyond the ice wall, and yond is wherefore I have cometh to meet thee," assures the graceful individual.

"Wait, I thought celestial authorities did not intervene in human affairs. Why are you doing this? Who sent you?"

"C'rrect, the celestial ones doth not receiveth involv'd in human affairs since the nonce in the garden. But at which hour thither art men like thee, able to connect with the secrets of heaven, then, Grand-Abbadi sends us to protect thee, f'r thy true purpose on Earth is did fulfilled."

The young guardian cannot help being perplexed. He never imagined himself standing at the sight of a being like Maikeru. His heart beats so hard; it threatens to pierce through his muscular chest.

Ikhabot says to himself.

How is this possible? I do not even know where I am.

The celestial listens to Ikhabot's thoughts as if they were his own. His eyes, sapphire blue, are fixed in the eyes of the Tenshian.

Ikhabot feels a warm air caressing his face. Involuntarily, he closes his eyes and sees Maikeru's face telepathically. The celestial being speaks to the Tenshian inside his mind.

Thou art whither thee shouldst be, but't is time, thee needeth to train and becometh a Thakaiken. Doth not waste a single minute, the end of t'Era is near, and the final batt'l fr the souls of humanity is at hand. Maikeru explains. Once thou art eft, my own army and I shall be thither under thy hest and command.

Ikhabot is thunderstruck—he cannot recall the last time he was this nervous.

"It is a great pleasure to meet you, great Maikeru!"

"No, the hon'r is all mine, Ikhabot, firstborn of The Younger Sibling. Thou ought to wend to the Sea of Sorrow. Thither thee shalt swim to the center of

Yond Ocean and amid the vicious storm, climb most wondrous Stone of Shōkan."

"What is the Stone of Shōkan, great Maikeru?"

Maikeru smiles at the young guardian, "It is the place whither the hath lost and sorrowful souls has't their last chance of coming back to Ghanedén—the paradise f'r souls. Shouldst they cross the Sea of Sorrow in bawbling rafts, facing forty feet waves under a scorching electrical storm, then they shall be cleans'd of their transgression. I shouldst mention, only a few art brave enough t' tryeth this, and most of those who have doth, has't been devour'd by the Sea and taken to the abyss to be destroy'd."

The honey-skinned Tenshian becomes pale; a chill runs down his back as he listens to the celestial. The look on his face changes abruptly. Once, he heard Arwind mention this unforgiving place, but he never spoke of it ever again.

Maikeru continues, "The Sea of Sorrow is a condemnation spot. Shouldst thee make shift to swim across the water without being drag'd by the hath lost souls, 'r being swallow'd to the abyss by the water itself, then thee would have finish'd the first grise of thy training. Thee shall swim f'r hours in this sinister sea and amerce thy body in order to succe'd. Thither is n' challenge in the entire universe, such as this one."

"Okay! Tell me what I have to do once I get there!"

"Once arriv'd to the Stone and climbed to the top, thou shall findeth seventy-two letters in an ancient language carved in a silv'r plateth. The second grise of thy training shall be spiritual since the first grise wast mostly physical."

Ikhabot chuckles, "Oh, the first part is not spiritual?"

"Thy mind and thy soul art two separate things, mine young friend. Once enhanc'd thy body and mind, thee shall has't to increase the size of thy soul as well. To doth 'this, thee shall has't to meditate on the seventy-two letters f'r the entire time thee sitteth on the very top of the Stone. Remember my child, 'twill not be easy to concentrate and meditate whilst brutal waves hit the Stone, some submerging the Stone entirely. Not to mention the thunder striking not hundr'd feet hence from thy corse. Thy ability to focus and to findeth peace amidst the chaos shall determine the result of thy training."

"How will I know I am ready?" sights the Tenshian.

"Thee shall be eft at which hour thee reacheth Zorah. What I mean by this is, thee shall know once thee findeth who thee truly is in the timeless dimension. To achieve this, thee needeth to be capable of meditating the entire seventy-two letters betimes. From 'this eternal realm, nam'd Zorah, comes the power to modifyeth the creation and transform The Adversaries in thy world. Thee shall findeth who is't thee wast, who is't thou art, and who is't thee shall be. Shouldst thee achieve to receiveth thy true self in eternity, thee shall be invincible."

"What about my friends, Atmix and Silas, will they have to go through this too?" questions Ikhabot.

"At this precise moment, I am having the same conv'rsation with thy friends as well. Thee three shall face the same test, but shall not has't the same results. Each one of thee, shall have a completely diff'rent exp'rience. Shouldst all three becometh Thakaiken, thee shall findeth each oth'r at the top of the Stone of Shōkan in the endeth. Th're art only two rules f'r this task, young Ikhabot. First, thee cannot ener-travel, nor run ov'r the wat'r; the thund'r shall striketh thee if't thy corse is not submrg'd in the wat'r. And second, as thee swimeth, doth not ever look down!"

Concluding his confusing speech, the archangel vanishes along with the beautiful rainforest before Ikhabot's eyes.

The young protector is ready, he knows what needs to be done.

The deadly and grueling training could not wait. First, he needs to exceed the limits of human strength and punish his body and rule over the dark, violent sea.

Somewhere in the middle of the desert, Kharas and Merodak are back in Mizraim, where The Prince, anxiously, waits for them. The Specters walk through the granite corridors to The Prince's hall, where he sits on his carved ivory desk, with a Glencairn glass in his hand.

The Tsar of Mizraim impatiently taps his albino crocodile leather shoe when the Muhalif warriors walk in through the double doors. The look on his face changes, his smile could not be more genuine.

"My boys, tell me, was your little mission a success? Have you killed our underground fellas?"

The two Specters remain silent and avert their eyes as his Majesty's smile begins to fade. The Prince stands and walks around them. His pace is nerve-wracking.

"Where could Tartuross and Tiamat be? Are they done with their part of the mission and decided to take an unauthorized vacation?"

Only The Tsar's footsteps echo in the high ceiling hall. Merodak and his comrade are too scared to even speak.

"Your silence is intriguing—yet disappointing, my boys! Did something not go according to plan? Did four of my strongest warriors fail to kill three insignificant individuals? That would be a pity. You know, our success in entering the land of Tenshia depends on getting rid of its guardians!" yells The Prince. Kharas lifts his head slowly and closes his eyes.

"Your Majesty, if you allow me to explain—"

The Prince approaches the emerald-haired Muhalif and stands inches away from his face, "You know I don't care about explanations, Kharas! I only care about results!" he yells, "Where are the guardians' dead bodies?"

Kharas keeps his eyes shut while the Tsar yells at his face. Merodak hides his shame behind his ghastly golden mask, but the slight tremor on his arms and legs reflects the most profound fear. The mighty Prince returns to his desk, frantically reaching for the glass of liquor.

His mauve colored eyes seem to have a deeper shade than usual, and despite the cool breeze flowing into the hall through the open windows, a cold bead of sweat runs down The Prince's temple. With a gesture, he calls one of his servants.

He whispers something in his ear and turns to the window to look at the lower levels of his big city as he continues to delight in his one-of-a-kind single malt.

The butler addresses the Specters.

"His Majesty invites you two to spend some time

in the dungeons, maybe there you will be reminded how to do your job."

The Muhalif warriors leave the room writhing with anger, but without uttering a single word. They know the dungeons strip them of their powers and will be easy prey to Totsu—the underworld executioner. He will make them suffer under unimaginable tortures.   Without turning his body, he murmurs to the warriors.

"Ábaddon will accompany you during your stay at the dungeons. Now, get away from my sight, useless pieces of hell. I hope the other two arrive soon with good news—otherwise, they will join you down there."

Genuinely, the Specters wish they could kill Mizraim's Tsar with their own hands, but it would be like a ladybug trying to defeat a dragon. They look at each other in anguish.

They assume the punishment will be much worse once the Tsar finds out they almost killed Tiamat and Tartuross in their desperate attempt to eliminate Ikhabot

Beyond the ice wall, Ikhabot walks to the horizon in search of the Sea of Sorrow. Inside his mind, images of his friends, Silas and Atmix. He cannot stop

dwelling on his nephew either.

His thoughts seek to unbalance his soul and make him lose focus on what needs to be done. Ikhabot asks himself if he will survive his test. He wonders if he is ever going to see his friends again; his faith gives a twist to the negative thoughts.

"I trust myself, I trust my heart," says the tenshian to the cold wind hitting his tanned cheeks. He gets rid of his sadness and focuses on the mission he needs to complete.

Connecting with Grand-Abbadi's superior realms by meditating the seventy-two letters for forty days would give him the merit to manipulate the cosmos.

Only a few with enough strength and worthy courage to become a Thakaiken, could swim across the Sea of Sorrow and endure the meditation in search of the world of Zorah.

Soon, the ground under his feet has changed entirely. The horizon is no longer covered by the white blanket of snow covering the Ice Wall and the temperate forest where he found Maikeru has disappeared.

Instead, he walks on a dark and slippery rocky ground toward the Sea of Sorrow. The wind is cold, colder than the wind in the Antarctic.

The sky is frighteningly somber, as the atmosphere, entirely covered by clouds, drops violent thunderbolts in the middle of the water.

Thunderlight illuminates the crest of the high, unforgiving waves as they hit against the cliff. The rumble in the distance is deafening, but the Tenshian does not fear.

He finally reaches the edge of the cliff and looks down. The wind blows strong, almost tearing the fabric of his embroidered tunic.

At the slightest carelessness, he will lose his balance and fall more than two-hundred feet, having to face the sharp stones at the bottom of the cliff.

He peers out to look at the base of the ridge for a couple seconds, then raises his eyes and stares at the Sea of Sorrow. His heart accelerates when he hears the enraged sea roar with the force of a thousand lions.

Lightning bolts dazzle the black tide where hundreds of souls sink in the enormous waves. Everything in that place represents death.

Taking a long-lasting breath, Ikhabot decides to start the last phase of his hard training and dives into the Sea of Sorrow. The water is freezing, but also full of sadness.

Its name is appropriate.

The guardian thinks. He feels drowned in tears of others, in someone else's misery for whom he cannot do anything at all. The blue-haired protector does not know in which direction to swim, but in a split-second, the sea opens between one wave and the other.

In the distance, he spots the massive Stone of Shōkan. He closes his eyes and, without delay, begins to freestyle stroke in the horrendous and intoxicating sea.

The water feels like hundreds of knives cutting his tanned skin. His muscles cramp due to the cold and the soreness; they threaten to leave him paralyzed. Ikhabot quickly shakes off the uncomfortably raw sensation and continues to swim with all his strength.

The waves hit the young guardian's body with such ferocity that an average human would be knocked-out instantly.

The sea forces him to swallow several mouthfuls of bitter-salty water, burning his throat and lungs. The raging tide casts pieces of broken rafts against the guardian while swimming amongst the steep waves. Despite the storm, the frigid water, and the pain, Ikhabot struggles desperately to keep track of the Stone of Shōkan.

Lightning strikes everywhere, but the real danger appears when one bursts against the crest where the brave guardian swims.

An intense beam blinds him completely, and electricity runs through his body, rendering him unconscious, at the mercy of the sea hungry for souls.

Ikhabot sinks into the depths without being able

to help himself. Seven minutes later, he regains his senses to discover that the darkness surrounding him is swallowing his body into the abyss. He swims upwards, following the sound of the waves crashing into the wrecked rafts and the flashing of thunder over the surface.

He is tempted to look down but remembers Maikeru's warning. The Tenshian keeps kicking his way up for air. Breathing is as challenging as swimming in that place of death and desolation.

Being underwater for so long has made the water plagued with souls to seep into Ikhabot's chest, causing damage to his lungs and other internal organs. He hurts for Atmix and Silas; he wonders if they are suffering as much as he is.

Doubting whether he will see them at the end of the quest as Maikeru promised, the Tenshian pushes himself to find the strength to keep going. But the tide seems to drag him back to the cliffs the more he tries to swim.

Ikhabot has always thought he has the strongest determination among his mates. If he is having such a tough time, he cannot imagine his purple-haired friend's physical enervation, nor Atmix's ego being shattered by each relentless wave.

Exhausted, the protector floats for a second to catch his breath. His mind is weak, his body even more. The aching in his arms is excruciating, and he no longer feels his legs. However, he tries to concentrate on the peace Ghalaban's hills make him feel. The warm breeze caressing his hair. The sweet but refreshing taste of Tenshia's fresh water.

He sobs in silence as lightning bolts impact a few feet from his enfeebled body.

I am going to die, humanity will perish, and all this is a big waste of time.

More than two hours have passed since the blue-haired Tenshian jumped off the cliff. A weak breath comes out of his mouth.

"I can't do this!"

His nearly lifeless body floats away, giving up all hope of survival. After a while, and finding himself abandoned to his misfortune, a gigantic, providential wave wildly pushes the Tenshian's body on top of the magnificent Stone in the middle of the sea. Ikhabot lies facing down, unconscious.

An hour later, the Tenshian comes to. His mouth is drier than it has ever been.

The salty water must have dehydrated my body from the inside out.

He sticks his tongue out, making sure he did not gulp sand instead of water. The burning in the young guardian's chest returns when he tries to catch his breath after sitting on the algae-covered rock.

The blue-haired man looks around the place; it is murky and humid, chaos still scourges the rough sea around him. The gravitational pull of the moon and the sun seem to combine beyond the Ice Wall, making the tide a lot more aggressive.

Ikhabot is astonished.

I have never seen salt water behave this viciously before!

His five senses overwhelm him, cold and hunger make it worse. It is the first time the young guardian has to face such a situation.

When Arwind told them the training was going to be challenging, he never thought that the suffering would be immeasurable. The Tenshian's stomach aches in hunger; the last things he ate were some leaves and roots of a tree in Tristan da Cunha.

And on the Stone of Shōkan, it would be impossible to satisfy his appetite.

Amid massive waves that threaten to throw him back into the ruthless sea, Ikhabot stands up and begins to look for the inscription of the seventy-two letters he must meditate on.

The Tenshian guardian finds a high ledge and leans on it, trying not to lose balance, but the deplorable state of his body makes everything more complicated.

Not to mention, the mind of the guardian is

worried about his nephew and not being able to sense his friends.

He remembers Maikeru's words, "It is all about dominating the body; you have to subjugate the physical realm for the next few days while your soul achieves an unbreakable bond with the powerful world of Zorah."

Ikhabot finds the seventy-two letters; he looks at them, slowly tracing each one with his gaze. The seventy-two letters make up a name that few on Earth know exists. It is Grand-Abbadi's highest name; it is the name of secrets.

The young guardian takes advantage of the light flashing over the metal plate. In the middle of the storm, he lays his hands on the sides of the scripture.

His tunic, half-destroyed, is soaked by the rain falling incessantly. The Tenshian's blue hair covers his wet face, and the drops trickling down each strand of hair seem to light up with the rhythm of the storm.

He scans each letter, memorizing them in order. Then, he hikes to one edge of the Stone of Shōkan and sits down with his legs hanging.

Closing his eyes and resting his hands on his lap, the Tenshian guardian starts his meditation. He visualizes each letter, illuminating the outline of the letters in the dark background of his thoughts.

Soon enough, his external senses lose power to his

mind, and his soul takes command. The strenuous thunder and the chaos around him become insignificant.

Every nerve in his body seems disconnected from all physical sensation; his whole being is now immersed in the astral realm.

Without Ikhabot noticing, his body lifts from the surface of the magnificent Stone of Shōkan. Ikhabot is levitating, far from the reach of the fearsome waves, and protected from the electrical storm by a strong shield of energy emanating from his very heart.

As the powerful meditation continues, Ikhabot adds letters of Grand-Abbadi's name in his internal visualization. The more letters the guardian connects, the more his soul ascends, visiting spiritual worlds looking for his true self in eternity.

On his journey, he meets different celestial authorities. Some of them question his presence in their realms, others welcome him. Some even challenge the Tenshian guardian but are defeated by the power Maikeru bestowed upon him.

There are no shortcuts or easy ways to ascend to the world of Zorah from the physical realm. In fact, only one man has achieved it in human history, and He shares the very nature of Grand-Abbadi.

Their meditation requires an effort of such magnitude that Ikhabot, Silas, and Atmix have trained for decades for this moment. The astral journey each of them is performing is the most personal thing in existence.

A journey to these worlds must be experienced privately by the soul of every being in the universe. Zorah and the secrets it offers to those who reach it are unfathomable.

There are as many paths to reach Zorah, as there are stars in the sky.

On day thirty-four of Ikhabot's meditation, the soon to be Thakaiken has mastered fifty-eight letters out of the seventy-two. He visualizes every single letter as radiant as a winter morning sun.

His connection with Zorah is outstanding, even though he has not mastered the entire name yet. Nonetheless, his knowledge of the cosmos is massive. He understands now how each letter of Grand-Abbadi's name is capable of creating and modifying an entire universe. He has finally met his eternal true self.

The Tenshian's physical being, still levitating over the Stone of the hostile place, begins to suffer a quantum change he would have never imagined possible.

Every carbon atom, forming his physical body, is

transformed by the energy of his cosmic self. The brave guardian sheds his body's mortal traits and transfigures into an incorruptible organism.

In the middle of the darkness, a natural sheen magnetizes the guardian's tanned figure. His skin, dried by the salty wind, is now moisturized and healthy, and his bronze skin tone is no longer dull.

The muscles emaciated by the lack of water and food return to their slender and toned shape, and his hair regains its shine; his cosmic experience is about to end. Slowly, Ikhabot's perfected soul returns to his renovated body. With his eyes still shut, he feels the energy running through his veins. He feels strong. He feels invincible.

When he opens his eyes, he is surprised to see he still floats above the wet rock, and his whole skin shines brightly in the gloom. The young Thakaiken does not feel hunger, nor thirst, no physical need, nor any sensations that imprison a mortal body.

His vitality now emanates from the timeless dimension; his source of energy is Zorah. Quickly descending to the Stone, he feels immeasurable joy when he sees his two brothers standing in radiant bodies just like his.

Ikhabot does not hide his relief and runs to hug them. Silas clings to his friend with immense bliss.

"Brother!"

"I can't wait to hear every detail," says Ikhabot trying to hug Atmix. The blond Tenshian stops him even though he is glad to see his friend, "Don't get overly excited, Ikhabot! You first! Tell us how was it, why did it take you so long? You are the last one to come back."

"What do you mean, I am the last one?"

"Well, this moron here became a Thakaiken seven days ago, and I joined him four days ago. Right, Silas?" Atmix pats Silas in the back, almost making him fall to the ground.

The lilac-haired Tenshian replies, "...Moron? You are jealous because I was the first one to complete the training!"

"Why did you wait for me in this horrendous place? You should've left a long time ago!" queries the blue-haired Thakaiken.

"It is not like we had a choice, brother. Atmix and I don't have the amount of energy needed to break out of this dimension. We had to wait for you whether we liked it or not!"

Atmix nods, agreeing with his friend, then asks, "So Ikhabot, how many letters were you able to visualize?" always interested in being better than his peers.

"What do you care, it is not like that will make you better than Silas or me!" Ikhabot's sharpness always manages to neutralize his competitive friend's ego, but not happy with the answer, Atmix insists.

"Oh, come on, just out of curiosity. I'll start! I visualized forty-nine! Not bad, huh?"

"Forty for me! I barely made it, but forty was enough to reach Zorah," Silas's humbleness always present in his words encourages Ikhabot to continue with the conversation and tell his friends about his experience.

"If you really want to know! Fifty-eight letters, my friends. It was captivating to visualize each one of them. I felt wrapped in infinite love, a kind of love older than stars, older than the creation of the universe. I felt in a different time and space. Then, I saw it, the name above all names. The code that makes the impossible, possible. The key to modify and transform energy and matter!"

The blue-haired Tenshian says with his eyes fixed on the dark bushy clouds.

"The only important thing right now is we all completed our training. Even though we did not achieve the seventy-two letters, we now possess the everlasting name which allows us to use the power of the universe. So now, before going home, what do you think if we purify this place and finish with all the suffering these souls most definitely do not deserve?"

Silas smiles in relief; his heart hurts when others

suffer, "I am sure most of these souls in this sea want and deserve another chance. I got your back Ikhabot, let's transform this horrid place once and for all!"

The three Thakaiken stand in a circle and look up to the gruesome sky, and they declare in unison, "Ascendit!"

The sorrowful souls in the rafts become beams of light and begin to ascend, crossing the stormy clouds up to the heavens. Then, the guardians get down to where the sea hits the rock and submerge their hands in the frigid liquid. The glow on the Thakaiken's palms purify the water, and the entire scenery, the clouds, thunder, and gigantic waves, begin to dissipate before their eyes.

Sooner than they expected, they float in the middle of a peaceful pool-like ocean, surrounded by infinite oneness. In front of them shining bright, the Stone of Shōkan is still intact, revealing its true essence. It is one of the columns that hold the universe together.

What they first saw standing in the middle of the Sea of Sorrow was just the tip of the immense pillar whose base rests in the underworld.

The young-looking protectors look at each other, fulfilled and curious at the same time. Ikhabot and his friends discover that once the waters were purified, the abyss is left exposed. A desire to transform the underworld grows in the Thakaiken's hearts, but they lack the power to do such a thing.

At least not without the Thakaiken from the surface.

However, they decide to swim down and take a peek at the unclean and debauched scrapyard of souls.

THE DUNGEONS

Tiamat and Tartuross, the Tsar's warriors, travel back to Mizraim. Upon their arrival, they are taken to see his Majesty immediately. The Prince has been impatiently waiting for them. He cannot wait another minute to go by without an explanation, "What the hell took you two so long, my cherished warriors?"

The red-eyed Specter turns to Tiamat, hoping he does not come forth and tell The Prince precisely what happened. The Specters agreed not to mention anything about the recent events with the Tenshians and their fellow Specters.

It is easier to avoid explaining the situation to The Prince, so they choose to swallow their pride and thirst for revenge. Time will come for Merodak and Kharas to pay for what they did with blood.

Without hesitation, Tartuross comes up with a much clever answer, "We were badly injured, sir. The underground visitors are stronger than we anticipated!"

Mizraim's Tsar tries his best to control his temper. "Really?" He gets up and walks toward his subordinates, "I didn't think the cads were strong enough to hurt any of my warriors."

Terrified that The Prince could sense his lack of honesty and retaliate against the two, Tiamat decides to tell him the truth about what Merodak and Kharas did to them.

"Those two idiots attacked us and left us behind, sir."

"I already knew that, Tiamat! The two worms are being tortured in the dungeons as we speak!" The Prince states, squishing a grape in between his thumb and finger, "...and despite the fact you failed as well, at least you fought bravely till the end. Please get out of my sight and get those maggots out of the dungeons; they will be relieved to see you are alive. Go now, all six of you, and I are going on a trip."

Tartuross follows Tiamat down the spiral staircase into the dungeons. Then knocks on the heavy iron door, "Guard! The Prince has sent me to get Merodak and Kharas; they must be brought before him immediately."

The masked Specter is the first one to hear Tartuross's voice. He shivers fearing his comrade is there to kill him; after all, that was the perfect place and time to get revenge.

"Yes, my lord," answers one of the prison's putrid servants while kneeling before the formidable Muhalif warriors. From the shadows, appears Ábaddon—the warden of the dungeons. He walks toward the gate as he sharpens a blade stained with dark crimson blood.

"Ya dare come to my domains and boss my servants around Tiamat? What bad manners you have. I wonder if they would improve if ya joined me someday and pay for one of yer misdeeds," says the stout man placing his cold hand on the Specter's shoulder.

"Get your filthy hand off of me unless you want to lose a limb, Ábaddon," grinds Tiamat holding the warden's wrist with one hand and pushing the other against the fat man's throat. "You are not to touch me, small-time minger. Pray The Prince under no circumstances sends me here, as he sent the two losers you are about to release, for the first thing I will do before entering my cell will be to rip out your tongue and tie it around your fat neck. Now, do as I say and fetch those two backstabbers for me."

"Ya seem pretty tough when The Prince's got yer

back, don't ya? Better hope he doesn't let ya down as he did with these two ya came to take!" Ábaddon smirks, walking to one of the cells with a rusty ring full of keys in his right hand. Opens the door and drags Merodak and Kharas out.

The Muhalif warriors look pathetic to Tiamat's eyes. Flinging them to their ginger comrade's feet, the beaten Specters quiver. Tiamat could hurt them badly if he were to attack them in that condition.

Totsu's prolonged tortures have bruised, not only their bodies but their minds; they look painfully insignificant and vulnerable. Tiamat cannot help but humiliate them, "Look at yourselves cowards, I pity you. I will not have my revenge while you are in such a disgraceful shape. Once you have regained all your power, Tartuross and I will skin you alive. Get up! This is not the time to fear for your miserable lives; fortunately, The Prince still needs all of us. That will keep you breathing, for now, bastards. I want you to know that, when the time comes, you would have preferred to stay here for eternity."

Upstairs, The Prince waits for Tiamat and Tartuross to return with Merodak and Kharas. He stands in front of an enormous gold-framed mirror, buttoning up his silk tunic.

On the couch across the room, sits a man, and another one stands by the door to the terrace.

Mizraim's Tsar laughs as the gentleman in the pearl-colored armor tells him a joke, "that is hilarious, Kaiosel!"

Kaiosel is the friendliest Specter; he cares about his comrades and The Prince's wellbeing. He often tells jokes, anecdotes, or references philosophical quotes, always out of place.

A long silky mane, pearl-toned, with stray light chestnut strands of hair falls over his shoulders. His turquoise eyes brighten up when his four fellow Specters walk into the room,

"Hey! You guys just missed one of my jokes."

Tartuross walks into the room with the masked warrior on one of his shoulders. The Muhalif warriors are indeed in bad shape. Redhead Tartuross tosses Merodak on the couch next to Kaiosel.

The masked Specter sits himself up and nods at The Prince out of respect and fear. Tiamat drags Kharas across the room and leaves him lying against the wall next to the main door.

The ginger Specter shakes hands with Minos and walks out to the terrace to get some fresh air. The stench from the dungeons lingers on his clothes. Minos follows Tiamat outside.

Being the tallest of the Specters, Minos is not as fearsome as his height and build would suggest. The warrior, unlike his comrades, does not wear an armor.

Instead, he only wears forest-green slim trousers leaving his upper body uncovered.

Minos's perfectly toned abs are adorned by light chestnut strands of hair falling over his shoulders down to his waist. His jade eyes, rest flirty under his chestnut thin eyebrows, and his smile would charm to death any woman who crossed paths with him. The sun caresses his tanned torso while he and Tiamat talk about the Tenshian guardians.

Now The Prince's army is complete. The six Specters are again reunited under Mizraim's roof and ready to fight under the Tsar's command. They will join The Prince and Henry, and will soon head to Ghalaban to retrieve Minerva's remains. Tenshia's underground cities have never faced anything like what is about to happen.

Weeks have passed since Henry told The Prince the location of his mother's body. The amber-eyed boy begins to lose his patience, for he has already made up his mind about having his beloved mother back. The intense overindulgences start to make a dent in his body.

His flesh gradually begins to grow weary of banal pleasures. The teen never imagined that someone could get tired so quickly of having everything they wish for, whenever they want it. It is as if little by little, the spell the place has on him is fading away. The fleeting happiness of having everything starts to bore him.

The Prince still does not communicate to the boy the decision of when to recover Minerva's corpse. He plans cautiously with the Specters every detail of their visit to Ghalaban.

The wait is agonizing.

The Prince said if I stayed here, I could have anything I wanted! I want my mother back! That is all I need.

Henry cries to himself, sitting in the guest room. His anxiety starts to take control of his mind and body; he walks from one corner of the room to the other and rubs his hands together. He believes he has been wasting time without results and sits against the balcony's sliding door.

I'm done! I'm nobody! I don't want to be...

The door opens, interrupting Henry's thoughts. It is The Prince.

"My dear Hen, care to go for a walk with me? There are some folks I'd like you to meet." Young Schulze and The Prince walk through the mansion's extravagant hallways escorted by one of the butlers. Up in the terrace, six shady men expect the teenager.

The boy has never seen any of them in the city before.

Without further ado, the desert city's Tsar introduces Henry to each one of the strangers.

"Hen, allow me to introduce you to our companions; Tartuross, Minos, Tiamat, Merodak, Kaiosel, and Kharas. They will come with us to retrieve your beloved mother's body."

Henry stares at each one of the Specters with noticeable distrust.

"I see, but I thought you and I were enough to get this done."

"Oh, nah! We need these gentlemen's cosmic energy to find what wants to remain hidden, like the land of Tenshia, for example. Besides, we need to be sure that recovering your mother's corpse will remain a secret. I have been told your underground friends demonstrated great power here on the surface the other day, so we need to be prepared. We don't want snitches catching you and I alone, taking something from their land, do we?" replies The Prince hiding that his warriors had been after the Tenshians already, mainly because they failed to prevent the guardians from completing their training.

"It is a preventative measure, Henry," says Mizraim's ruler with irony. "Taking into account the Tenshian's strength, I have been advised not to take this matter lightly. They could be expecting us for all we know. I want to be ready. You get me, right?"

"I guess I do, but I see that you are well-informed; maybe more than I thought," murmurs the boy.

"I always know more than it seems, and always share less than I should. Remember this, Hen!"

"Why? Because you are Mizraim's Prince?" inquires the boy.

"I am much more than a Prince, I am afraid. Frighten you with my true identity is not on my to-do list, boy. Your soul is not ready to even fathom who I am!" The Prince's demeanor shifts, he becomes cold, and his skin turns pale.

For the first time, Henry is so close to The Prince enough for him to see something strange in the ruler's eyes. Apart from the extraordinary color of his eyes, when he blinks, his eyelids resemble those of a reptile. The boy, predisposed by The Prince's words, notices how his pulse accelerates.

Maybe what he just saw in the Tsar's eyes is nothing but a product of his paranoia. Henry has been questioning his judgment since the whole thing started.

The boy mistrusts his ability to reason; even more, now that the desire to see his mother again has blinded him from everything else around him.

"By the way, Henry," adds The Prince, "now that you know our companions' names, it is just fair that I tell you mine. You have been calling me '*your Majesty*,' which is very kind of you, but please, forgive my bad manners. I hope you understand that I have no clue how the vibration of my name is going to affect you," he states, looking at his comrades. The warriors kneel when they see the shine emanating from The Prince's fair body. Henry is humiliated by the feeling of not knowing why they kneel. He ignores who the ruler truly is, but not for long. The charismatic and mysterious hierarch evidently enjoys that kind of attention. He continues to talk to the boy without revealing his name.

"You see, boy, knowing the name of something or someone can give you power over it, or even allows you to borrow its power." The mauve-eyed Tsar smirks, "…but I believe I have nothing to worry, right boy? After all, we will always be family. It has been a pleasure to meet you, Mr. Schulze—my name is NaHash!"

After The Prince says his real name every granite tile covering the terrace floor shudders. An inexplicable wave of energy pushes the Muhalif warriors to the ground, and some are hauled back to the pillars supporting the terrace.

Henry, still standing, has the weirdest sensation inside him, like his body does not belong to him anymore. His soul seems to detach from his flesh and his blood to evaporate. His mind surrenders to the blowing wind. However, the boy is still alive. He does not understand what is happening.

The horrible feeling bends him over, and he falls on his knees. Time seems to stop, and the teenager's thoughts float in an infinite void inside his skull.

What kind of power is this? Who is this man? Did all this happen by solely pronouncing his name?

Henry regains some control over his body and pulls his thoughts together. The Prince looks at him with excitement. He waits for the boy to come to focus and congratulates him, "you are exactly who I thought you were, young friend. A mere mortal would have suffered, at least, unstoppable internal bleeding. It would have been fatal, but you, my friend, are still here. So, tell me, why is your physical nature so fascinating?"

Henry knows he is not an ordinary human; he carries

Khazios's genes. The naive boy, underestimating his own powers, asks The Prince in awe, "Is that your name's power by saying it out loud!?"

"It does if it is me who speaks it!" explains The Prince, "You see, boy, a single syllable carries the power of the voice which pronounces it. In other words, a meaningful word is even more powerful, depending on who voices it. Now, if you have no further questions, how about we go get your mother?”

"Alright!" the boy agrees, "but, your Majesty, even though I know your name now, I'd rather not say it!"

"You are wise, little human, you don't want to hurt yourself with the things you ignore," suggests NaHash, "Let's go to Tenshia!"

The six Muhalif, Henry and NaHash, are ready to go to the subterranean world of the Thakaiken. The teenager's heart pounds inside his chest out of fear and excitement at the same time.

Not utterly conscious of his choice, the boy does not realize he is willingly about to walk into a bonfire. The prevailing desire to see his mother, clouds any other thought suggesting otherwise.

Mizraim's Tsar is standing by, "Listen, boy, hold on tight to Tiamat's and visualize the place your mother is buried clearly in your mind. Aim to picture it sharply; Tiamat will take us there."

Ener-traveling is not new to Henry, but The Prince does not know that. On several occasions, the boy ener-traveled with Ikhabot, so he became somewhat used to it. The feeling of the drowning void does not bother him anymore.

Tiamat does not succeed. His power fails after the teenager struggles to picture the place. Henry tries to focus on his breathing and begins to meditate.

Deep in his thoughts, he begins to see the luminous

grass and feel the warm wind blowing his hair.

The crystals in the cave's ceiling become vivid, and the hill where Henry buried his mother, Minerva, appears before his eyes, "I got it!" says the kid.

Instantly, the unexpected visitors arrive at one of Ghalaban's majestic hills. Everything is quiet; everything remains beautiful and as serene as the last time the teenager was there.

His soul aches as he sees in the distance the grave of his deceased mother, but the feeling of being back in Ghalaban calms his grief. The rush of getting his mother's remains and seeing her alive again shakes his being.

"Up there, in that cave," points Henry with an uncomfortable foreboding of what he is doing.

"Well done, boy!" says the Specter's leader, "Merodak, scan the place. We don't want interruptions while we carry out our job here!"

"As you wish, master," the masked Specter closes his eyes and falls into intense silence. His body fades.

After a short while, the warrior returns.

"I have covered the entire land of Tenshia; I have seen the freshwater ocean, it is splendid! It will be a great addition to your assets, sir." The Muhalif bows before NaHash, "...also, there are six big cities; all at our disposition to do as we please."

"Is there anything or anyone that could represent an issue for us?" questions The Prince.

"No, sir, I didn't notice anything you should worry about. Six beings have a significant amount of energy but are not a danger to us. You have nothing to worry about, your Majesty."

"Splendid!" yells The Prince, then turns at the boy and pats his back, "my boy, what can I say except thank you? Thank you for bringing us here!" celebrates the magnificent Tsar.

Henry does not take long to figure out what is really happening. Now he comprehends everything.

Darn... I handed Tenshia to NaHash on a silver platter! He is going to take the ocean for his own. What have I done?

The boy knows he made a huge mistake. A mistake he will have to bear his whole life. "I will never be able to fix this," laments young Schulze.

NaHash walks barefoot on the hill of the sacred place. After each footstep, the luminous grass loses its brightness and becomes wilted.

The Prince's mere presence sucks the life out of what once was beautiful.

He seems to enjoy the destruction that he leaves in his path. Filling his lungs with fresh air as he looks at his comrades, and with a diabolical face, he turns to Tiamat.

"Open the grave now. Grab the woman's body."

The ginger-haired warrior walks to the cave, and by tapping the boulder blocking the entrance, it disintegrates into a million pieces. Henry stares astonished.

His powers seem to be menacing, and far superior to those of Ikhabot. They are monsters, maybe even demons.

A pervasive and unexpected smell comes out of the cave. The scent of aromatics herbs Tenshians use to bury the dead has not yet been dimmed by the stench of a decomposing body. The Prince and his followers act surprised and get closer.

"Well, well," says Tiamat walking inside, "how curious that your mother's body does not smell bad after all this time."

"Truly intriguing," mutters NaHash while Tiamat comes out of the tiny cave followed by a levitating motionless body wrapped in beige fabric. Former S.E.N.'s spokeswoman's exhumed body lays outside the cavern undefiled.

"I wonder what kind of person she was," inquires Tartuross. At the same time, Henry stares from afar under the tranquilizing leaves of a violet Olanín tree. He refuses to get any closer to his mother's dead body.

Deep inside, the teen is still in denial of his mother's unfortunate passing.

"Well, what are we waiting for?" continues the redhead warrior, "we have the body," he says with a satisfied look on his face.

NaHash addresses his comrades, "Alright. Tiamat! Take the boy and his mother back to Mizraim," he commands, "we will now do what we came here to do. Destroy Tenshia! Leave no one alive! The freshwater ocean is mine!"

TENSHIA FALLS

H enry is shocked, "what have I done? I have been tricked. I placed this peaceful land in criminal hands," shrieks to his insides, "...these demons will do away with this beautiful place, and it is all because of me."

Young Henry reaches inside his mind to warn his uncle, "Ikhabot, please, listen to me!"

Shame drowns his inner-self. The anguish and suffering he feels for his actions are more tormenting than any physical pain he has ever experienced.

The teenager realizes he needs to stop feeling sorry for himself and do something to help with the situation he caused. Henry runs downhill to the city of Ghalaban, seeking shelter from The Prince, "Ikhabot!" Henry screams.

NaHash sees the inconsequential human boy run for his life, and laughs, "Who are you calling, boy?"

The Prince's voice torments the youngster's mind. Henry sprints faster as NaHash's hissing still tortures his head, "...is that one of your underground friends? He won't help you now; he is dead. No one will save you or this place. Thank you, boy, for you have done a wonderful job. You should be proud of how far you have come."

Henry stops and yells back at The Prince, "Ikhabot is not dead, you liar!" and watches Tiamat vanish with his mother's body in his arms.

The boy's heart shatters, nothing went according to his plan. To make matters worse, the other five warriors are on their way to the rest of the Tenshian cities.

And now, not only is his life in danger but everyone's life in Tenshia as well.

He runs as fast as he can, in an attempt to warn Arwind or somebody else.

The clumsy teenager trips on a rock and starts tumbling down the hill. Not only the grass but also stones and branches of the Olanín, tear the boy's tunic and cut his skin.

Still having four miles to reach the town of Ghalaban, he stands up, and despite the burning on his scraped knees, he keeps on running.

When he reaches the edge of the valley, the muscles in his legs surrender, his lower back hurts so badly that he cannot take another step.

The kid falls to the ground and notices the marble houses less than a hundred yards away. The pain is excruciating, but he must go on, even if it means crawling all the way to the old Satrap's house.

Lacking the energy and pulling his own body across the meadow, young Henry manages to reach the front yard of one of Ghalaban's beautiful buildings.

The blood coming out of his elbows and legs stain the white marbled sidewalk. He recognizes the gardens neighboring the house and sees a silhouette approaching him; it is Aurora.

"Henry? Is that you?"

"Aurora," screeches Henry in agony. He is relieved to hear his friend but feels guilty for betraying her in a handful of ways. Not only did he leave and did not come back, but he fell in love with someone else. The beautiful Aurora comes running to the screaming teen, "For heaven's sake, Henry, what happened to you?" stutters when she sees her friend covered in his own blood. She is shocked, the Tenshian girl had never seen so much blood in her life. She tries to comfort Henry, and lays his head in her lap, "Henry, talk to me, please, what happened to you?"

Young Henry is thankful to see Aurora again, "I didn't remember your voice being so sweet," he says, struggling to smile. Atmix's sister hugs her friend gently. Her hands are soothing; some of the discomfort in Henry's muscles goes away immediately. For a minute, he forgets the reason why he is there.

Young Schulze's inner voice breaks him out of his trance, "Aurora, her voice, and this place meant nothing to me minutes ago; I was blinded by the desire of having my mother back. How could I be so stupid?"

"I am so...sorry Aurora," he stammers.

"What happened to you? Why do you apologize? Who did this to you?"

The pain in young Henry's chest makes it hard to speak, "Tenshia is in danger!" he coughs, "...they are going to destroy it."

"Who is *they* Henry?"

"Some powerful monsters! We need to tell Ikhabot! Now!" says Henry trying to sit on the luminous, silky lawn.

"Why is Tenshia in danger?" questions the girl, "Ikhabot is not here, he left with my brother and Silas to finish their training and become Thakaiken. There is no one here with such power as theirs, Hen."

The throbbing in the boy's ribs makes his voice hard to understand, but he tries to speak slowly, catching his breath in between words, "Where is Arwind? There is no time to lose!"

Henry does not understand how tumbling down the hill caused that much damage to his body. The Prince must have done something to him.

Blood starts coming out of his nose and lips; the taste in his mouth makes him barf, "Hurry Aurora, we must tell the people of Ghalaban, we need to get out of here. It is too late for me, but you need to save yourself!"

"I am not going to let you die, Hen," shrieks Aurora with tears in her eyes. She stands and runs to her house. From behind the backyard, Aurora pulls up in a hovering vehicle. She helps Henry climb into the back seat, "Okay, we will take the velokar to Arwind's house. Hold on tight!"

Henry babbles in the back of the velokar; his words are confusing. Aurora presses the accelerator and leaves at full speed. Velokars became rarely used in Tenshia because of the magnetism they require to navigate.

Even though the minerals under the marble streets were abundant, the Satraps agreed to use them for emergencies only, instead of disturbing the earth's core magnetic fields.

Riding in the velokar is smooth enough to not hurt Henry any further despite Aurora's high speed.

She turns each corner so quickly that the velokar tilts almost all the way.

The grey-eyed girl notices through the large panoramic glass that the cavern's ceiling is cloudy, and not with ordinary clouds, but similar to the ones on the surface before a tornado strikes.

What is happening here? This is not normal.

The girl knows the phenomenon only used to happen in a few places on the surface. Pressing down on the velokar's pedal, the magnetic revolution engine boosts the vehicle reaching one hundred miles per hour with ease.

Henry and Aurora arrive at the Aghora, Arwind is inside the great hall meditating. The brave Tenshian girl strides down the hallway with the deathly injured boy on her back.

How is it possible Ghalaban's great Satrap is not aware of the situation? Does he even suspect what is about to happen?

Henry wonders as Aurora runs to the great hall. She kicks the doors and screams, "Arwind!" shattering the peace of the sacred building.

"Great Satrap, we are under attack, Tenshia is about to be destroyed!"

Arwind opens his eyes, and the first thing he gazes at is Khazios's son covered in blood, "What happened to the poor boy?"

"Henry!" she says, trying to catch her breath, "...suffered an accident on his way to warn us about the danger. Tenshia is at risk, Arwind!"

"Danger?" asks the wise old man, "Tenshia is in danger, you say?"

"Go outside and look for yourself, the cavern's vault is overcast with weird clouds! It is obvious this is someone else's doing, we have no clouds in Tenshia," claims the girl in a desperate tone, "...Henry was mumbling in the velokar on our way here; there are six evil beings, called Specters, under the orders of a Prince. They are down here to kill everyone and steal the freshwater ocean!"

The wise Satrap walks to the window and stares at the vault's ceiling. Worried, he turns back and says, "The first thing I must do, is to heal this boy. Follow me, to the apprentice's chambers, quick!"

Aurora lays Henry in one of the firm beds. Arwind examines the injured boy and finds he has several broken ribs.

"His left femur is fractured, his right arm dislocated, and he might have one or two broken vertebrae," fears the old Satrap as Henry shivers in pain, "Aurora, Henry told you he plunged down a hill? I do not think so!"

"Yes, Arwind, that is what I thought. Maybe one of those monsters he mentioned did this to him," says

Aurora, enraged as Ghalaban's Satrap places his hand on the boy's forehead, and he falls asleep.

Then, Arwind skillfully readjusts young Henry's dislocated bones and heals his broken ribs. The old Tenshian gets up from the bed and walks toward a beautiful marble dresser to grab some bandages from one of the drawers.

Sitting gently beside the boy, and with Aurora's help, Arwind wraps the curious silver bandages around his thigh. The bindings dry instantly into a silver cast returning his crooked, broken leg to its original form.

"Henry is out of danger, Aurora, do not worry. You did a splendid job bringing him here," says the Satrap, placing his hand on the kid's chest to pronounce with his eyes closed, "Accelerium!"

Fifteen minutes later, Henry recovers consciousness and opens his eyes. Mysteriously, the pain is gone. Arwind's healing energy worked wonders on the teenager's body.

He sits on the edge of the bed and hears Aurora and Arwind chatting in the hallway.

"Aurora? Is that you?"

The Tenshian girl runs inside the apprentice's room and hugs her friend tightly, forgetting about his injuries, "Thank goodness, Henry Schulze, you scared me. I am glad you are okay," she cheers, giving him a gentle kiss on his cheek. Henry blushes and smiles as he sees Arwind standing on the doorway.

"Arwind!" grins Henry, "why is the pain gone? How long have I been out?" effortlessly moving his arms and legs.

"Not more than half an hour, dear boy!" says the Satrap.

"Arwind healed you, Hen," explains the girl.

"Really? The last thing I remember was feeling Arwind's hand on my forehead. Thank you, but ...How did you do it?" sighs the teen.

"I stimulated your cells for them to heal quicker. The human body has the ability to heal itself. I boosted your healing nature by giving you a small amount of my energy," explains the old man taking the silver cast off the boy's leg. Henry is thankful for Ghalaban's Satrap; in the end, the old-man owes him nothing. It is still a mystery how he got injured so severely by rolling down a hill. The boy understands now more than ever that there are things in the universe that reason will never comprehend.

The world is not necessarily how regular people see it on the surface. Henry concludes. *Supernatural events happen every day and are as real as I am.*

Arwind approaches young Henry one more time after cleaning up all the wounds and removing the bandages, "you brought those demons here, right?" Henry's soul tears, leaving him pale and wordless.

"Why did you allow greed and lust to take over your heart, boy, and bring destruction upon us?" laments Arwind with trembling voice, "Ikhabot and the two other guardians left Tenshia to finish their training. They will not be back until they have become Thakaiken. No one here has a mind powerful enough for a message to reach them where they are. We are alone and defenseless! This could be the end of Tenshia," a glistening tear finds its way down the Satrap's wrinkled cheek.

Henry is speechless, he knows they are in trouble. The teen brings his fists to his temple and presses his head while tears fall on the white sheets.

Disappointment takes over every feeling of happiness for being back in Tenshia with Aurora. The shame and disgust for his own actions are overwhelming. Arwind leans against the wall. The wise Satrap is dismayed, as he has never been before.

"I am afraid, my children, there is not much we can do now. I might know who is attacking us. We had been trying for centuries to stay hidden, but he is finally here. We cannot alert the citizens of the great danger, if we do, our enemy will learn of our secret place and will follow us. We shall never allow, for no reason at all, that our adversaries find where our hidden city is located. It would be catastrophic for the whole world if they find our most sacred possession here in Tenshia. It could mean the end of everything; the end of our mission to transform the universe."

Each word coming out of the old man's mouth crosses a maze of uncertainty. The pain in his eyes is impossible to ignore.

Aurora cannot believe Arwind is not going to warn the people, her eyes flood with tears. The Satrap walks toward the bed where the teenage-looking girl and Henry sit and places a hand on her shoulder.

"It is more important to protect Tenshia's holy secret, than saving the cities around the freshwater ocean, my dear girl. You will soon understand why this is the best choice, despite the lives that will be lost."

"What secret?" asks Henry while he hugs the girl.

"We need to save as many people as we can; we need to do it in secret. Just the three of us. We need to do something now, there is not a second we can waste!" urges Arwind, pulling Henry out of bed and hurrying both of them to the door.

Once outside the Aghora, Ghalaban's Satrap grabs their hands, and they ener-travel to the central plaza. People gathered in the streets are frightened; they talk to each other about what could be the reason for the strange weather inside the colossal cavern.

The breeze is no longer warm or gentle; it is more a hurricane wind blowing the leaves off the trees.

In the distance, waterspouts rise to the cavern's ceiling. The sight is terrifying to the locals who are used to looking at the horizon and seeing a calm ocean. No one knows what is happening, but the unruly tide and the aggressive winds do not offer a promising future.

The menacing clouds approach Ghalaban's shore while Arwind, Henry, and Aurora run to the crowd gathered in the plaza. Everyone in the city stops their activities to observe the unusual and wild phenomenon in complete perplexity.

Suddenly, a threatening voice resounds in the middle of the apocalyptic clouds.

"People of Tenshia, I am sure you have never heard of me before, so allow me to introduce myself. I am Kharas, one of the celestial generals. By order of the Planetary Prince, my comrade and I are here to destroy this land," threatens Kharas as Kaiosel grins.

"...And let me tell you all something; it is useless to run or hide. All of you will perish. Hail The Prince forever!"

Following his words, the emerald-haired Specter releases his toxic gas, and the waterspouts lash out against the beautiful city. Everything starts flying everywhere like leaves in a gale, and the water ejected from the spouts' vortex travels the air like piercing arrows.

Henry, like the rest of the Tenshians, has no choice but to close his eyes and cover his face.

Kaiosel's hands start shaking, and his turquoise eyes turn black. The thunderbolts harnessed in the palms of his hands begin to fall over the marble streets with such power that the people of Tenshia shudder violently. Chaos and desperation take over the peaceful Tenshian city. There is nowhere to hide; there is nowhere to run.

The strong winds whip hundreds of Tenshians as their cry for help resounds in the town that, little by little, falls apart by the hand of Kharas's atrocious power.

The beautifully carved houses are torn down by the toxic gas while washed away by the water along with Ghalaban's inhabitants.

It is a matter of seconds before Arwind and the teens are drowned by the pool, too; time is running out.

"Hold on to the rope!" yells the wise Satrap, taking off through an alley toward the hills. Aurora and Henry try to keep up and cling to the rope tied around Arwind's waist, even though the boy finds no sense in it. Fighting to run in the water up to his knees, young Henry tries to understand the older man's purpose with the rope. The two teenagers run and scream desperately while the wind thrashes dozens of people running behind them.

Thunder strikes on each side of the crowd sprinting toward higher grounds, fleeing from the strong water current.

Arwind shouts while pulling the teens by the rope, "Aurora! Tell the people to hold on to it!"

The Tenshian girl turns and helps people beside her, grasp the silver twine, "hold it tight, do not let go!"

Suddenly, Henry and those holding the rope find themselves suspended in the air. Arwind uses all of his power to lift a dozen people off the ground and keep them alive.

The majority manage to hold on despite the wind, others fall off in different directions losing themselves in the blurry horizon, and a few others are absorbed by titanic columns of water.

Those still avidly clinging to the rope, disappear behind a sharp flash of light in the middle of the mysterious and unnatural storm.

TENSHIA'S GREATEST SECRET

S econds later, the survivors wind up in a gorgeous garden. Henry lies face down when he regains his breath. The boy's amber eyes take time to adjust to the brightness before he can see the grass almost caressing his nose.

Rubbing his eyes to relieve the slight pain caused by the light, he opens them to see the pale mint meadow under his bare feet.

Young Schulze wiggles his toes and brushes the grass with his fingertips; it feels soft to his touch as if it were the most delicate feathers.

He raises his head and cannot help but open his mouth in amazement. At about thirty feet, a gigantic white root emerges from the ground to become a white trunk of immense proportions.

The boy looks up and sees in the distance the

precious branches thousands of feet long, covering the firmament of the place in all directions. The wood of the gigantic tree is smooth, without any bark or fissure, to disturb its perfection.

Millions of luminous white leaves embellish the daunting branches of the beautiful tree. Any mortal would find it difficult to digest the grandeur of the natural wonder.

Orioto is a hidden city in the depths of the freshwater ocean in Tenshia, host to one of the most precious mysteries of humanity.

It's never been seen nor been fathomed by any man on the face of the earth. The inhabitants of Orioto dwell in the shade of a tree that covers all directions.

Its sturdy trunk is as thick as the base of the Great Pyramid of Giza. It is held by outer and underground roots that furrow everything that surrounds them like strong walls.

The houses, also made of marble, border the roots in a way that makes the landscape something extraordinary to stare at.

Henry looks around and sees Aurora to his left end; his heart fills with peace. He covers his eyes to clear his weak vision and manages to locate Arwind, who is already standing and comes walking toward him.

In other parts of the garden, different groups of

Tenshians have come to this place too. The Satraps, along with the survivors from the other five cities of Tenshia; Üversa, Alzamak, Olu, Gémeaux, and Burh. All of them have also been destroyed by the Specters.

The teenage boy is surprised to see there are several people who, judging by their appearance, come from the surface as well. He immediately understands the Tenshians have brought them there as refugees. He spent so much time in Mizraim he forgot about the outside world.

"What is going on?" he asks himself when Ghalaban's Satrap places his freckled hand on his shoulder.

"My boy, I shall go back to the city now, I ought to save more of my people!"

The teen feels he is in debt with the Tenshians since all of it is his fault. His laden conscience forces him to choose others above himself, He decides to go help Arwind instead of staying in Orioto away from NaHash. Without a second thought, he speaks his mind.

"I am coming with you, sir! Whatever happens, I want to help," begs the boy. Aurora's sweet voice sounds in the background.

"Me too! Henry, you are not going alone!"

"Oh, no, no, and no! There is no way you two are coming with me. You have done enough, and I thank you, but it is time for you to rest and stay safe," states the old Satrap.

"Sir you know you won't be able to do it alone," insists Henry, "…please let me help you, I swear to my mother's memory that I won't let you down. Not again, at least!"

The Tenshian sage notices the youngster's sincere and strong will, so he holds him by the wrist, and they ener-travel back to Ghalaban.

Back in the cavern, the Specters continue to destroy the cities. They have trashed the place completely, crumbling everything in their path. Arwind and Henry wander through the cracked streets, hiding from the Muhalif warriors.

They search the houses looking for survivors, but the only things found are the drowned corpses of the Tenshian people. The beautiful capital is in ruins: the entire city dissolves as the water recedes to the ocean carrying hundreds of years of memories and technological advances with it.

With his eyes full of tears and great pain in his heart, Arwind looks at the hills of his destroyed city and turns to the boy. Stares at him sorrowfully and his hoarse voice breaks, "Let's go back to Orioto, Hen."

"I am so sorry, Arwind!" cries the teen holding the silver twine fastened around the sage's waist. He looks over his shoulder one more time to see the massive destruction he provoked.

"Taxidi!" howls Arwind a second before one of the Specters reaches for the rope, but it is too late, the word has been said. Henry screams in vain, and they vanish in the static air. Back in Orioto's garden, the teenager stares in fright; Kharas holds Arwind by the neck with his strong left arm.

The specter's emerald hair waves mighty in the breeze that flows through the roots of the magnificent tree. Now Henry has something else to worry about; not only Arwind's life is in danger, but Kharas will inform The Prince about his location any minute.

Kharas closes his bright eyes and calls his comrades. Arwind knows this is the end; Tenshia's secret will be revealed, and everything will be lost.

NaHash and his warriors will discover the great tree's true nature.

"Comrades, you need to come to see this. There is a city under the ocean, a huge dome on the seabed. And the best of all, you have yet to see!" whistles Kharas in amazement.

The five Muhalif warriors are destroying the remaining cities when they hear Kharas inside their heads, and one by one, the Specters make their appearance in Orioto's garden. With great agility, each of the warriors captures a Satrap.

All six Specters seize Tenshia's six Satraps and

stand in a circle looking up, waiting for something to land in the middle. The Tenshian survivors lie on the grass crippled with fear. Henry and Aurora stand behind the specter holding Arwind.

The only thing to be heard is the Specters' labored breathing trying to adjust to the air density of the underwater city.

The merciless Prince appears close to the branches of the magnificent tree. He descends gently to the center of the circle, where the Satraps are held captive by the impish beings.

NaHash looks around and takes a deep breath. The grin on his face when he spots Henry makes the boy feel the most profound guilt. The Prince slowly approaches Ghalaban's Satrap and frees him from Kharas's grasp to address him with unexpected kindness.

"Dear friend, allow me to introduce myself. My name is NaHash, the planetary Prince," the dome jolts when Mizraim's Tsar pronounces his name. Orioto's floor rattles, and the roots cringe; the people quiver in fear.

"Would you care to explain what this place is? This tree is so curious! What is this stunning tree that covers the whole of your peculiar dome? Huh?"

"I do not have to tell you anything. You will get no piece of information from me. You are wasting your time, ancient serpent!" groans the Satrap.

"The secrecy bothers me, old man, what is it about the tree? It looks familiar. I believe I have seen it before; a long, long time ago! Even though its appearance is slightly different, its essence lingers. Is this the everlasting Vạkkai-Maram that once stood in Ghanedén before the foundation of this material realm?"

Arwind's eyes betray his conscience and give him away. The Prince is right; he confirms his doubts after the involuntary and inevitable reaction of the Tenshian.

"How is this possible?" babbles The Prince, before talking to the old Satrap again, "I feel how fear runs through your veins, old man. There is no doubt that you have a powerful thing under your domain. That explains a few interesting things about you and your people. Am I right? This is enthralling!" pauses and meanders around, whispering to himself, "... but you are not allowed to eat its fruit, are you? No, no, absolutely not; that would mean living in rebellion against the Creator. I know the tale by heart; experienced it actually. Aren't you ashamed of having to hide under its shade?"

The Tsar's pace around the garden scares everyone close to him, even the Specters. He has not been so anxious in centuries. His mauve eyes volley side to side as if he were reading a book, and his fingers snap offbeat.

"Now listen to this, stinking human, because I care little about Grand-Abbadi's bylaws, I am going to go up there and take a bite of one of those juicy yellow fruits. My body shall forever be, and I will obtain the power to break the barrier of Third Heaven. The universe will be mine!"

Arwind loses control and throws himself at The Prince, "Oh no, you won't! Not a single being will live under your oppression forever; no one will be enslaved by the astral powers anymore. You will be sent to the abyss and shall perish. This is your fate! There will be no reason for your existence!"

NaHash opens a crack in the garden's ground and buries the sage up to his neck while the Satrap boasts in frustration. Tears of defeat fall ceaselessly from the wise man's eyes.

"I and each one of my Specters will eat the fruit. Then we will burn the Vākkai-Maram to ashes so no one else will ever eat from it again. And last, we will grind up the last city in Tenshia, and there will be no one left to tell the tale!" threatens The Prince.

Arwind centers all his power in his mind. His old body is weak; there is no way he can fight The Prince. While his bitter tears keep falling from his eyes, he tries to talk to Henry with his mind.

The sage knows he is going to die soon, so he has to give Henry the last advice to become a Thakaiken and come to be strong enough to defeat NaHash. Arwind's last words to the kid, shall not be known by the evil Prince.

Hen, can you hear me? Can you hear my voice inside your head?

The boy gazes at the tormented elder and nods discreetly.

...pay close attention, my boy, you need to run away, fast, and take Aurora with you. You are the world's only hope now. Go to the surface and find a guy called the Myth-Keeper; he will teach you all you need to know to become the Thakaiken of the surface. Do it, Hen, do it for Tenshia, for your mother, for the friends you found here, for Ikhabot and all of humanity. Make your miracle happen!

The Tsar sees Arwind looking directly into the boy's eyes. He understands that he is saying something to him, but the barrier inside the wise man's mind is hard to penetrate. Slowly, the old man feels a lack of air.

The earth around his chest tightens around it, and the air he breathes no longer oxygenates his body. The Prince is suffocating the great Satrap of Ghalaban.

Now panting, Arwind's body gasps for air. The loving elder's lungs try to inflate forcefully, but the blood that runs through his veins no longer has the will to keep him alive. Everyone sees how their caring leader dies slowly.

Henry looks wide-eyed, red in anger, and full of tears. The boy's heart is downtrodden; his throat closes, and his insides burn. The boy cannot endure more suffering. His soul breaks down, knowing all this pain is his fault.

First, his mother, then Tenshia, and now Arwind. His mind questions whether the cause of all that evil is his very existence.

The naive teenager believes maybe everything would be solved if he died there and now. At the same time, he realizes that not even his death would stop The Prince. The only thing left to try is actually to become a Thakaiken, whatever that means.

When Arwind's heart stops beating, The Prince lets out a wicked laugh. Many of the Tenshians who thought they had no strong bonds toward anyone, lay crying for their kind leader.

The wise man's head sticks out from the ground, already lifeless. His blue eyes stare steadily at the big tree with love, while his last tear rolls down his cheek.

"My angels of the power of the air, the tree of life is ours!" yells The Prince as the Specters cheer in victory, "...we shall eat the Vakkai-Maram's fruit and will be freed from this mortal body. There will be no more reincarnations; these will remain our bodies for eternity. Enjoy your new incorruptible nature, my dear comrades. No water or food will you require, no time or sleep will burden you from now on. We are invincible! Now please, slay 'em all!"

The Specters rush to end the Tenshian leaders' innocent lives and then toss their bodies next to Arwind's. They head to reach the branches of the Vākkai-Maram. The survivors cannot believe what they witness; their leaders are dead, and they soon will be gone too.

Henry holds Aurora back when she attempts to run to Arwind. The girl sobs hopelessly while Henry hugs her tightly. He closes his eyes and tries to connect with Ikhabot.

Where are you guys? Tenshia has been destroyed by these hellish creatures; why aren't you here?

In the meantime, NaHash raises his hand and grabs a yellow fruit. The ambition in his eyes is overwhelming; he has waited thousands of years to hold a fruit from the tree of life. He slowly takes the fruit to his mouth and takes a bite. His Muhalif warriors do the same.

That could be the beginning of a cruel destiny for all humanity; there was nothing Henry or anyone could do about it. The Prince and his Specters delight themselves in the tree's fruit; they savor on eternal pleasure.

They all eat one fruit after the other, but there seems to be no immediate effect on them at all.

Suddenly, sparks of energy materialize on their backs. Wings of light grow out of nowhere. The Muhalif stare at each other ecstatic; they feel pleased and prosperous. The emerald-haired Muhalif yells, "We are invincible!"

The Specters cheer and laugh. The Prince smirks, looking at the boy who handed him a comfortable victory and toasts with the juicy fruit on his hand.

Tartuross suddenly remembers that there are hundreds of survivors still looking at them. He believes it is only fair to put them out of their misery as well, now that all their leaders are dead.

"Listen, people, after our unexpected but welcomed finding of the Vākkai-Maram, I feel compelled to perform a merciful act," he pauses briefly to organize his thoughts. He looks at NaHash, who nods back in approval, "...I will grant you all a quick death, no suffering or pain. I will create a wave so powerful that your hearts will pop inside your tiny chests. Let's see, who wants to be the first one to put my new power to the test?"

The winged redhead snaps his fingers, and the dozens of survivors are lifted off the meadow. The Tenshians flit in the air while the rescued humans yelp.

The sinister specter extends his left arm out. He points with his finger at the floating victims, and, one by one, they are left lifeless and plummet to the ground like inert dolls. The corpses crash against the immaculate garden's luminous grass.

NaHash walks facing the terrified teenager, bragging about his newly restored wings. His mauve eyes shine with pride as he starts sharing his thoughts with the boy.

"My dear Henry, you too will eat from the tree. Don't be scared; I am interested to see what effect the fruit has on you. Although your girlfriend won't have the same luck!"

"I want nothing to do with you. I will eat no fruit you wish to give me. You are cruel and ruthless; you sacrifice innocent people without regret, and destroyed a venerable man like Arwind, just because you have the power. You are nothing but a coward!" vents Henry with bitter tears flooding his amber eyes, "...you brought me here based on lies; you gave me hope to see my mother again. But the truth is, you never meant to do that, you had your own agenda. You have blinded me since I arrived in Mizraim, and I forgot who I was. I won't rest until you are destroyed!"

"Think and say whatever you please unthankful little wimp. You want to destroy me? You will find out how impossible it is; you will die trying. You are useless, weak, and good for nothing. I tried to change your destiny, but I see that you are a putrid waste of time. We will wreck this place after eating every single fruit of the tree of life, or until we are satisfied. And if you and your friend are still here when we are done, you two will perish with this city."

Aurora, who listens carefully to each syllable of the conversation, challenges The Prince bravely.

"Henry, the boy you look down upon today, will become the strongest being in the universe. Then he will turn you and your entire celestial army into dust. There will be no memory of none of you!"

The boy acts surprised when he hears the faith Aurora has in him. He does not understand how someone other than his mother, and Ikhabot could believe in him with the same love and conviction.

"Who do you think you are to address me, insolent brat?" growls NaHash, instantly slapping across the girl's delicate face. The Tsar's strength makes Aurora fly through the air and hit one of the tree branches.

Henry runs to aid her and gently lifts her head off the ground. She has a drop of blood sliding down her forehead. Henry aches, Aurora is the only real friend he has ever had.

The boy is fuming and stunned; he turns his head, the people's muffled screaming, the piles of dead bodies, and Arwind's blank eyes bring more discomfort to his soul. The meadow is stained in red, and pain has infested every corner of Orioto's garden.

Young Henry wipes Aurora's forehead with his tunic's cuff. The girl comes back to her senses, and her silver eyes open bit by bit to find her friend's amber eyes staring back at hers.

Despite being a Tenshian, Atmix's young sister lacks physical strength, and now that Arwind is gone, it is not possible to know what internal wounds her body could have. She is in pain; her eyes close again slowly, and she falls in a deep sleep.

Henry cannot take his eyes off her and feels a big emptiness in his chest. Suddenly he realizes the deep love he feels for the wounded girl lying in his arms. Many have died, but the boy's lips tremble at the mere idea of death also taking Aurora.

"Aurora, please hang on!" Henry weeps leaning his head against hers, "don't leave me, please," he hugs her delicately and rubs her tanned cheek with his thumb, "not you, please! Not you, I need you," the boy's voice starts to break, "don't you dare leave me, Aurora, hang on!

The future guardian's tears slide down his face onto hers. She opens her eyes again, and there is her friend, caressing her cheek as nobody has before. She smiles and lifts her sprained hand and wipes the boy's tears.

Her eyes are still the most beautiful thing Henry has ever seen.

The love inside his heart grows every second. He feels the need to express his emotions, but he cannot find the words. He must do something before it's too late.

Looking at her lips, Henry closes his eyes and gently kisses her mouth. Aurora, somehow relieved, accepts the kiss.

"I will be fine, Hen, I promise! It takes more than this to hurt me," mumbles Aurora with a smile on her face and passes out.

Henry, trusting her words, smiles back and kisses her again in the forehead, then tries to contact Ikhabot. The boy knows that his uncle is the only option to save the city of Orioto and its people. He focuses all his energy and sends a cry for help.

Uncle, listen to me! Where are you?

Quickly, the boy receives a flash of Ikhabot. He is walking in a gloomy place. Silas and Atmix walk by his side, but none of them seem to hear him. He tries one more time.

"Ikhabot!" shouts the teen in his mind.

The blue-haired Thakaiken stops abruptly and turns back at the unexpected wind blowing his hair from behind. Ikhabot visualizes his nephew and sees the scene through his eyes.

Henry is glad to have finally reached his powerful uncle. The guardian's face turns pale, and he stares petrified at the floor.

"Silas, Atmix, we ought to go back immediately! Something horrendous is happening in Tenshia; NaHash and the Specters discovered the Vākkai-Maram and have destroyed all Tenshia! Arwind is dead, and so are the other Satraps and hundreds of people!"

"What!?" Atmix growls.

"How do you know, who showed you this, Ikhabot?" questions Silas.

"My nephew is back in Tenshia, and unfortunately, he brought the Specters with him. I am not aware of the details, but I am certain he was played by NaHash. Let's go!"

Atmix stares at Ikhabot reproachfully but surprisingly decides to keep his thoughts to himself. The three guardians are ready to leave the abyss and go to the rescue of their beloved underground nation.

Back in Orioto, the Specters continue to feast on the yellow fruits from the Vākkai-Maram. They rejoice in their victory and suspect nothing about

Henry's attempts to communicate with the Thakaiken.

Before they can react, the air turns dense, and a peculiar magnetism wraps the Muhalif warriors, leaving them immobile. They do not understand where the fierce energy is coming from.

A warm breeze flows from the crown of the tree of life, and three figures descend from a dense white fog. The Specters stare astonished, who could they be?

Ikhabot, Silas, and Atmix levitate down slowly. Their hair and tunics wave amaranthine in the breeze. A gorgeous silver aura surrounds the Thakaiken's bodies as they land gently on the mint-colored grass and look around. It is worse than any nightmare any of them has ever had. The three powerful guardians take off to help those who are still alive.

The Specters, still frozen by a wave of magnetic energy, have no other choice but to look at the guardians. Silas, checking for live victims on the piles of bodies, sees Arwind's head sticking out of the ground.

His eyes are still open!

Silas approaches the Satrap. He covers his gaze to avoid looking at him, and gently closes the old man's eyes, for he has seen the angel of death. Then, Silas kisses him on his forehead and whispers to his ear, "we will make this right, I promise you! Rest in peace!"

On the other side of the garden, Atmix pounces

knee first on Tartuross's chest. The redhead Muhalif flies through the air and lands tumbling down the garden, leaving a crack on the grass in his path. The ruthless warrior is knocked out in one fell swoop.

"I don't know if you can hear me, you coward, but I told you I was going to crush you when I saw you again!" laughs the blond Thakaiken, reminding the warrior about their last conversation in Mont Ross.

The remaining Specters stare petrified at the guardians' new powers. Filled with hate and somewhat fear, the Muhalif warriors see how Atmix is about to kill their redhead comrade.

Rage invades their minds; they are supposed to be the most powerful creations of all, and now, the Tenshians are capable of injuring them in one strike.

"Silas! Ikhabot! I got this! I alone will deal with this vermin! I will make them pay for what they have done," the blond Tenshian grumbles before he sees his sister lying unconscious on Henry's arms. He runs toward them and snatches his sister off the teenager's hands. "How dare you touch her, you nasty piece of work!" shouts Atmix at the boy, handing Aurora to Silas and getting ready to smack Henry on the head.

"Calm down, Atmix, I understand your frustration; your pain is mine too, but you are much more powerful if you stay calm. The perfect balance between rage and serenity helped you cross the Sea of

Sorrow, remember?"

"Leave me alone, Ikhabot, it is not time to nag!" he snaps back at his blue-haired friend and takes off to grab the rest of the Muhalif warriors.

The guardian hits the celestials hundreds of times, leaving each one of them knocked down, with no chance whatsoever of attacking him back. The wicked celestials squirm on the ground staring at the blond man with the most deep-seated hatred.

NaHash watches the fight standing still inside a force field he created for himself, Mizraim's Tsar's power is inconceivable.

He is untouchable, even here in Tenshia, where its inhabitants regulate all events. His expression is not that of surprise nor doubt or fear, and Ikhabot is watching him rejoice with the defeat of his warriors.

The Thakaiken decides to strike the orchestrator of the devastating episode.

"Infinite-Mayımdın" hails Ikhabot whipping his finger in the air. A gust of wind forms around the sphere where The Prince hovers. The fierce wind lashes the leaves of the Vạkkai-Maram, but its branches hold firm. When the wind stops blowing around the force field, Ikhabot notices he barely jumbled the implacable Prince's hair.

"Drats!" rumbles the blue-haired Thakaiken as NaHash stands with a scornful smile while being no more than an onlooker of the circus around him.

"Nice try, tiny guardian! But you need more than that to impress me," The Prince chortles, "...to those who don't know me, I am delighted to meet you, gentlemen. Allow me to tell you that you have incredible powers, but I shall not slaughter you here. It would take away all the fun! Moreover, I won't kill you myself; there is no need for me to filthy my hands with rivals such as you three. My Specters will end you on the surface where their strength is not this limited. None of you are a match for my warriors up there," he laughs. "Once my generals finish you off, we will come back here. The freshwater ocean will be mine, and the Vaḻkkai-Maram burned to ashes!" argues NaHash floating down to the lawn and strolling in the garden gazing at his warriors.

He wants the Thakaiken to understand they do not pose a threat to him.

Dragging his bare feet on the meadow, the Tsar looks at Ikhabot and adds, "...Should we continue with the show on the surface? That puny girl dared to say Henry will destroy me when he is ready. I gladly accept the challenge. I am more than eager to see what that useless piece of work and all of you can do. What do you say, huh? I intend to complete my millenary plan and will crush whoever chooses to oppose us. My warriors will turn Second Heavens' columns to dust;

the Epsilon barrier will fall; the universe and Grand-Abbadi will be mine!"

The three Tenshian guardians pay attention to what The Prince says with great conviction. Atmix looks at him with disgust, while Silas and Ikhabot stare at each other. Leaning over Tartuross, The Prince places his right hand on his shoulder, and the glowing energy heals all of his wounds.

Quickly, the redhead specter recovers consciousness. One by one, the warriors stand up after being restored by their leader. Silas knows they are in great danger; he saunters, trying not to be seen and discreetly pulls on Ikhabot's tunic sleeve.

"What are we going to do?" whispers on his friend's ear.

Ikhabot grabs his wrist and talks to him in his mind.

He might be right. We are no match for them, at least not without the fourth Thakaiken!

Atmix sprints after The Prince, willing to attack him despite his intimidating speech. NaHash turns around and glances at him with disdain, then raises his hand and snaps his fingers.

The blond Tenshian darts violently toward the dome that shelters the submarine city, breaking several of the white tree's sturdy branches in his path.

"Hopefully, that will teach him to be polite with

his guests!" rasps The Prince and the Muhalif laugh, "farewell, guardians!" shouts NaHash and takes off flapping his incandescent wings followed by his six warriors. After the roar of a lightning bolt, the seven destroyers of the sacred cities disappear before the Thakaiken's and the few survivor's eyes.

Silas runs to aid Atmix, who lies terribly injured on the grass. In spite of the blond Thakaiken's incredible strength, both his left leg and collarbones have been fractured, as well as multiple ribs. His right wrist also looks out of place.

Thanks to the infinite providence that protects the Tenshians, Atmix is still alive.

Not being able to speak, the blond guardian limits himself to stare at Silas, trying to alleviate his misery.

"Brother, don't you worry. I will ease your pain right away, and we will get your bones back in place. As long as you're still alive, there is much we can do. Unwind your thoughts and rest, you have lost some blood and have several fractures, stay still before you puncture an organ..."

The beaten Thakaiken stops his friend's on-going speech with an annoyed look. Silas interprets the gesture and places his hands on Atmix's torso to make the pain go away.

With help from a couple of survivors, they carry him to one of the homes not too far from the garden.

Silas takes his time to clean his brother's open wounds, and using Arwind's techniques, bonds his shattered bones back together. In a matter of minutes, Atmix is as good as new.

"How are you feeling?" asks Silas as soon as he opens his eyes.

"Thank you, brother. You did a decent job. I feel good enough to go to the surface and finish NaHash on the spot!"

"Oh, you will not. I understand how you feel, and I am glad you recovered, but you need to think things through the next time. Maybe you won't be lucky enough for me to be around and save you again!" taunts the kindhearted Thakaiken.

"I hate to admit you are right. I never thought that guy had such power as to hurt our renovated bodies. I wanted to gauge how strong he was and almost sent me to the other side. I am not the smart-type of person, but I promise you I will be more careful," thanks Atmix, patting his brother's back. They walk together outside looking for Ikhabot, who sits on a bench talking to Henry and Aurora.

Spotting Henry, Atmix loses his temper and attacks the boy, "I am going to kill you, traitor!" howls holding him by the neck and slamming him twice against the marble sidewalk. If he wanted to kill him, the Thakaiken would not need to touch him. He just desires to punish the inept teenager.

"Atmix, stop! What are you doing? Killing him won't fix anything," shouts Silas pushing Atmix away from the fragile boy.

"Control yourself, you fool!" Ikhabot steps in with a stern voice, "...what will you accomplish hurting the kid? Do you want to kill him? Is that going to bring Arwind back? Or the others? Use your brain for once!"

"Take that traitor out of my sight! Imbecile! Get away from my sister!" fumes the blond Tenshian.

"You know we need him to overthrow NaHash! Grow up, Atmix, we don't have the power to defeat him by ourselves. We had providence on our side today; the Vakkai-Maram protected us. On the surface, we won't stand a chance of beating them without Hen as the fourth Thakaiken!" spouts Ikhabot slapping Atmix on the head.

The arrogant Tenshian lifts Aurora from the bench and ener-travels to the ruins of Ghalaban without uttering a sound. Silas looks troubled at Ikhabot, who tries to comfort Henry.

"I am sorry Ikhabot, I am truly sorry," bawls the teen in his uncle's arms. Silas helps Henry sit on the sidewalk and checks for injuries from Atmix's recklessness.

"Ikhabot, power is getting to our brother's head. You know he won't be accepted in the new era with that attitude!" assures Silas.

"Let him be, Silas, he will let it go; you know how he is; his heart is kind, deep down, at least. His soul is wounded, and he hasn't taken the time or put any effort whatsoever into healing his heart. He is afraid, that's all," laments Ikhabot dusting his tunic.

"...and that is precisely why I am troubled," says Silas, making a gesture to walk with him to one of the houses, "...he has the main ingredient that feeds NaHash and his demons; fear. On the other hand, I must say I don't trust the kid either. I don't see how he can become one of us!"

Henry, ashamed enough, has nothing to say against Silas's statement.

"You'll see brother, his success will be greater than his mistakes, and his soul will grow bigger than his ego. He will make his miracle happen! Right, Hen?"

The boy turns to his uncle with hope. His mother's phrase brings peace and comfort to his heart.

"That is what my mother used to say," he nods, shedding a tear. Ikhabot puts his hand on the back of his neck and encourages him to lift his head, hopeful for what the kid needs to become.

"I hope you are right, brother. Otherwise, we will never beat NaHash, and we will all die in vain. Dire circumstances have reached their peak now. The temporal dimension continues to tear faster and faster," states Silas.

"I know, right now, there is something else we have to do; let's bury our brothers and sisters and have faith that they will rest in peace!"

It seems to be a difficult thing to do. Still, Silas, Ikhabot, and young Henry start digging along the roots of the Vākkai-Maram to lay entire families to rest for eternity.

The situation is new and brutally uncomfortable for Henry since he never had to dig a hole on the ground and put a body in it. He pushes himself to help and try to ease his guilt.

The remaining survivors gather in the garden to help with the burials and share with Henry the Tenshian burial traditions. Once done, everyone meets by the white trunk and places their right hands on it.

Henry stands by his uncle uncertain of what to do, but Ikhabot holds his hand and encourages him to do the same. The boy closes his eyes and senses the energy flowing from the Vākkai-Maram into his body as Silas sings a traditional tenshian song.

There is so much I don't know about this world.

Henry feels the warmth in his right palm.

Ikhabot taps Henry's shoulder, letting him know it is ok to open his eyes now, but the teen holds on to the tree a bit longer. The boy has never experienced that amount of peace and sense of belonging.

"Come on, Hen, we must go!" whispers Ikhabot in his nephew's ear.

, Henry, and Silas ener-travel together, leaving Orioto behind, to visit the fallen Tenshian cities. The minute they appear on the shore, the scene of desolation takes its toll on the emotions of the two guardians.

They cannot look around without tears streaming down their cheeks. The boy keeps his chin down to his chest. He does not want to be tormented one more minute by his guilt. Ikhabot interrupts the uncomfortable moment.

"There is nothing to be done here, Silas; it is not time to rebuild quite yet. First, we need to meditate and visualize everything that is going on the surface and, especially, in the heavens. The Prince and his comrades ate from the Va̱kkai-Maram, but it is not too late. We need to know how things look up there! We ought to find this hidden city in the desert and stop his wicked agenda. There are lots to be done, shall we get started?"

"What about Atmix, where did he go?" the lilac-haired Thakaiken asks.

"I am not sure, I haven't been able to feel his *sharah*; neither can I find Aurora's. Wherever they are, they don't want to be found. Anyhow, we can't count on Atmix in his current mindset. His rage and resentment toward the people on the surface won't allow him to see clearly," explains the Thakaiken to his friend.

"To make matters worse, we have little time to stop NaHash," Silas points out anxiously. Ikhabot nods and takes a few seconds to look at the demolished city one more time. "Well, from what I can see," he sighs, staring at his nephew, "...you are against the clock to find the Myth-Keeper, Hen. You need to find him as soon as possible. He is the only one capable of showing you the path to the power of Zorah, now that Arwind is gone!"

FRANKIE'S BUNKER

H enry's mind is debating. His heart tells him he has to avenge all those he buried in Orioto's garden. Especially old Arwind, to whom, in the most literal sense, he owes his life.

His mind, still ignorant and naive, tells him he is not worthy enough. He fears he will never be able to be as strong as his uncle and his friends and defend the world as the fourth Thakaiken.

Perhaps this time, he will embrace his thirst for revenge against The Prince and all Mizraim's citizens to become stronger.

The events in the last couple of days hurt him to the bone. The situation seems so dark and complicated, he almost disregards his deceased mother was taken by the Specters. His heart is demanding him to make amends for his mistakes.

A new path has been laid before him, and he needs to follow it. He feels he ought to become a Thakaiken and take revenge in the name of the lost cities. The teenager is ready to become a man.

With his uncle's support, he will manage to transform pain and frustration into determination. Now he is willing to give up his life to grow wiser and tougher with the sole purpose of destroying The Prince's plans.

Ikhabot does not have to try hard to read the kid's emotions. He is glad his nephew finally found a reason to fight for others. The guardian places his right hand in Henry's boney chest and starts to explain some of the details about the journey that awaits him.

"Listen carefully, son of Khazios. Your path to becoming a Thakaiken will be unlike ours. You have been in this world for a short while, so you will have to transcend the veil differently. You have been taught to see life as a one-way road, but that is not how it works. The time you spent in Tenshia taught you about meditation, delayed aging, rapid cell reconstruction, and other things you didn't consider possible, right?"

"It did, Ikhabot!"

"Okay, there will be things that will blow your

mind farther shortly! Most of what you knew before discovering Tenshia, you ought to unlearn; all that information is rubbish. On the other hand, I don't know what you did while in Mizraim, not that I want to know, but you need to use everything you learned about NaHash against him. You must find the darkness he planted inside your heart and eliminate it. Every time you bring good and evil together, good always wins. Like the small flame of a match can illuminate a large dark room; you can turn all darkness around you into the most radiant light."

Ikhabot explains, then takes a step closer to meet Henry face to face, "…and the most crucial thing you need to do, is to forgive yourself. We forgive you for every mistake you consider you made, and you can be sure that Grand-Abbadi forgives you as well. Free your heart from all guilt!"

Henry breaks down in tears. He has seen so much destruction and suffering in the past hours that he cannot keep it together.

The young man wishes from the bottom of his heart that Aurora is alive and that her brother forgives him someday. Ikhabot allows him to cry it all out before adding a few more things.

"Hen, I love you! You are my nephew, and Tenshia is your home now!"

"You mean what is left of Tenshia? Right?" sighs

the teen.

Silas soothes the boy and places his hand on his head, handing him a cloth to wipe off his face, "We all love you, Hen!"

"You see," whispers Ikhabot, "...hold us close to your heart in the same way you hold your mother, and our love will take you far. Now, let me hug you before you leave; I want to show you the love I have received from the world of Zorah!"

The brave guardian brings his nephew's head to his chest and wraps his arms around him. Henry hugs him back. Without letting him go, Ikhabot looks into his amber eyes and caressing his head, he says proudly, "You have your father's eyes!"

"Do I?" asks the boy.

"Without a doubt, his love is within your heart as well!" Continues the guardian as a tear slides down his tanned cheekbone, "I will see you soon, fourth Thakaiken, your quest will be lonely, and neither of us can help you any further. Silas and I will take you back to the surface. Find the Myth-Keeper; he will know who you are. Now go, do your best, and take all the power Zorah will give you, and bring it to this world. Remember, NaHash, and his Specters want to attack Third Heaven to avoid Grand-Abbadi's revelation to the world. They will continue to enslave humanity if you don't come back in time," stresses the guardian.

"I understand, uncle, I won't let you down!"

"I know you won't," Ikhabot cheers.

Silas encourages the boy, "...and the next time we see each other, you will be a Thakaiken, and we will fight side by side as brothers!"

Henry smiles when Ikhabot nods, "So, son of Khazios, where do you want to go?"

"...to the only person I know who can help me find the Myth-Keeper; Frank Waltz!"

The moon is at its zenith when Henry ener-travels to the courtyard of the musician's house. The boy enters stealthily to find the house empty and full of dust. The sofas in the room have been covered with white sheets, and the famous composer's piano is missing.

Henry enters the kitchen where the pipe drips under the sink giving him the creeps. He leaves the kitchen and tiptoes down the hall to Frank's room.

The shelves in the study reveal the shadow of dust left by the books that are no longer there.

Swiping his finger through the dusty furniture, Henry wonders where his godfather could be. Trying not to make much noise, he enters the room and whispers, "Frankie? Are you there?"

The wood of the floor creaks with every step he takes, and the quietness in the house is more frightening than the idea of putting his life in danger. With his heart echoing in his ears, he decides to sit on the floor of a large closet full of fancy suits.

Maybe Frankie hasn't been here for a long time. Maybe he's running away. Maybe, Frankie is dead? No, it can't be.

The teenager analyzes the situation.

The truth is, there could be a million people looking for him or Frank all over the world. The S.E.N. has eyes everywhere, and there are very few places the musician could be hiding.

Henry stands and decides to search inside the nightstands, the dresser, and the bathroom cabinets for clues.

He finds nothing.

Tired and disheartened, Henry chooses to sit on Frank's king-size bed. The young man takes a deep breath, and it seems to resound in the entire house; he closes his eyes and lies back on the bare mattress.

"I haven't had a minute to just, be..." whispers to himself, exhaling all the air in his lungs.

Mindful of his breathing, his skinny body sinks in the dusty pillow top.

He rests for no more than five minutes. Young

Henry has a hunch and opens his eyes. There, on the edge of the Dalbergia wood nightstand, a familiar face in a picture smiles back at him. It is Minerva Goldsmith, his dear mother.

The boy grabs the picture frame and holds it against his chest. To his surprise, there are still tears in his eyes to shed for his dead mother.

The miserable teenager is tired of crying. It seems to be all he has done since the earthquake at the excavation site for the *AQUA-DE-VITA* project.

All alone, he tries to motivate himself, "Come on, Henry, you need to be brave. You are almost a man; calm down and focus!"

Saying this, he decides to take his mother's picture with him and leave the house. The frame is too big to carry, so he turns it over and takes the frame's back cover off. Young Henry, clumsy as always, drops the glass to the floor, and it shatters into hundreds of pieces.

He looks up to the bedroom door, worried somebody might have heard the noise. A minute later, after trying to clean up the broken glass, he notices a piece of parchment taped to the back of Minerva's picture.

"I knew it," the kid gushes, "I knew Frankie would leave something behind!"

Dear Henry,

If you are reading this, then I was right to assume you would take your dear mother's picture. The S.E.N. androids and a handful of bounty hunters have been around the hills looking for you, so I have decided to go to a safe house hardly four kilometers from here. I am eager to see you and hear all about your adventure. I sense things in this world are not going well, and I am sure it has something to do with your uncle's people. Okay, I am writing too much. Walk out through the garage, and grab a red backpack I left for you with some fresh clothes, water, and a pair of hiking boots. Then walk about three kilometers north into the mountains. When you pass the creek, you will see a white mark on one of the pines. It means you're close. You will notice a clearing between the pines, in which you'll find ten young pines in a row forming a snake. Knock seven times on the second trunk, and I'll know it's you. See you soon!

Love,

Frankie

Henry walks down the stairs to the garage and finds the backpack. Leaving the Tenshian tunic behind, the boy puts on the clothes the musician left behind for him and folds the picture along with the note and shoves them in his left sock.

Finding the safe house will not be a problem for the teenager; six months ago, he did not know where the North was and surely would have been complaining about hiking three miles. But then again, life has taken him on a very different route.

Aurora had taught him to find true North on the surface, even during the day. She told him how, by burying a stick straight up in the ground and using rocks to mark where the stick's shadow ends, he could find his path.

She showed him the world through her silver eyes. He misses her so much, but the beautiful girl is in better hands with her stubborn brother.

By Henry's side, she would only be in danger.

Opening the garage door, young Schulze sees a figure standing about a quarter-mile east from Frank's house. The boy knows the person is looking straight at him, but fear is not going to stop him now.

He might be a bounty hunter. He thinks. *What am I going to do now? Running would not be a smart choice if he has a gun. And now that The Prince knows where the freshwater is, they might not need me alive!*

Standing still is not the best choice either. That would make Henry an easier target for a skilled shooter.

The teenager decides to run downhill as fast as he can towards the tree line and thus lose his pursuer.

Upon entering the dying woods, young Schulze does not hear any gunshots, so perhaps they are trying to capture him alive.

The crackle of the dried leaves trodden by the one running behind him grows louder. He finds it shocking that the individual standing a quarter-mile from him, less than a minute ago, is nearly stepping on his heels.

Or it could be a second man hunting him. Whoever it is, is closer, and the teen's life is at risk.

Henry zigzags through the pines trying to lose his hunter, but it is useless. Whatever it is, it is faster and smarter than the boy. The predator finally reaches the teenager, and pounces on his back, pushing him to the ground.

"Shhh…" a feminine voice whispers, "… be quiet, don't scream. I am sorry, I won't hurt you. You don't want to alert anyone looking for you in the forest!"

Henry turns around, "Aurora?" he yells, "…oh, sorry," he whispers, "what the hell are you doing here? Your brother will kill me if he knows you are with me!"

"My brother doesn't own me, Henry! He cannot tell me who I can be with. I want to be by your side for better or worse," mumbles the girl. "I realized that in Orioto when you stepped forward to protect me from The Prince," she says, trying to catch her breath, helping Henry up from the ground.

"I see, but anyway... you will only get yourself killed!"

"Hush, don't say that! Words have a lot of power" she reproaches, "The last time you left Tenshia, I thought I was never going to see you again; I was going crazy," sweet tears of joy run down her blushed cheeks, "...and then, that kiss!"

The teen interrupts the girl's emotional speech with another passionate kiss. She surrenders in Henry's arms and hugs him tightly.

"How did you find me?" questions Henry fixing a strand of hair covering her beautiful sterling grey eyes.

"Ikhabot told me, so it was easy," replies Aurora, kissing his cheek one more time.

"Okay, it is not safe to be here in the middle of the woods. We need to find Frankie."

The couple walks further north holding hands. They reach the group of pine trees, and the snake-shaped row stands ahead.

"I need to knock on the second one," shouts the boy running to the second tree.

"How do you know that is the second and not the ninth tree, Hen?" puzzles Aurora.

"Then we will try both," argues the anxious boy.

Henry knocks seven times on the trunk, but nothing happens. Then Aurora runs to the other end and claps seven times on the bark of the ninth tree.

Instantly, a dozen feet behind the peculiar line of trees, the ground opens, leaving a narrow stairway down to a shiny steel door.

"We found him, come on, Ro!" babbles Henry. They step down the stairs, and the heavy door opens.

"Hen!" yells Frankie hugging his godson. He seems tired and thinner than the last time Henry saw him. The boy had never seen a beard grow in the famous musician's face; it is obvious he has not shaved in a long while.

"It is so good to see you, son, I have been terrified for heaven's sake; you have no idea. I started thinking you were...well, dead. We have lots to talk about. Tell me everything; Conner helped me get this hideout some time ago. In a world under constant surveillance, this kind of place comes in handy. Where is Conner, by the way?"

Aurora stops at the doorway staring at the two. It is curious to her how humans from the surface interact with each other. Aside from Henry, Frank Waltz is the first human she meets on the surface.

"And who is she?" asks Frank, intrigued by the girl's beauty.

"This is Aurora, Frankie, my... hmm, girlfriend," he stammers, "she is Tenshian, you can trust her," explains Henry and invites the blushed girl to walk inside. The musician shuts the heavy bulletproof door behind her and shows them to the living room.

"So tell me, son, I want to know everything that happened since I left you at the hangar. Did you find the answers you were looking for?" questions Minerva's lifelong friend.

"Well, is there anywhere we could speak in private?" asks Henry, turning to the Tenshian girl tucking her hair behind her ear. "If it is okay with you, Aurora, I would like to talk to my godfather alone."

"Absolutely," nods the girl and sits on a leather couch, grabbing a book from the coffee table.

Henry and Frank walk to an office clustered with books and unopened boxes.

"Okay, first of all, she is beautiful, son, but we can talk about her another time," taunts the musician.

Henry chats with Mr. Waltz for more than two hours. The boy tells his godfather every detail of everything that happened in the last month. Minerva's faithful friend listens in amazement to everything the boy recounts.

It makes him sad to know that Conner is still in Mizraim. Who knows if he is still alive now that Henry has turned his back on the Tsar.

Frankie tells the young fugitive that the authorities have been trying to find him for further interrogation as a possible accomplice.

The choice to move to the bunker was the musician's best option; nobody will know he is there. At least not for now.

"We have nothing to worry about, son, this underground bunker is made of military-grade bulletproof steel. Top-notch technology and communication systems. Beds, clothes, water, and food to last us for years. I even bought a custom-built magnetic generator in case the wind generators stop working," brags Frankie.

"It seems like a safe place, but not safe enough for the ones who might be looking for me. It is just a matter of time before The Prince finds me here. He won't leave me alone until he has my loyalty or my head. The Prince won't admit it, but he fears the day I come to be a Thakaiken," Henry explains to his godfather, "...I can't stay long. I need to find the Myth-Keeper; he is the one to help me with my training to become a guardian. You see, I am running out of time. I need a favor, Frankie, I need cash and some food. I ought to find this man soon." The boy urges.

"And, how are you going to find him or know who he is at the very least?"

"I have no idea. The only thing I know about the Myth-Keeper is that he is some prophet that has roamed this Earth for more than two thousand years!"

Frankie opens his eyes wide. He is passionate

about being part of the unearthly event, "fascinating... just fascinating! This individual sounds interesting. I might have an idea of how we can find him!"

"How?" Henry inquires keenly.

"If this individual has been alive for that long, let's search the internet for information about paranormal experiences. That is ghosts, miracles, angels, etc. Those things that ordinary people talk about all the time, but nobody pays attention to because nobody understands what is going on," Frankie continues. Henry nods, showing that his cunning friend's suggestion makes sense.

"Clever!"

"Follow me, the laptop is in the living room; besides, I want to take another look at your new girlfriend," teases the musician.

"Stop it, Frankie," Henry giggles.

They walk out of the office while Frank murmurs, "once we read various stories on the internet, we can narrow our search for the Myth-Keeper. I can assure you some people have seen this mystical man."

They both sit down on the leather couch and start reading numerous chronicles, every single one of them, regardless of how absurd they may seem.

After two days, they have a group of urban legends from around the world, which have a curious detail in common. The accounts describe a mysterious man who talks about things no one has ever heard of, appearing and disappearing without a trace.

Nobody knows what his name is, nor do they describe the way he looks. Witnesses say he has healed many people. Some claim to have seen this man speak to corpses and return them to life immediately after hearing his bizarre language. The last event chronicled matching these characteristics happened in a small community near Bhutan just over six months ago.

"Sounds like the place to go, what do you think?" Henry turns to Aurora, and she shrugs, smiling. The boy knows if he is close enough, the Myth-Keeper will recognize his *sharah* and find him, as Ikhabot told him before leaving Tenshia.

"Fine, I am coming with you two," shrieks the excited musician.

"Are you serious? It will be dangerous, Frankie," asks Henry.

"I have missed most of your thrilling events, my young friend. Besides, it sounds far more interesting than staying hidden in this metal box!" Frankie gabbles, running around and throwing random things in a backpack. Henry stares at him, happy but worried at the same time.

"Okay, but we will need something to defend ourselves; just in case we come face to face with someone unfriendly," highlights Frankie.

"Weapons might help us against androids, but not against the Specters!" explains Henry doubtful of bringing Frankie along. The boy does not want to put anybody else in danger, "...this is why we need to travel light, and cautiously; we don't want any trouble. At this point, any encounter could be fatal. In case something goes wrong, we have Aurora with us," states the teenager gazing at his beautiful, strong girl. She smiles back. Frankie, on the other hand, looks at her and sees nothing but a pretty girl, not a warrior who can protect them.

"Say no more, son, let us gather everything we need and get ready to depart at dusk. We need a vehicle," rattles the musician wandering around the bunker, like a lunatic, "a fast and reliable vehicle! I will drive this time, we can drive it off-road to the hangar!"

"Sure, Frankie, what do you have in mind?"

"No worries, Hen, everything is set. I have a powerful four-wheeler that will do the job wonderfully. The only problem is," says concerned,

"...we have to go back home to get it, along with some false passports. It is risky, but it is our only chance if we want to get out of here fast," explains Mr. Waltz.

"We won't be needing fake IDs," interrupts Aurora.

"What makes you so sure," inquires Frankie.

"Humans and androids are easy to mind-control. I will have them see whatever I want them to see," she says confidently.

"I already love this girl, Hen," Frank tattles and gives Aurora an effusive kiss on the cheek, while she looks confused, "with friends like her, there is nothing to fear then," cheers Frank.

One hour after Frank has finished packing, they are ready to leave. The musician leaves his safe bunker behind to join Henry, in what could be his life's most exciting adventure. They walk outside on the sly with the moonlight as their only guide.

Crickets and cicadas sound everywhere in the still forest despite the drought. The sky is clear, and the moon shines bright; anyone walking through the leafless woods could see them effortlessly.

Trying not to make noise, the travelers tiptoe through the pines' fallen branches. Walking three miles on a chilly night does not seem to bother the composer. In a different situation, Frank believes it would have been a lovely evening hiking with his godson and his new girlfriend.

Nights are so silent in the Swiss countryside; even the most insignificant sound is naturally amplified due to symmetrically aligned trees. They reach the hills, and some lights from the other houses dimly light the entrance to Frank's mansion garage. Everything remains quiet as they walk inside the side door.

"Hen, let's take the four-wheeler and leave immediately; there is no time to lose," rushes Frank fearing someone could be around.

They hurry out of the house to the hidden airport in the middle of the hills. There is one more jet in the hangar waiting for them. Despite the off-road vehicle's electric engine, the wheels' grind is heard through the forest.

A ranger patrol in the area hears them, and the officers react immediately. They are curious to see a buggy at that time of night traveling at high speed. They quickly undertake the chase to find out what it is.

The occupants of the sophisticated rover notice the bright lights and sirens that pursue them. They look at each other, trying to decide what the least risky thing to do is.

"We must lose sight of them now!" howls Henry.

"No, it is stupid," Aurora contradicts, "...if we try to run away, they will simply call reinforcements, and it will be harder to get out of here. As I told you before, I'll take care of it!"

"Ro, I couldn't stand if something happened to you," he says, stroking her beautiful long hair, "they will know you are not from around here as soon as they see you."

"Everything will be fine, Hen, I can take care of myself. They are not a threat. Please believe me! Frankie, stop the car, you two can trust me," assures the Tenshian girl.

The Swiss musician stops the vehicle, and the ranger sitting on the passenger side gets off and walks to the buggy, pointing at the musician with a flashlight.

"Evening, sir, documents?" says the man in uniform.

Frank looks at the girl, and she nods her head. The composer takes his wallet out and shows the ranger his identification card.

"Thanks, let's see who we have here, Karl Marx," reads the ranger, "Where are you going alone this time of night through the forest, Mr. Marx?"

Frank, astonished by Aurora's hypnosis abilities,

decides to play along.

"Alone?" chuckles the musician, clears his throat before coming up with an ingenious response, "Animal emergency down at the reserve, our last bear, not an uncommon case of poisoning. Now, if you'll excuse me, I need to leave, or the bear will die if I don't get there in time," scorns Frank.

"I understand, Mr. Marx, I apologize for the delay. I am just doing my job, please, have a wonderful night! Good luck with the bear!" mutters the numbed ranger returning to the jeep.

"Phew!" He exhales, "interesting display of mental control, you beautiful girl," flatters Mr. Waltz.

"I told you human perception was easy to deceive," Aurora says, happy she could be of help.

"...and creative on top of that, Karl Marx," he laughs, "...it is genius! No one in this society would know who he is! I like her, Hen," says Frank, starting the buggy's engine.

Right before dawn, they get to the hangar and prepare the jet for take-off.

"I didn't know you could fly, Frankie," the boy praises.

"There are a lot of things you don't know about me, son."

Aurora and Henry buckle their seat belts as they

taxi through the runway. The boy stretches his hand toward the Tenshian girl, and she holds it tenderly.

The crew of three begin their quest, confident that Aurora will outwit the S.E.N.'s aeronautical security. She will be in charge of altering their coordinates on the enemy's radar until reaching their destination.

THE MYTH-KEEPER

A week goes by as they stop in several countries to rest and restock. Eventually, the jet lands safely in a rural area near Bhutan, in the southern foothills of Eastern Himalayas. Henry has done a fantastic job guiding Frank to the right spot after meditating for almost the entire trip. Hopefully, his inner-self has confirmed the right location to find the mighty Myth-Keeper.

With Aurora's help, the boy finally learns the mind is like a magnet. With the correct use of meditation, he has managed to generate the necessary cosmic resonance to be able to get the mysterious character's attention.

Bhutan is a lonely place now that its inhabitants have been wiped out by S.E.N. soldiers. Henry and his companions know no bounty hunters, or soldiers, are hanging around the area. The three explorers decide to stay in a desolate village and wait for a sign to lead them to the Myth-Keeper.

On the third night sleeping more than four thousand miles away from home, Henry receives a vision during his sleep. This vision invites him to climb to the top of a mountain near the village of Dechen Phrodrang. The young man abruptly wakes up, sweating and bewildered.

Young Schulze jumps out of his sleeping bag, and runs to get a warm coat from his backpack, puts it on, and then walks out of the abandoned cottage.

Frank hears the young man gasping in the middle of the night. He gets up and looks for Henry, who sits outside shivering.

Henry tells his godfather the vision he just had. The musician immediately offers to go along with him. Aurora, who guards the perimeter of the deserted house, overhears their conversation and insists she will come as well.

She will not leave her beloved Henry's side at any time. Both Aurora and the musician think that it could be a trap.

"Hen! The Prince is powerful enough to influence and manipulate dreams," warns the Tenshian girl.

"You are right, but," Henry hesitates about the idea of Aurora coming with him to the mountain. He believes it would be better if she stayed with Mr. Waltz, so he attempts to persuade her "...Ro, I don't want you to join me; this is something I need to do alone. Besides, this could be very dangerous; I couldn't stand putting you and Frankie at risk. If something were to happen to you, I would never forgive myself! And your brother! He would kill me this time!" blurts Henry.

"I told you not to worry about me, I won't let you go on your own; whatever happens, I will be there," thunders the girl.

Henry stares deep into Aurora's eyes. He has a bad feeling, but it is pointless trying to convince her otherwise. They go back inside the cabin to shelter from the cold wind coming down from the Himalayas.

The Swiss composer falls asleep the moment his head touches his small pillow. The two youngsters lie side by side and whisper to each other.

"Okay, you can come with me, but first tell me something, why does Atmix hate me so much? He doesn't even know me, and he hates me since the first time I set foot in Tenshia," the boy questions.

"He does not hate you, Hen, he holds a deep grudge against anything involving the S.E.N. and the surface. You see, our father and yours came together to the surface years ago. When your father died, ours decided to never come back. We didn't hear from him for a couple of years. Atmix was up here looking for him on various occasions, but he didn't find him. It was not until he sent a message to Arwind explaining that he had fallen in love with a woman from the surface and had started a new family with her. He wanted nothing to do with Atmix or me," Aurora weeps telling Henry their story. "It was hard; it was like he had turned into another person. Atmix never forgave him or got over it, as you can see. He blames this world for our suffering," explains the girl.

"Blimey! I am so sorry, Ro, I didn't know," whispers Henry and holds her hand, trying to cheer her up. Aurora interrupts the boy's attempt to make her feel better.

"It's okay; I am not that bothered about it anymore. My mother and I let go of it years ago. My father made a choice he judged was best at the time, that's it. Now, let's sleep, we have a big day tomorrow. Have a good night!"

"Goodnight, and thank you for sharing that with me," murmurs Henry, kissing her forehead.

At sunrise, Henry wakes up to the smell of food. Aurora sits outside, in front of a small pit roasting Himalayan Kumaon roots and cutting some other fruits she found to share with her companions. The teenage boy joins Aurora and gladly accepts the breakfast she has put together for them. Shortly after he sits on the ground with her, Mr. Waltz walks out.

"Frankie! What are you wearing?" giggles Henry.

The European composer, accustomed to dress in expensive suits, wears cargo pants, a safari hat, and long white socks with a pair of hiking boots.

"These were my dad's when he used to hunt way before most animals went extinct," brags the musician and joins them for breakfast.

"You look, well, a bit ridiculous," says the boy and chuckles trying to fade the anxiety in his heart.

The Thakaiken candidate feels optimistic about his journey to the peak of the mountain. He hopes he finds a clue leading to the Myth-Keeper, or better yet, the Myth-Keeper himself.

Two hours and a half up the mountain, and about five thousand feet above sea level, the inexperienced hikers find a valley full of Himalayan wild roses. They sit to delight in the gentle smell; it is soothing to their senses.

The sight is gorgeous, regardless of the chilly weather. Frank Waltz was not expecting it to get so cold so quickly.

He worries about the youngsters feeling cold and hands them a thin throw he carries in his backpack.

The musician shivers, "we might not have the appropriate attire for this weather."

Henry and Aurora walk side by side under the blanket, trying to keep each other warm. The teenager begs the heavens for a sign before reaching dangerously cold temperatures. He longs for answers and hopes they do not have to return to the village empty-handed.

Not a mile up from the wild rose valley, the amount of static in the atmosphere becomes abnormal. It gets so fierce it almost shocks their skin. The edges of the deodar cedars light up due to the sparks of energy.

"Is this normal?" Frank asks anxiously.

"No," alerts the girl, "stop! Don't move,"

They do as she says, and they stand closer together. After a few seconds, the electricity around them is strong enough to immobilize their bodies.

Their muscles become numb when three entities approach them. Henry sees the gracefully slight figure of a young woman accompanied by two towering men walking on each side.

"It can't be," he stammers. Adrenaline floods the youngster's entire body. He feels sick, "It is Cristabella," he panics, "...and Tiamat and Tartuross!"

Aurora is trapped as well; she cannot move an inch. Frank freaks out and writhes in fear. He wants to run, but his muscles do not respond to his brain's commands. Henry has told him about the Specters, but he never thought they would be as terrifying as they are.

No more than ten feet away from him, the red-eyed celestial stands with a buzzing spear in his left hand. Henry, struggling to stay calm, hears himself say, "Tricked again! Curse my luck! We are going to die."

"Long time no see my dear Hen. I've missed you so much I even decided to come looking for you myself," murmurs the woman sensually walking toward young Schulze. "Honestly, I thought I lost you forever. When my dad told me what happened, it was hard to believe. Have you forgotten about me so quickly? About us?" she asks, landing a kiss in the corner of his lips.

Henry feels as if losing control over his emotions. The warm sensation in his chest impedes his breathing. Speechless, the boy tries to focus on the feelings he holds for Aurora while Cristabella hovers over his cheek with her soft lips.

True love battles lust, and desire.

He looks at the Tenshian girl and feels that something genuinely pure and special unites them. On the other hand, he cannot help but contemplate Cristabella's body.

Her lush attractiveness brings a cascade of memories from the nights of passion and debauchery. Even though the choice is obvious, the boy flounders to make the right decision. Deep down, he knows a life with Cristabella is not what he wishes for his future.

Let alone the fact that the world would be in The Prince's hands to enslave and destroy.

"I am sorry, Bella," Henry grunts, "…our paths don't lead to the same city, so to speak. I shall follow my destiny, and you are not part of it. Whatever happened between you and me was incredible, but it is also in the past. A lot of things have taken a toll on me since you last saw me; I will never be the boy you met, ever again. I apologize for letting you down, but this time, I am not coming with you," he declares.

Cristabella looks disappointedly at Henry's face and then examines Aurora from head to toe, belittling her, almost humiliating her.

"I see what's happening here! You are in love!" she crows in laughter, "Can you believe this, Tiamat?"

"Pathetic! They are meant for each other, my lady," chuckles the ginger-haired warrior.

"In love? Please! You will forget her name the second you have me in your arms again!"

"My decision has nothing to do with her; it is bigger than any of us. We should leave now, it was a true pleasure seeing you again, though, and I can't say the same about your father. Please, Bella, let us go," Henry asks.

"You can't possibly believe I am going to let you go. Your naivety doesn't cease to amaze me," Cristabella giggles caressing the boy's neck, "things are a bit more complicated than you think. You see, you are coming to Mizraim with me; dead or alive!" forcing a passionate kiss on his lips.

Aurora, fed up by the taunting woman, closes her eyes and focuses her energy into breaking the magnetism binding them together.

She breaks free, and the first thing she does is try to strike Tiamat's face. The evil Specter grabs her leg and sends her flying several feet in the air.

Cristabella laughs. "Your girlfriend is not useless, after all. She managed to escape. Still, it is not enough as you can see," she teases as Tiamat walks straight toward the Tenshian girl. "Tiamat will tear her apart!"

The ginger Muhalif brutally pounces over the weak girl and beats her. Aurora tries to defend herself, but it is pointless. She howls in pain.

"Take me! Please! Leave her alone, Tiamat, I beg you!" Henry whines, incapable of moving one bit, "please! Please! Hit me instead!"

The musician stares shocked at the scene. His eyes show the deepest of terrors while the warrior savagely wallops the innocent girl. Tiamat stops and lifts

Aurora by her ankle; blood trickles up her face as she hangs upside down. She is unconscious.

Henry is surprised his reaction is not the same as many times before. He feels the pain and the need to help, but the desperation and torment are gone.

Now, young Schulze focuses on what he can do to help. The difference is that his mind has not lost its ability to reason, and that is a huge game-changer.

There is nothing I can do right now! Even if I tried, my feeble skills are nowhere comparable to their powers. The boy thinks. Tiamat will kill my sweet Aurora, and then Atmix is going to kill me for it! I can't allow anybody else to die for me.

Time slows down as the red-eyed Muhalif runs toward the musician. The Specter grabs Frank by his neck and stands in front of Henry.

"Let him go, Tartuross! He has nothing to do with any of this!" yowls the teenager enraged with tears in his eyes, "Let Aurora go too, Tiamat, please stop! I beg you! Bella, please," he screams, turning to the woman in the red dress.

The redhead warrior, fed up with the boy, growls, "You are nothing but a coward, boy, and you are a piece of trash! I honestly do not understand why The Prince needs you alive; otherwise, I would behead you right here, insignificant bug. You are worthless! Your friend will die, and there is nothing you can do," rumbles the Specter.

Henry looks at Frank and mouths, "I am sorry!"

"Do you want to know what is going to happen to your dear friend? Let me tell you—" he says as he begins to generate white sparkles a couple of yards on the ground ahead of him. "I am taking your friend to enjoy one of the most beautiful sights on planet Earth—the peak of Mount Everest. His body won't last more than ten minutes in the cold. The altitude will deplete his lungs from oxygen, and he will die at more than twenty-nine thousand feet above sea level!"

The Specter voices something, and a gale of frigid air and ice rushes up through the pit on the ground.

Frank keeps his eyes fixed on his godson's eyes while the Specter walks to the energy portal. Hanging by his neck held by the Specter's muscular arm, the Swiss musician yells at the boy.

"Remember, Hen, make your miracle happen!"

"Frankie! No!" Henry yelps.

A minute later, the Specter in onyx armor returns unaccompanied. Henry knows that was the end of his godfather's days on the planet. Instead of sadness, the teenager's heart bursts in anger. He finally understands why he needs to become the Thakaiken from the surface. He is determined; there is no other way. He is tired of being weak and losing those he loves the most.

"Tiamat!" says Cristabella, "time to go!"

"Yeah, stop fooling around! Kill that girl once and for all!" grumbles the redhead Muhalif.

The warrior on the metallic sarong is ready to crash the girl against the stone path when a loud rumble comes from the east. They all turn, but none of them sees a thing; stunned by the sound, they look at each other somewhat confused. Suddenly, from above, an ordinary-looking man descends amid a light blue glim. "Kill her quick, Tiamat" rushes Tartuross, "this dude is making me uncomfortable, hurry up!"

The mystical man lands on the mountain and starts whispering words in an ancient but powerful language. He saunters toward Henry with his eyes looking up to the heavens.

Tiamat, Tartuross, and the beautiful Cristabella try to snatch Henry, but an invisible barrier protects the boy. Perplexed, they watch the strange man getting closer. Somehow tied with invisible ropes, they are incapable of reaching young Schulze.

Tiamat opens a portal in their midst, and the three disappear instantly along with Aurora. Henry watches helplessly as Cristabella and her two warriors abduct his girlfriend.

"Hello, Henry! Follow me. Right now, there is nothing we can do for your friend," requests the stranger approaching Henry looking right into his amber eyes.

Henry's soul crunches to the idea that the stranger man is right. There is nothing he could do to save the girl. The static field that kept him imprisoned has disappeared.

He falls to his knees, and his screams echo in the immaculate beauty of the Himalayas. All he can do is let his anger out by furiously pounding the ground. He is sick of whining and not being able to face the enemies that have taken everything away from him.

The stranger interrupts Henry's violent tantrum, "The girl is strong; she is alive. Come with me, and you will be able to rescue her soon!"

"Who are you? Why are you helping me?" Henry inquires.

"I am who you are looking for," replies the man.

Henry, distrustful, stares at the man from head to toe, trying to understand how the stranger resembles what he thought the Myth-Keeper would look like, and asks, "Are you the Myth-Keeper?"

"My name is Yohanán," he grins, "... the Myth-Keeper is a name people have given me after listening to my stories. Why are you staring at me like that, Henry? Am I not what you were hoping for?" laughs the stranger.

"It is not that you are not what I was hoping for, but I never imagined a powerful mystic wearing jeans, canvas sneakers, and a long-sleeve t-shirt!" Henry explains, embarrassed, smiling at the Myth-Keeper regardless of his pain. The boy feels an instant connection with the man that will guide him to the most important milestone of his life.

"Thanks for saving me from the Specters. How did you manage to control them? What language were you speaking?" asks Henry.

"It is Aramaic; those words truss beings such as them. Well, it is time to go! We have a lot of work to do in no time. I know you have a lot of questions, but don't worry, I have a lot more answers. Let's go, my friend," declares the Myth-Keeper.

A blue beam of light lifts the two men to an ovoid-shaped ship. The particular spacecraft is entirely smooth and white on the outside, without windows or any other apparent hatch. Young Henry hovers silently, staring at the clouds around him. The sights are beyond anything the Swiss boy ever imagined.

A small sliding door opens at the bottom, leading them into a large and comfortable room. Neither the furniture nor the walls of the place have an array of many colors.

Everything looks sober with shades of silver, blue, black, and white. The ambiance inside the hovering home is peaceful, pure, and stable.

It seems like any sophisticated house back on the surface. Inside the space home, Henry forgets they are thousands of feet above the sea level. He is certain it is a space capsule designed with technology from another world.

"Welcome aboard the Mattriozka; this has been my home for more than two thousand years. Please, get comfortable; feel yourself at home! You are free to walk around whenever you want it, but first, you need my faithful friend's approval; Aki?" calls the Myth-Keeper.

A mid-size furry pal appears from behind a couch, wagging his long tail. Aki, a chocolate Labrador retriever, runs toward Yohanán and avidly licks his face.

"Aki! Stop!" The bearded man laughs.

Henry cannot believe what he sees, "I have never seen a dog like this with my own eyes!" he whispers.

Aki comes close to the boy drooling all over the teenager and then sniffs his shoes. Panting and wagging his tail, Aki is enchanted by the visitor.

The gorgeous furry creature runs to the living room, and his snout goes around the modern centerpiece table.

Henry stares at the dog as he looks for something. Suddenly, the pup comes back running with a bone in his mouth toward Henry and throws the bone at the boy's feet. Yohanán laughs.

"He wants to play *fetch*!"

"What?" asks the boy, rather confused.

"Just toss the bone, and you'll see," giggles the Myth-Keeper.

The blue-eyed Labrador captures Henry's attention for a few minutes but does not take his mind away from everything he has been through.

Yohanán notices the sadness in the youngster's eyes and sends the pup away to his bed. Soothingly, the Myth-Keeper approaches the boy.

"I believe you are not sure why you are here, right? Should you not find answers in the time you and I spend together, you will be lost forever!" he explains.

"Why do you say that?"

"...and you will probably die ignoring the true purpose of your existence," the Myth-Keeper continues disregarding the boy's question.

"Right now, all I care about is finding out what happened to Frankie, and know if Aurora is still alive," he replies.

"My mind is capable of tracking every living thing in this realm. Your friend is no longer with us, but the girl is still alive. I am not sure where she is, though. It looks like they took her to a place outside of this dimension," Yohanán tries to comfort the distressed boy, "we can still do something for Frank if you want. We can give him a proper burial in an unconventional perpetual way. If that makes you feel better, we can go get his body, and I will do the rest!"

Henry nods, and the Myth-Keeper commands the Mattriozka to go to the highest point on planet Earth; Mount Everest's summit.

Once there, the two men descend from the Mattriozka with the appropriate equipment to survive the hostile conditions of the twenty-nine-thousand-tall peak.

Frank Waltz's body lies lifeless curled up in a fetal position. Rigid by the temperature and with his skin burned by the deadly frigid winds, Henry believes the musician's last minutes on Earth must have been terrifying.

Then, more than ever, the youngster reassures himself he must become the Thakaiken from the surface and defeat The Adversaries. There is no other way.

Yohanán grabs handfuls of snow and starts covering Frank's body. The Myth-Keeper asks Henry to do the same, being careful not to touch Frank's dead body. Both work for several minutes until the body is covered entirely.

The sage places his warm hands over the piled snow, and it turns slowly into a shiny, robust block of ice. Henry observes baffled how the Myth-Keeper has total control over the elements of nature.

After five minutes, the famous composer's body

rests in the middle of a crystalized ice coffin. Frank Waltz will rest untouched for as long as Mount Everest's everlasting snow exists.

Henry loved his godfather so much, and the least he can do to honor him is to fulfill his destiny. Standing in front of the ice casket, the future Thakaiken remembers his mother's best friend's last words.

Make your miracle happen!

Henry feels ready to live under the legendary Myth-Keeper's guardianship.

"Let us go, Henry, there is no time to waste. NaHash's attack is coming, and you have years of training ahead of you!" rushes the Myth-Keeper.

The eccentric mystic's words make no sense to the boy.

"Years of training? What do you mean by that? I don't have years Yohanán! I have to rescue Aurora as soon as possible and go back to Ikhabot and the others. They need my help!" reproaches the boy.

The mighty Yohanán places a hand in Henry's left shoulder and briefly explains what kind of training he is about to begin,

"In this temporal dimension, we will be gone for a month, or two; while on the beach of Nazarah, where you and I are going, it is years. Remember, time is an illusion inside people's minds, my young learner. I understand you are anxious; answers will come, I promise. Now!" says the Myth-Keeper with excitement, "It is time for you to meet Lemayhan!"

ZORAH

THE CELESTIAL SANCTUARY

A new S.E.N. Secretary-General has been appointed after Mr. McArthur got coldly murdered at the meeting with The Prince. The S.E.N.'s high executives are terribly aggravated by the overwhelming conflict with the Tenshians.

Even after stripping all the purgatories of their last freshwater reserves, the Elite knows they will not last for long. More than ever, world leaders desperately need to find Tenshia and get the freshwater ocean by force.

Not long after the cruel Elite sacrificed most of their underpaid and marginalized workers in the purgatories for water, peaceful daily life in the S.E.N. has been rattled by turmoil. More and more people inside the invisible walls have heard a rumor or two about how bad the water crisis really is.

Despite the restrictions on classified information, a few unknown civilians have leaked details about the monumental failure of the 'Aqua-de-Vita' project. The wealthy nations' inhabitants are becoming aware that drinking water might run out any given day without any previous government announcement.

Groups of people in several cities around the globe are turning to the streets with banners demanding the truth, and even threatening the elitist regime.

The increasing upheavals have the S.E.N.'s high council under pressure. Big corporations and world banking consortiums, the ones who actually brought about the establishment of the new ruling power on Earth, demand to know how such sensitive information got out to the public. Tired of the impediments the riots represent to their agenda, the S.E.N.'s high council has decided to request the Regents of nations to get directly involved.

These embodied celestials of lesser rank, who answer directly to The Muhalif, took the place of presidents and prime ministers from the old democracy. There are seventy Regents in total around the S.E.N. territories, each one per every original nation on planet Earth.

To their disadvantage, the high council completely ignores The Prince's ego has gotten in the way. He will not yet allow the world government to know he has already found Henry, the freshwater ocean, and ravaged Tenshia.

The Tsar of Mizraim cannot wait for his Specters to tear the Thakaiken apart in an epic battle on the surface of the earth. He is extremely confident about his warlords' victory. The mighty Tsar is sure he will soon take control of the last standing Tenshian city.

His one and only purpose is to show himself to the world as a hero worthy of praise and adoration. Thus, defeating the guardians from the land of Tenshia, and bringing clean water to the thirsty nations is his top priority.

The surface dwellers are still being brainwashed day and night by newsfeeds on how dangerous the Tenshians are. Everybody in the S.E.N. territories, from servants to lords, seems to be silently demanding the authorities to capture the outlaws and punish them.

With Atmix and Aurora still missing, Ikhabot and Silas continue to scan the surface through meditation and, against all odds, have spotted more survivors around the purgatories. These afflicted humans are about to die of dehydration; the Thakaiken will not allow it.

However, they have second thoughts about leaving Tenshia, since they cannot trust back-stabber NaHash, who promised to wait for them to fight the Specters.

In the meantime, the Mattriozka invisibly furrows the skies at an unmatchable speed, always beating all radars on the surface. Young Henry and his mentor, the intriguing Myth-keeper, hope to reach the Beach of Nazarah soon, where the apprentice will be initiated in the mysteries of heaven.

K. Emerson is a writer, elementary literacy teacher, and author of Book 1 of the Zorah series, The Adversaries. With over a decade of teaching, writing plays, and publishing award-winning articles for his alma mater, K. Emerson finds his true calling in writing young adult fiction novels. Despite being born to sandy beaches in the Colombian Caribbean, K. Emerson is often seen enjoying a coffee somewhere in the Colorado Rocky Mountains, at a Rock n' Roll concert or listening to the particular sound of a home run hit at Coors Field. When not absorbed in Epic Fantasy page-turners with his fifth graders, K. Emerson loves taking his dogs on walks while beholding gorgeous Colorado sunsets.

www.ingramcontent.com/pod-product-compliance
Lightning Source LLC
Chambersburg PA
CBHW031617100726
47898CB00006B/1821